URBAN SHOTS
LOVE COLLECTION

Born in Kuwait, **Sneh Thakur** has an MBA from the Symbiosis Institute of Business Management, Pune. An innovation enthusiast, she has worked with FMCG majors like Perfetti, Wrigley, GSK Consumer Healthcare and Nestle and has several business excellence awards to her name. She now lives in Dubai, writing by the beach and dreaming on abras.

URBAN SHOTS
LOVE COLLECTION

Edited by
Sneh Thakur

RUPA

Published by
Rupa Publications India Pvt. Ltd 2015
7/16, Ansari Road, Daryaganj
New Delhi 110002

Sales centres:
Allahabad Bengaluru Chennai
Hyderabad Jaipur Kathmandu
Kolkata Mumbai

ISBN: 978-81-291-3712-8

First impression 2015

10 9 8 7 6 5 4 3 2 1

The moral right of the author has been asserted.

Contents

Foreword

SNEH THAKUR

I must have been six when I first fell in love.

We were in Sister Sophia's art class and I was trying to draw a pink pony. Catastrophe struck when, in an exaggerated effort to colour within the lines, I broke the tip of my pink pencil. My Minnie Mouse sharpener refused to work and soon the tip of my nose had turned red and tears threatened to spill over my half-painted masterpiece. Seeing my unhappy face, a messy-haired little boy reached out and offered his sole pink crayon. We exchanged a gummy smile and in that moment I was introduced to the euphoria of love.

Love. An emotion that captures the world's imagination.

Perhaps some of life's most vivid memories come from being in or losing love. That sunny, high feeling of a first crush, to glancing at your watch every five minutes, waiting impatiently for your date to arrive. The magic of a first kiss. The sunken feeling of rejection. The sky-high exuberance of emerging from pain. We've all been there.

It's no surprise that the various dimensions of love have inspired artists and cultures around the world. Through decades, music in all its genres and languages has paid ode to 'a crazy little thing called love'—Edith Piaf's soulful melody *L'Hymne à l'amour*, to celebratory tunes from The Beatles or the more recent magic of Adele. In art, themes of love have been immortalized on canvas in a thousand vibrant hues. Celluloid, in recent times, has had a marked departure from the portrayal of love in mainstream cinema to accommodate for new twists in the tale like Dev D. Gone are the days when letters were penned and the wait mind-numbing; social media today keeps us adequately 'posted' on who's moved on from being 'single' to 'in a relationship'!

Fiction itself is no stranger to memorable lines etched in love. So when Grey Oak collaborated with Landmark in a unique initiative to showcase new writing from India, the response was overwhelming. Weaving through the expanse of emotions that make up love, first-time writers and familiar authors bring you a collection of stories that are sure to pull at your heartstrings. Stories in this collection traverse themes of young love, betrayal, marriage, humorous accounts, and translated regional literature—all set in the context of the Indian landscape.

Within these pages you will find fresh voices with a new take on love. But even more so, you may find yourself reliving many familiar, bittersweet and uplifting moments.

Written in the Stars

R. CHANDRASEKAR

Tripunathura Mahalingiyer Shivasubramaniam, known as TMS to his colleagues, Chinna Mani to his parents and Bank Mani to his other relatives, banged his head on the windowsill every morning. This was part of his daily morning routine. Pain and suffering were a way of attracting the Almighty's attention, earning him brownie points which would, in due course, deliver him from the cycle of lives. He took care not to bang his head too hard. A cracked skull would mean hospitalization and endless complaints from the neighbours who would be responsible for bundling him into an auto and to a hospital. Neighbourly feelings went only so far. The worst-case scenario, death from over-enthusiastic contact with the windowsill, was likely to arouse divine ire. So he knocked his head hard enough to cause some discomfort, just enough to get the Almighty's attention.

He would then bathe and go to the temple clad in a crisp veshti. He was a regular there and didn't take any short cuts. He observed the daily, weekly, fortnightly and monthly rituals punctiliously, divine pleasure and displeasure never far from his thoughts. He would then have breakfast before setting off for the bus stand.

Once a week, Mani met his astrologer. They usually discussed the weather, the cricket scores and politics before settling down to the business of astrology.

'Sir, they are not giving Manikandan a fair chance.' Manikandan, Tamil Nadu's sole representative in the national side, had been making heavy weather of things, leading to concern and consternation among his many fans. That morning he had been dropped.

'His stars are not in correct alignment. Saturn is in the ascendancy and his horoscope has some dosham in it.'

'How do you know all this, sir?' The astrologer smiled mysteriously and said nothing.

'You are actually aware of Manikandan's horoscope, sir?'

The smile widened just a touch.

'You mean…you mean…Manikandan is your client, sir?'

The astrologer cleared his throat. 'There are ways of countering the dosham in Manikandan's horoscope just as there are ways of countering your dosham. In your case for instance, I see that the number twenty-nine is a bad influence. You should avoid the number twenty-nine.'

Mani had a hundred questions for the astrologer as he did every week. He just nodded, though, and walked away after making his weekly donation. He held the astrologer in high regard and felt at times that he was in the presence of a superior human being. Asking for clarifications would only expose his ignorance. In addition, he was always conscious that he might be wasting the astrologer's time and left as soon the week's advice had been given.

All the buses that took him to work and back directly were numbered 29. Mani took the astrologer's advice as seriously as his head banging: fate was capricious and there was no point tempting it. Avoiding 29 meant a great deal of inconvenience. He had to take a circuitous route, which cost him time and money, to work. It meant a considerable amount of footboard travel with all the unpleasantness that it entailed. But he felt good.

'I felt that I was doing punyam for my past sins,' he told the astrologer when he met him the next week. He even added more than the usual amount to his weekly donation.

The astrologer felt guilty when he saw Mani. He had been a bit annoyed the previous week at the time Mani showed up (for reasons that had nothing to do with Mani). All the stuff involving the number twenty-nine was bunkum. He knew that Mani took one of the 29 series to work and it made him feel a bit better seeing someone else's daily routine thrown a little off-kilter. He had decided to make amends the next time Mani showed up.

Years of experience, and some advice from his father (who had practiced astrology for over seventy years), had made him aware that the successful practice of astrology revolved around three basic principles. First: know your customer. Then you knew what he (or she) wanted, and gave it to them in dribs and drabs. The second principle: too much of a good thing was not good. If the customer felt too good, he would feel that his life's problems had been sorted out and wouldn't come back. The corollary to this formed the third principle: too much of a bad thing was not good. Too much negativity and they changed astrologers. The idea, therefore, was to string the customer along and keep him (or her) slightly off balance.

But here was Mani with a smile on his face. The inconveniences of the past week had not put him off stride. This was an odd situation, one that needed delicate handling. Weekly paying customers were not exactly thick on the ground and the astrologer was loath to lose Mani's custom.

The weather, cricket and politics done with, they got down

to business.

'See, the number twenty-nine is still exerting an influence on you. Less than last week, for sure, but it is still a matter for concern. Avoid number twenty-nine for another week.'

Mani's face fell slightly.

'But,' the astrologer hastened to add, 'I think I see something good coming.'

'This week?'

The astrologer frowned as he consulted his dog-eared almanac. 'Perhaps,' he replied, 'but things are not entirely clear at the moment. Next week it might be clearer.'

The annual accounts closing meant that Mani had to work late into the night. By the time he was done, most buses were off the road and he looked around for an auto. Mani hated autos and their drivers: they ripped you off; they drove like madmen; they insisted on chatting with you. At this time of the night, though, he had no choice. Some fifteen minutes later a lone auto came limping along. Its license number was 2933. He hesitated, and then waved it on. No point tempting providence, even if 2933 was not exactly 29. By midnight he had resisted temptations bearing the numbers 4293, 3529, 1729, 3290, 929, 2929, 7297 and finally, momentously, 29. He knew this had to be a sign. He had been tested and not found wanting. Someone, somewhere, was keeping a close eye on him, and he hoped that his forbearance had been noticed. He walked home, arriving rather weary in the limb, but feeling very virtuous.

Mani half thought of walking to work the next day, but his legs were not up to it. He had gone through the head banging and the temple rituals perfunctorily. The number 29 was burned into his brain: what had happened the previous night was clearly an omen. He scrutinized the bus licence plates, the bus number and the route number of each bus with care and finally got a toehold on a barely vacant footboard of a bus which met all his criteria. The physical discomfort he felt was amply compensated for by the sense of mental calm he felt for having stared temptation in the face without giving in.

Mani's thoughts turned to the astrologer. Clearly the man was special. There was something to this 29 business. Just what it was wasn't clear, not least whether 7297 was really 29. Did those extra sevens matter? These were deep matters he needed to discuss with the astrologer. Then there was the weekly donation. He had been handing over fifty rupees each week, more from habit than out of complete conviction. He now felt remorse at his stinginess. The man was a genius and deserved better. There couldn't be too many such geniuses; theirs was a precious science that deserved generous support. Momentous changes might well be in his future and he wanted to be sure he missed none of them. Better to visit the astrologer twice a week. That way there was less chance of his doing something wrong during the week, less chance of something falling between the cracks. The future was not something to be trifled with.

The astrologer was surprised to see Mani on his doorstep. Even as he ushered Mani in, the astrologer was worried. Mani was a Wednesday client and here he was, showing up on a Friday. Had something gone wrong? Perhaps he should have stopped that 29 rubbish after a week. But Mani had been so eager, keen almost, to continue his 29 penance. The astrologer peered at Mani's face as they sat down. Know your customer, his father had told him, and now he wished he had a way of knowing what was going through Mani's mind.

Mani, mindful of the presence of a Superior Being and a genius, kept a straight face. Levity, ardour, good cheer, any form of overt enthusiasm on his part, would be inappropriate here. What few words he had were stanched by the sight of the astrologer's eyes boring into his innermost self. He stared at the floor silently, unable to meet the astrologer's stare face on.

Both stared silently as long minutes ticked by. The suspense built, became palpable. Unable to take this anymore, the astrologer cleared his throat.

The floodgates loosened, and then broke.

'Guruji!' began Mani, falling at the astrologer's feet. 'You are a genius! A genius not just of this world, but of all worlds!'

The astrologer heaved a huge sigh of relief. Thank God this hadn't ended as a big screw-up.

'I must tell you all that has happened,' continued Mani.

'Yes, yes,' sighed the astrologer, his voice weak with relief. 'Get up and sit down. Make yourself comfortable. It was the number 29 wasn't it?'

Mani shook his head in awed disbelief. He really had underestimated this man. 'So you do know all about it.'

'I endeavour to look into the future Mani, and the Almighty God sometimes gives me a glimpse at things that are to come. But you seem eager to tell me the story as it happened to you. So go on, I am a good listener.'

The astrologer listened and scratched his head in puzzlement. This was all very nice, he could see that this would mean an increase in his emoluments, but he hadn't the foggiest idea what to do next. Astrology, after all, was psychology practised with one's fingers crossed. It wouldn't do to have someone felled by a heart attack a day after good health was prophesied. You tried to get things out of the customer. Had he seen a doctor? What had the doctor said? Had he been asked to undertake any tests? Did he feel breathless when he laughed along with his morning Laughter Club friends on the beach? And so on and so forth, but with some cunning and subtlety. And when you did venture a prophecy, you kept things vague and open to interpretation. Those nine autos with the number 29—that was just his luck. A prophecy that was too good was just as bad as one that was completely wrong.

Mani, on the other hand, clearly saw a sign in all of what had happened to him. Now he wanted the astrologer to tell him what it meant. Something good, something auspicious, obviously. He had heeded the astrologer's advice; things were ripe for him to earn the fruits of his forbearance.

The astrologer closed his eyes and sat still in what he hoped would be taken for a meditative pose. When he spoke, it was in a sibilant voice which he felt conveyed mystery.

'Fortune is about to smile on you,' he said. Mani listened in rapt attention, eagerness suffusing his face like that of a sage receiving favours from a grateful God after years of penance.

'Thank you! Thank you so very much!' gushed Mani. 'But could you tell me a little bit more? Am I going to get a promotion? Is my luck in the lottery going to change? The Sikkim lottery is having its draw next week. Should I buy a ticket without a 29 on it?'

The astrologer frowned. Mani stammered and stopped. I shouldn't annoy the great man, he thought. I mustn't get too greedy. After all, he has saved me from some major disaster. He bowed his head and waited for the astrologer to continue.

The astrologer sat silently, his tongue searching out a grain of rice that had lodged itself awkwardly between two teeth. Just how do I send this blighter packing, he wondered. Years spent as a very modestly successful practitioner of his art had not prepared him for anything like this. He had spent his career dealing in ambiguous generalities and platitudes which, after the fact, could be interpreted as predictions of a sort. He sensed that his clients did not always believe him, but came back out of habit, superstition, or a desire not to break an old, comfortable routine. The donations he expected were reasonable, the pinch felt by his clients minimal. And here, now, he was being asked to interpret an omen, to find a way out of a trap of his own making.

Think hard, he urged himself. What does this chap want that he is likely to get anyway? Not the lottery: the odds against the Sikkim lottery were prohibitive. And certainly not a promotion. None of his regulars was likely to get a promotion, in this lifetime or the next. That is probably why they come to me, he realized in a flash of insight. What, then? His eyes bored into Mani's, trying by sheer force of will to pry out the secrets that hid there. Suddenly, inspiration struck: he knew just what he had to say.

'Not the material,' he intoned in a solemn voice, 'but the spiritual. That which you want, but know not that you want. That which you need, but know not that you need.'

Puzzlement, fear and awe crossed Mani's face in turn.

'Seek not what is incorrect,' continued the astrologer, 'and you shall be delivered of it.'

With that the astrologer closed his eyes, brought his hands together in a namaskaram and stopped. I hope he doesn't expect any more of this nonsense he thought, since I've run out of things to say.

Mani puzzled over the conundrums set him by the astrologer as he half-heartedly entered numbers in a ledger and later on his way home. Absentmindedly he boarded a bus and finding a seat empty, sat down. Just what did he want that he didn't know he wanted? And what was the incorrect thing he was supposed to avoid? Why was it that things were never simple or obvious? The astrologer knew something, that was certain, but he also wanted Mani to look deep within him and discover it for himself. All this deep searching was tiring and, lulled by the random lurches of the bus, Mani dropped off to sleep.

'Excuse me, sir. You are sitting on the ladies' seat.'

Mani woke up with a start. There was a woman glaring at him with intent. She was short, her pulled-back and plaited hair added to the severity of her expression, her build suggested easy familiarity and facility with a rolling pin and her glasses magnified her wrath. Several impressive-looking volumes perched under one arm, others peeked out of a cloth bag slung over her shoulder. From a storyteller's perspective, not promising at all.

'Oh, the men you see these days,' she added, addressing the other occupants of the bus, 'no courtesy at all you see. They sit on the ladies' seat even when ladies carrying books and babies and vegetables and all are standing for want of a seat.'

There were murmurs of sympathy from the chivalrous Tamilian crowd.

'Terribly sorry madam,' said Mani rising hurriedly. 'I was having a short nap by mistake and I did not notice your good self. Kindly sit. May I carry your important books so you are not further inconvenienced?'

'Of course not,' she said huffily as she arranged herself on the seat along with her books and bag. 'Men nowadays are not to be trusted at all. You, sir, would probably abscond with the books and sell them in the second-hand market.'

This hurt.

'Madam,' said Mani with a pained expression, 'you have completely misunderstood my good intentions. I am a hardworking clerk in the Indian Overseas Bank and only try to help others when I can. I am a regular temple goer. I humbly apologize, madam, for occupying a ladies' seat in this bus. But kindly do not insult me.' Having regained the moral high ground, he pushed his way through the throng and stood elsewhere, well out of the sight of his tormenter.

Two weeks went by. The astrologer counselled patience and, judging that he was on firm ground, gently berated Mani for not looking far enough into himself. 'This,' he told Mani, 'is something you have to see and acknowledge for yourself. If I tell you everything, the Almighty will not be pleased and might well nullify and change His plans for you. Things will never happen that way.'

Never intellectually minded, Mani puzzled over this as he walked to the bus stop. The abstract and the metaphysical had always been closed books to him and now it appeared as though his very happiness depended on those very concepts. He tried hard to relate those mystical allusions to his mundane existence. What connections there were eluded him completely.

The lady with the books was at the bus stand. Seeing her, Mani looked away and stood at a distance.

'I am sorry about the other day, sir.' She had moved to his side and was looking contritely at her feet.

Mani had not forgotten the insults. He swallowed hard, looked the other way and moved on.

'There are indeed many bad men on buses these days and you will pardon me if I mistook your intentions.'

Mani blinked hard. He was not used to being spoken to by women. He shuffled away some more.

'Sir, my mother is an account holder at Indian Overseas Bank and she says that the clerks are helpful.'

'Which branch?' he blurted out.

'Perambur branch, sir. Only last week a clerk pointed out an error and corrected her passbook, sir.'

'Oh. Ah. Yes. Customer friendliness is our motto. We are always waiting to help and assist valuable customers. Like your good mother.'

'You are which division clerk, sir?'

'Third division. I am always telling my friends, heaviest responsibilities resting on Division III clerical staff. In fact I am turning down promotions even to continue to discharge heavy responsibilities.'

This was a blatant lie, his conscience twinged and he tried to remember the astrologer's words. Had he asked him to seek not was what incorrect or to say not what was incorrect? Either way, it was best not to take a chance.

'But yes, as you were saying, many bad men are riding the buses these days.' He looked at her: the hard edge had gone and something approaching feminine softness touched her features. 'You must have experienced many trying moments on the bus. So many chain snatchers and pickpockets and rowdy college boys. Only good thing is that politicians don't travel by bus these days.'

'Yes, sir. But we also have Division III clerical staff from IOB to help us when we are in difficulty.'

Having undergone the trials and tribulations of bus travel for many years, they proceeded to share their experiences, each more gruesome than the other, at length. Shared experiences are as strong a basis for friendship as any as Mani and Pushpalatha, his new friend, proceeded to demonstrate over the next few weeks.

A visit to the astrologer helped, of course.

He smiled knowingly when Mani mentioned his new acquaintance at which point Mani knew that what had been prophesied had come to pass without his even realizing it. Never one to miss belabouring a point, the astrologer added that the bus they'd had their beginning on was entirely 29-free. He ensured a big fat donation for himself and the seat of honour at their wedding by reading their horoscopes and announcing that never in his long years as an astrologer had he seen two horoscopes so perfectly matched as those of Bank Mani and Pushpalatha. And, by announcing that a wedding feast consisting of thirty-three items would be triply auspicious, he also ensured a good dinner for himself.

Rishta[1]

AHMED FAIYAZ

Imtiaz Rehman walked in feeling fatigued from the heat and dust he put himself through as he walked back from Mr Chaudhari's home. Imtiaz was a history teacher at the Good English High School in Sultangarh, where he had worked for over thirty years. He also tutored the district collector Mr Chaudhari's dull sons to earn extra income. Of late, given the rise in food prices and with his son in school, he found himself under financial strain with the added burden of an unmarried daughter—Aaliyah.

Aaliyah was the apple of his eye. Like him, she was a teacher at the Hummingbird English Nursery, a job she had taken up after completing her MA in English in Kanpur two years earlier.

'You've come back, I've been waiting for you,' Fatima, his big-built nagging wife of twenty-five years said as she watched him enter and put his jhola[2] down on the table. The tiny living room was filled with ramshackle furniture that was falling apart. They

---

[1]Proposal
[2]Bag

had an old diwan and squeaky sofa set bought second hand from their neighbours a few years ago.

'Rahil, turn off the television now and go study. All you do is watch cricket all day. Keep fooling around and you'll be left behind in this godforsaken town for the rest of your life and you'll suffer like us…' Fatima warned, pointing her finger at little Rahil who was engrossed in the game on the television set.

Imtiaz sat back and quickly finished a glass of water before wiping his brow with a towel.

'Only ten minutes Ammi[3]! Sachin is batting…' said Rahil pleadingly.

'No! Get up and go now,' Fatima said turning off the television and dragging Rahil out of the room.

'Take this nimbu-paani[4] Abba[5]; it will help to refresh you. I made your favourite kadi-rice today,' Aaliyah said walking in with a smile and handing him a tall glass of the drink. 'Thanks beti[6], sit down. How is your new bunch of rascals this year? Are they much like the unruly bunch of last year?'

Sultangarh was an industrial town and the political bastion of Sanjay Shukla, a wily old politician from an aristocratic business family. The Shuklas ran a leather goods factory, a steel mill and a number of businesses from petrol pumps in the district to schools, a hospital and convenience stores.

'They are no different from the last one Abba. The parents are keen to see their children educated but it doesn't help when they themselves have little education. The child's development at

---

[3]Mum
[4]Lemonade
[5]Dad
[6]Daughter

home suffers...all they do is run around and play in the streets.'

'True, I don't know when our Sultangarh is going to change. Most of these children drop out of school...the few that pass the state board exams do not go to college. Look at Salim's son, Shakir. He finished school with you but he is repairing mopeds in his father's shop despite being a top ranker in our district. What can we do?' Shakir and Aaliyah were fond of each other but their blossoming affection went kaput after she left for Kanpur to do her Masters and he stayed back to work in his ailing father's garage.

'You don't do anything! Go to your school, come home and complain about the rest of the world going to the dogs. Worry about what's happening in your own home...' Fatima snapped at him as Aaliyah got up to go inside.

'What happened now? I'm doing the best I can to meet the expenditure,' he said, exasperated by her constant nagging.

'I'm talking about our daughter,' she retorted, cornering him into a discussion.

'What do we do? There is no one in this community as beautiful, well-mannered and easy-going as our Aaliyah. Very few girls are as educated and intelligent as she is.'

Aaliyah was standing behind the curtain in the next room listening to her parents discuss her future. Over the past couple of years, many young men and their families had come to see her. Though a lot of them showed interest initially, they all backed out given that her father had little to offer in the form of dowry. Of late she had begun to get proposals from divorced men in Kanpur through her aunt, and there was a rich widower in Sultangarh whom her father had turned down.

'You turned down Rahim's proposal. What is wrong with him? He's only thirty-five. At least she can live a comfortable life.' Fatima spoke accusingly, not in favour of Imtiaz's decision.

'It is not about him being a widower—he is uneducated. My daughter is an MA gold medallist. She deserves better,' he said.

'Yes, you sit and keep dreaming all your life! That Rahim has three cars, his own factory and four servants at home. At least she won't have to break her back like I have to in this house. So many boys have come and gone. MBAs, engineers, doctors and lawyers, but we have nothing to give!'

Aaliyah felt flustered and began to get upset. She blamed herself for the stress that her parents were going through.

'If they are so great, why do they need money from us? Why can't they earn their living?' Imtiaz asked, scratching his beard.

'Yes, you keep making your comments on society. In another year or two even the proposals we get will stop coming!'

'What do you want me do? Rob a bank or kidnap someone?' he asked with some frustration. Fatima looked at him and smiled. She took out a photograph from the drawer and handed it to him.

'Who is this young man? Where did you get this photograph?' he asked looking at it with interest.

'Imran Karim. His family runs a number of shops in Dubai. Saba tells me he's a very good boy and his family is looking for a suitable match. They funded the repair of the mosque in Rajgarh last year and they do a lot of charity,' she said with a portly grin.

'But we don't know these people. Yes, I've heard of the Karim family and their good fortune but we don't know what these people are like. Send our little girl there … I don't know.' He leaned forward, looking worried. Thinking of his delicate and innocent Aaliyah leaving the country was too much for him.

'He is only thirty; he runs a business of his own and the family lives together in a big apartment. Saba says they are well-to-do. Her cousin is married to his older brother.'

'Why doesn't your sister-in-law get her own daughter married to him?'

'She is trying to help us and here you begin accusing Saba! What is there if our daughter can go away and lead a better life?' she asked persuasively.

'I don't know. Let them come down and meet us. Let's get to know who these people are.'

'Saba says all we can manage is meeting his uncle who lives here. If we want to, we can go to Dubai. The family just made a trip here last year and they won't come for another year or two.'

'This is a big decision in our daughter's life. What are you suggesting?'

'Imran is busy setting up a new business. If we accept the rishta then the nikah[7] has to take place on the phone...'

'That is outrageous! I don't know who this boy is and what he does. Besides, he is thirty while our child is only twenty-three. It is a big difference! Why can't we wait?'

'Wait for whom? Look at this picture, he looks so young. He doesn't look a day more than twenty-five,' she said with a raised eyebrow.

'We cannot do the nikah on the phone! Why can't he fly down for the wedding? We haven't met these people and you expect me to pick up my daughter and send her away like that...'

'Because you know how expensive it is! The entire family has to fly. Saba tells me it costs more than ten thousand for one person to come and go! Look, they are not even asking for any money. They took Aaliyah's photograph from her and they really like our Aaliyah. It is her good fortune.'

Imtiaz sat back and looked deeply worried. He gazed at his

---

[7]Wedding ceremony

wife with confusion. He scratched his beard again and sat back folding his arms. 'What about Shakir? His father has already asked me and I told him I'll think about it. He has lived here and he went to school with Aaliyah; it will be easier. Our daughter will also be close to us.'

'Nonsense, what did he do after school? They have no money at all. They are also indebted to a lot of money lenders. What kind of a life can he give her?' she asked challenging him.

'He is a sincere boy; at least they are of the same age. With her working as well, I feel they'll manage fine.'

Aaliyah smiled, thinking about a future with Shakir. She still ran into him a few times on the way to the school or in the bazaar and they exchanged greetings. She began to blush, thinking about her future and the prospect of a life with Shakir whom she found dignified and attractive.

'That's what I believed! That we'll manage and we will be okay. What happened?' Fatima asked bitterly.

Imtiaz turned his gaze away from her to the old bookshelf on the other side of the room. 'Well, in that case let our Aaliyah decide then. I will agree to whatever she decides. It's time for my prayers; I'm going to the mosque,' he said submissively, getting up to leave.

Fatima went into her bedroom and called out for Aaliyah to join her. Aaliyah had overheard the discussion and made up her mind to say yes to Shakir's rishta. She was uncomfortable with the prospect of getting married to someone unknown who had grown up in a land she had just heard about.

'Aaliyah beti, see there is this offer from this boy Imran in Dubai. His family is very well-to-do and they don't want anything from us. You are very fortunate; his aunt saw you at Hajira's wedding and sent your pictures to his parents in Dubai. They really like you and have told Saba that they don't want their son to marry anyone but you.'

'But Ammi, how can I say anything? It would be different had I met him and his parents. Besides, I feel Shakir…' she began meekly.

'Nonsense, don't talk about Shakir! You'll end up working like a dog to feed him and his large family. They are under a lot of debt. He's got two younger sisters and a younger brother, a lot of responsibilities! Look at Imran's picture, he looks so young despite being thirty and you can lead a comfortable life.'

'It's difficult Ammi! Going so far away…to a different country,' Aaliyah said, looking confused.

'I left Adilabad and came here with your father twenty-five years ago. I saw him and his family for the first time at the nikah. There is nothing wrong; we all go through it! Your father is a good man but we have struggled so much. As a mother, I'm suggesting what is best and most comfortable for you. You won't even have a room to yourself in Shakir's home.'

'Let me think about it, Ammi; I'll give you my answer tomorrow,' she said taking Imran's picture and gazing at it intently. He was not good-looking like Shakir but had pleasant features and didn't seem like a bad prospect.

Aaliyah said her prayers and got into bed after dinner but could not sleep. This was the hardest decision of her life. She had to choose between someone she knew and desired and someone who had better opportunities in life and prospects of a better future. She remembered the things her father had said and the advice her mother gave her. She twisted and turned in bed in a disturbed state of mind. She realised that with either of them she would face some type of struggle. She thought about which one would be easier to face for the rest of her life.

The next morning, while she served her father his cup of tea, he took her hand and gently beckoned her to sit next to him. 'Beti, with whatever you decide there will be challenges. Listen to your heart,' he said, gazing at her with affection.

'Yes Abba, I will think carefully and decide,' she said, managing to smile.

She went to school in a troubled state and thought about the choices she had and the advice her parents had given her. She spent an hour at lunch talking to Shilpa and Tasneem, who were her friends and colleagues in school, discussing her future.

She came home an hour earlier than usual and went up to her mother who was making dinner in the kitchen. 'Ammi, I've made up my mind. You can accept the rishta from Imran's family. I'm ready to marry him,' she said with some hesitation.

'Wonderful! You don't know how worried I've been all day. May God give you all the happiness and blessings you deserve! Let me go to Premchand's shop and call Saba to give her the good news!' she said after embracing her daughter and kissing her. 'You better start eating properly; people in Dubai will think we don't feed our daughter.' Fatima smiled at an emotional Aaliyah before leaving the house.

◆

The wedding date was scheduled a month after Aaliyah had made her decision. Her parents pulled out all stops to ensure they were doing the best for her and were busy organizing a reception for over two hundred guests. Most of them were from Imran's family and would be coming in to celebrate and participate in the wedding from nearby towns. Her father had taken six months' advance from Mr Chaudhari to meet the mounting expenses related to the wedding while Aaliyah was spending all her savings on buying a wedding dress and the little jewellery that she could afford.

While walking home through the bazaar after school a week before her wedding, Shakir stopped her by the grocery store.

'Salaam[8] Aaliyah, how are you? How are your Ammi and Abba?' he asked softly looking nervous.

'Salaam Shakir, we are all fine. How is everyone at home?' she asked with a friendly smile.

'They are the same. I wanted to talk to you Aaliyah,' he said turning his gaze away from her.

'Yes tell me,' she replied with an eager smile. He looked at her intently wondering whether to go on.

'I have never told you this but I really like you. I didn't know how to say it, given you know everything about our family's problems. I hear you have agreed to marry someone in Dubai. Please don't do that Aaliyah; please change your decision. I have got a job at a Honda Service Station in Kanpur for a salary of Rs 8,000. I was in Kanpur looking for a job when all of this happened. I came back this morning and heard about your rishta.' He spoke with sincerity and desperation to hold on to a dream that might be fading before his eyes.

'I don't know what to say Shakir. I wish this could have happened earlier, I don't know! Anyway, I have accepted the rishta and will be getting married to Imran next week. I'm sorry but my parents and I have given our word!' she explained with some difficulty. She could not bear to look at the pain in his eyes on hearing this. 'Take care of yourself Shakir; anyone who marries you will be lucky,' she said sweetly before walking away down the dusty track, while Shakir stood dumbfounded, watching her disappear among the many faces in the crowded bazaar.

---

[8]Greetings

◆

Four weeks later, Aaliyah walked out of the Dubai Airport with a trolley loaded with a large suitcase and a few small bags. She wore a bright pink outfit and jewellery from head to toe. Her mother had also got her to put henna again as she was a newly-wed going to her husband's home for the first time.

'Aaliyah, salaam!' She turned around to see a balding and pot-bellied version of the Imran she had seen in the picture. She stepped back for a moment in shock, unable to recognize him for a moment and then realizing how different he looked from the picture she saw.

'What's the matter? Don't you recognize your husband?' he said with a nervous grin. He now sported an unruly long beard and had puffy eyes.

'Salaam, Imran,' she said trying not to look disappointed while he pushed her trolley towards the car park.

'Hope your journey was comfortable. Let's leave quickly as Ajman is a little far away and traffic in the evening causes a lot of delays,' he said, while putting her suitcase in the boot of a dusty old Toyota.

'Ajman?'

'Yes, that is where our home is. It is thirty kilometres from here. Our family has a number of shops there.' She got in quietly cursing her fate.

'What kind of business do you manage?' she asked after a lengthy silence, while he navigated through peak hour traffic.

'I run a service centre for used cars. I also sell spare parts,' he said in a matter-of-fact way. She noticed the roads were getting narrower and the neighbourhood beginning to look more like Sultangarh back home.

For Convenience's Sake

PARITOSH UTTAM

'What hat strikes you most and what you will remember about it is the sheer magnitude of scale, the mammoth proportions involved. Imagine a bridge a mile long, carrying a road hundred feet wide for an annual traffic of millions of cars, another ten feet of walkways on either side for millions of pedestrians and the whole structure supported by two gigantic towers,' he said, sketching the suspension bridge on a paper for clarification. 'Made in the 1930s, mind you.'

'Wow!' Madhuri could not help exclaiming aloud, her eyes flitting momentarily to the sketch, but otherwise staying focused on his face, filled with wonder. The way he said 'mammoth' and 'gigantic' excited her.

'It's not just that. You would think that a colossal thing like that would certainly be imposing, but an ugly blot on the landscape. Nothing could be more wrong. From your vantage point on the bridge, which would be 200 feet above the water, you look up and see the azure sky, the turquoise-blue Pacific on one side and the San Francisco Bay on to other; you feel like you are floating with the clouds, no longer on terra firma. Indeed, you feel the whole bridge swaying…' he trailed off, his own voice shaking. 'Actually, it does sway, being suspended on cables. So that it can withstand earthquakes, you know.'

'And is it golden?' asked my Maddykins, coquettish as ever. It was the first time she heard someone using words like azure and terra firma in actual conversation.

'No, the Golden Gate is orange,' he said. 'That's funny, right? But it forms a good contrast with the blues, browns and greys of the surrounding landscape.'

I could imagine the bridge reflected in her eyes, its dimensions diminished a million times, but its grandeur intact, just as I could imagine their entire conversation, his voice clothing her dreams in gossamer. Hey Madhuri, Maddy darling, sweet Maddykins, in the name of all that was bright and beautiful, and warm and wonderful, why did you go?

'Are you listening, Prashant?'

'Huh?'

'I thought so,' Meghna said. 'You wanted to meet me, right? And now it looks as if I am boring you.'

The similarity to her sister was striking. I had invited her to meet me at Flury's, regarding it as a quiet and respectable place to suit the purpose I had in mind. The more compelling reason was that I didn't want to meet her at any of the other places that would remind me of Madhuri. There were very few places left in Kolkata that Madhuri and I had not been to, and Flury's was a notable exception. Meghna sounded suspicious on the phone, but I was both insistent and pleading, and she assumed nothing untoward could happen in a popular place like Flury's. Her voice had the same gentle, bullying tone as that of a pampered child, as her sister's, demanding to be placated. I hastened to do so, as I had done on countless occasions with Madhuri.

'No, not at all—I am listening. So she is now in California with her husband?'

'That's what I said. They went a month ago.'

'What does he do?'

'I don't know which company he works for exactly. But he did mention some start-up in the Silicon Valley.'

'What else?' I said, failing to keep the bitterness out of my voice.

She winced, as if she tasted the acerbity in the air.

'What do you mean?'

'Suppose we quit acting Meghna. You very well know what your sister meant to me.'

'I know Madhuri and you were friends.'

'Friends!' She could not have picked a more touchy word if she had wanted to. 'Just friends,' I shouted, as if by raising my voice and repeating, I could convey my hurt and sarcasm. 'What's wrong with you people?' I continued. 'That's what she wrote in her last letter—"We shall always be friends." From where do these "always" and "friends" come suddenly? What do they mean anyway?'

'Look, I don't—'

'No, you look here, Meghna.'

I could not stop myself now. This was not the way I had intended it to be. The vague picture I had in mind was of myself sitting composed and stoical throughout, my face depicting the self-restraint and forbearance of a tragic hero, with an untouched cup of coffee by my side. She would sense the suffering behind my impassive mask and realize with a shock how much I had been wronged and the baseness of her sister's act. But that was not how it was happening.

I found myself talking on and on without a pause as if each word that came out carried away with it some unknown weight from my heart. I uttered words, of which I became aware only after they had tumbled off my tongue. I spoke as if I would never be able to speak again if I stopped now.

'Perhaps it was just friendship that made us so glad to be in each other's company. And it was because of our friendship that we went to the movies so that for a few hours we could be hidden in our own world, alone in the crowd, shoulder resting against shoulder, palm clasping sweaty palm in the darkness. And the dozens of Hallmarks cards and letters with hearts and loves and dreams and wishes and darlings and sweetie-pies we wrote, each trying to be sillier than the other. And the unforgettable walks along the beach with the hot sunburnt sand under our bare feet swept away now and then by the chill white surf of the waves. And overhead the sea breeze that would suddenly push a massive cloud to block out the sun over us. And we could see that we were standing in the cool shade of the cloud while outside it the sand burnt as if our love was being protected from above. And as we walked, grasping hands tightly, she holding her sandals in her free hand and I carrying my shoes in mine, we did not speak because there was no need to speak to express our happiness because we knew we were happy. Oh God, that was the happiest moment ever in my life and words were so inadequate…'

In the name of all that was bright and beautiful, and warm and wonderful, why did you go?

As I spoke, my wounds appeared to me deeper and fresher. I grew convinced of the injustice I had suffered—as it happens when you are not sure of your opinions, the more you hear yourself reiterating them, the more convinced you become. Suddenly, it seemed so easy to surrender and be carried along in the torrent of self-pity.

'And now, my Maddykins becomes mature in a span of two months. This is what she writes, "…I was immature then. I see now that we can never be more than friends, since I have always thought of you only as a good friend. Your friend always, Madhuri."

'Why go through this entire friendship circus when she could say directly, "Look, I am going to throw myself at the first proposal that comes my way from USA, because I have to see the Golden Gate and the Empire State Building and the Grand Canyon and Las Vegas and all the skyscrapers and the highways. You, my dear friend Prashant, can go jump into a well because you like to live in your dirty, stinking hellhole called India. If you think I am going to share it with you, you are thinking wrong."

'And all the while poor Prashant is wondering what went wrong where. You know why your sister behaved like that? Just for convenience's sake.'

My monologue had deprived Meghna of speech for the past ten minutes.

'It's not all in black-and-white, as you put it,' she said, finding her tongue at last.

I carried on, as if she had never spoken.

'As if I could not have gone to the US had I wanted to? India might be a stupid frustrating country, but it's my stupid frustrating country. I don't mind living in the heat and dust and inefficiency. But she could not bear it; no, not when her eyes were clouded by the misty spray of the Niagara and her conscience drowned in its roar, in her imagination.

'On the one hand there is the beauty and attraction of the unseen and the unexplored and on the other there is disillusionment and the stark truth of life experienced and seen. Life here is sweating in the sun and choking in the smoke, there it is pleasant, smooth and noiseless. Of course, convenience wins hands down. So for convenience's sake, she kills her conscience, negates her own earlier feelings and even convinces herself that it does not matter who she sleeps with the rest of her life because that way she would be repaying him for providing her a comfortable life and—'

'Shut up!' Meghna was standing, self-righteous indignation glowering from her eyes. 'So what have you got against convenience? That anything obtained easily is undeserved and immoral?'

'Think of her this way. She could not have been independent either here or there, she would have to share someone else's happiness—either his or yours. You feel that she would not really be sharing his life or happiness, only reflecting it. There would be nothing of her own.'

'How would it be different had she chosen you? It's your decision based on your feelings and your principles that makes you stay here. Perhaps she did not think the same way as you. Perhaps you find it soothing for your ego when people point at you and say, "That's Prashant, he could have gone to the US, but he did not because he wanted to stay here." Would anyone say that she could have married and gone abroad, but she decided to marry and live here? It was always all about you, what was there for her to be happy about, except bask in your reflected glory?'

'You criticize my sister for seeking convenience and comfort,' she said, well into her stride. It was her turn to shut me out with her speech. Her voice was loud, and people at the other tables were beginning to turn around. This was not the usual scene at Flury's and I was getting flustered. 'But what about you? Since you opt for a materially less comfortable life, you feel morally justified in all your thoughts and actions. When you return home after work, you look for a doting wife to keep your home happy. Everything divided into neat, convenient compartments—this provides you moral satisfaction, that mental and physical.

'You seek appreciation and admiration at work and at home. Who would appreciate her? Not even you, for you would take her servitude and love for granted, as her duty. You might find satisfaction in seeing yourself struggling, plodding on against the odds, for the sake of your principles. You find some masochistic pleasure in your self-pity, playing the victim, the martyr who keeps up a brave front. Why should you expect her to do the same? You…'

I did not hear her last words because I had hurried out, even forgetting to call for the bill. An ego is a fragile thing; it needs all the protection it can get. It has to be packed in cotton wool for you cannot live with a fractured ego.

Outside the air-conditioning, the humidity was oppressive. I felt sorry for myself.

In the name of all that was bright and beautiful, and warm and wonderful, why did you go away forsaking me?

I stood on the sidewalk, deciding where to go next. The sun was still there and so were the trees. The sun did not feel as hot as it usually did, nor did the leaves look as green. But that's all right, a little coldness and a little dullness in the air won't kill me; I think I'll live.

You're Mine

SIDDHARTHA LAL

I make myself comfortable in a corner of the couch, my back resting against the arm rest. You're lying on top of me, an arm dropping loosely to the side, your face very close to mine. So close that I can make out the nuances of all the expressions playing across it, even the quizzical look in your eyes which seems to say, 'I do not know why you're saying this, but I love you too much to complain anyway.' Your breasts rest gently against my stomach and they make my navel tingle with nervous excitement. Several small beads of sweat glisten on your back in the warmth of the room. Some of them come together and, tracing symmetrical geometrical patterns, run down your spine to your hips. A cheap cigarette dies a slow death in my hand, ash waiting to be flicked to the ground. Every now and then, when you turn your head to find a more comfortable nook, your lips brush against mine, willing me to kiss them. But I hold myself back. I had sworn it would always have to be you.

I like the fact that my senses receive a new lease of life each time your head heaves gently on my chest, rising and falling slowly, in tandem with my laboured breathing. I inhale the woody fragrance of your freshly washed hair and marvel at its rich and luscious bouquet. You have let your tresses fall loose and they cascade in dark ripples, covering your bare arms with their modest silkiness, but exposing the nape of your neck. I absentmindedly run my free hand through them, thinking of all the conversations we had shared and all the promises we had never made to each other. None of us speaks and the silence seems to be emptying out the little space between us.

The curves of your body are all so sensual that I feel a force rising up inside me. And yet, you seem too preoccupied to notice any of this. I choke on my tears and pretend to cough a little in order to hide the obvious from you. Not that you would care. But you do. You look up, our eyes are locked in an embrace for a second, and I try to smile. Comforted, you shift ever so slightly and go back to your thoughts, the payal jingling in appreciation. It is the lone piece of jewellery adorning your body and I feel overwhelmed by its presence. I put out the cigarette and hold you just a little bit tighter, surprising myself, and you sigh contentedly in response, as if in a world of your own.

You look so serene that I hate to even touch you for fear of upsetting some delicate equilibrium. The turmoil in my mind is in sharp conflict with the peace you refuse to share with me. I kiss your eyes, rousing you. The light is dim, just the way I want it. It gently caresses your face, highlighting only the features I have come to accept as mine. And before Ghalib runs out of words, I decide to script a few of my own. I contemplate them, mulling over them as they come to my mind, before letting you know. You look at me expectantly, and so I begin my assault on your patience.

'We don't have much time left, Chandni.'

You rub your eyes and force the last remnant of half-dreamt dreams out of them.

'What do you mean? It's still one in the night. I don't have to leave till morning.'

I smile wickedly at your innocence (or is it ignorance?) and cup your face in my hands.

'That's not what I meant. It's time we went back to our lives. This cannot continue forever, you know.'

'I knew you had to pick up some subject like this. Why can't you just let us be? And who says it has to anyway Siddhartha? When we first started out, didn't you promise me you'd make things work? I believed in you then and I believe in you now.'

Saying this, you try to put an end to the conversation. But I am relentless and, holding your chin up to my face, kiss you tenderly on the lips.

'Yes, I did. And I would have, at any cost. But, you see, I am dying. And the strength to carry on has left me.'

This time you sit up, your legs entangled in mine. However, the discomfort of such a position does not bother you.

'What do you mean?'

'I'm dying. A few more months, maybe. It's cancer and, you see, I am still thirty-eight tonight.'

'Is this a joke? Because if it is, I do not want to be a part of it. I get enough of them where I come from.'

'I wish it was.'

I'm smiling now, and the tranquillity which I had envied switches bodies deftly. Your hair is trussed up and you look wild with passion.

'This is insane. It can't be. I can't let it be. I won't. And you're telling me this now?'

Tears well up in your eyes and I wipe them away before they can mar your beauty with their sadness.

'I had wanted to tell you earlier. But I was too weak, Chandni.

I could not bear to let you go. But I can't be selfish anymore. I won't let you suffer through this with me. I owe you that.'

'Oh, you're being so melodramatic,' you sob softly. 'Everything can be cured. I am sure you haven't tried hard enough, the tragic hero that you are. Uff. I will have to deal with this as well for you.'

'Believe me, I have. If not for my sake, then yours. But this is inevitable now. And since it is, it's best we do the right thing. For both of us. And that would be to put an end, not to our romance but to our story. Begin afresh. Don't feel guilty about anything, for you did nothing wrong. I never did get all your love and I still believe it's welled up inside, waiting for someone better.'

'And who would that be Siddhartha? Don't do this to me. Please. I deserve better than this. I want to be with you forever.'

'Shush. Don't be so tragic that you become a part of my tragedy. I won't be at peace if you cry. I can't say I will be if you're happy. But at least that will be something worth fighting for. Remember, learn to deal with memories without having to deal with the past.'

You're sobbing now. In short fitful bursts. The kajal is running down your cheeks in small rivulets. I clean the mess and some of it comes off on my fingers. You try to smile, but fail miserably. I smile instead and hold you closer still. You finally agree to rest your head against my shoulder and I begin.

'It's okay. You always knew my shelf life had an expiry date of forty years. Didn't you? When I'm here you think it's impossible. But when I am gone, moving on will be so much easier. So will letting go, I believe.'

'You know nothing about what you're saying. We wouldn't be here, dangling in each other's insecurities, if it was that easy.'

'Yes, I guess so. But you'll try. Won't you?'

'What options do you leave me with? You won't agree to anything I have to say. And I have always felt helpless around you.

Oh darling, this is so much more difficult than I make it seem.'

I feel jealous, for you've always been the person I could never be—strong, confident, resolute, happy and alive. But I detest my own pangs and continue.

'It doesn't have to be difficult, and the reason I am having this dialogue is because I will not let it be. I guess it'll hit you when you're least secure. But you'll be ready for it. Trust me when I say this. I've known you long enough. But before I let you go, I want you to tell me the story of our lives. In your own words. Start at the beginning, for that is always the easiest. Tell me everything. I want to relive it all. Paint it with as many colours as you can. Run wild with your imagination and don't leave out even the smallest detail. Could you do that for me?'

'What is this? Some kind of a game?'

'Humour me.'

You nod and, with a gentle sigh, plunge into your exquisite narrative. The details are fantastic and their quality surreal. It seems as if they're projecting a black and white movie on the canvas of my senses. Frame by frame, our story unravels—a story which I purportedly remembered so vividly, but had obviously relegated to some nondescript corner of my memory.

The people come alive and emotions are felt once more, their bite more tangible than ever. The plots, the subplots and their umpteen characters are sketched to perfection and it seems you had been lying all along, pretending to forget, so that you could goad me into telling my version of things. You sigh, you smile, you wish and you yearn. The night seems to dilate in order to accommodate the vividness of your narration and, by the time it ends, I have lived another life in the span of a few hours. You're exhausted and parched.

'Should I make a cup of tea for my lady?'

'Shut up and kiss me. And don't leave me wanting for more.'

I am agreeably surprised but I oblige, and for a few moments the world shrinks to the space that separates us. A buzzing sound disturbs this strange union. I reach out for your phone and recognize the number.

'It's your son. He says Avinash has been asking about you ever since he came back from work. Tell him you'll be home in half an hour. I'll get you that tea.'

I get up and start banging the cheap steel utensils, perhaps a tad too loudly, proclaiming my ineptitude with those alien objects to the world at large and to you in particular. Some of the tea leaves cling to the rim of the pot as the froth boils over. I pour the brew down the sieve to the sound of sobbing in the washroom. The toilet is flushed in order to mask the more violent outbursts. Three times. I grab the can of cookies you had brought for me last month and notice that it's empty.

'It's ready,' I say, re-entering the room, but you've already left. A green post-it note is stuck to my pack of Gold Flakes. 'You're mine. Not just yours. *Samjhe*?' it says. Overcome, I sit down and light up. Then, realizing the enormity of the occasion, I drink my first cup of tea.

The Girlfriend

NARENDRANATH MITRA

TRANSLATED BY ARUNAVA SINHA

After leaving his office, Bibhupada paused at the magazine stand at Esplanade. Several other people had gathered there too. All kinds of magazines in different languages—English, Bengali, Hindi and Urdu—were available. Different readers with different tastes, they were all to be found here. Most of the customers were leafing through the magazines; they did not seem to have any intention of buying them. Some had opened the film magazines to gape at the actresses' photographs inside. They wouldn't relinquish the magazines until the shopkeeper snarled at them. There were all kinds of people in the world. Some people were utterly shameless. But those who only looked discreetly did feel embarrassed. You could spot all sorts of characters if you stopped by such shops sometimes. Watching people's behaviour dispassionately could be quite interesting. Time flew by quickly and besides, you could add to your experience without much effort. But Bibhupada was not particularly interested in augmenting his experience at this moment. He kept scanning the roads. How could you relax when someone who was supposed to have arrived at ten past, or at most a quarter past, five was still not here at five-thirty? Bibhupada could not relax either. What was taking Sheela so long? She was never so late. In fact, sometimes she arrived five or six minutes early and waited for him. It was Bibhupada who was late at times. But it was just the opposite today; he had arrived first, counting the minutes and seconds as he waited, but the leader had become the laggard. Bibhupada glanced at his watch once more. Five-forty. No, Sheela probably wouldn't come today.

And yet Sheela herself had made this appointment two days earlier. She would meet him here at Esplanade at a quarter past five. They would cross the road and enter one of the restaurants on the eastern side, sit in one of the curtained-off cabins and eat something—a chop or a cutlet with tea—whichever Sheela preferred. There were days when her face suggested she was famished after a hard day's work at the office. On such days he ordered curry and rotis for her instead of a cutlet. He himself was a small eater. He didn't eat meat very often, since he neither enjoyed it nor digested it well. But Bibhupada loved to play host to those who ate well, those who loved eating. After the meal, they would take a walk by the river. Or stop at Eden Gardens to chat. Bibhupada preferred good old Eden Gardens to the modern Dhakuria Lakes. The memory of his youth was entwined around this garden. In his college days, he used to come here often with his classmates; they would argue about all sorts of things for hours on end. All those friends had become invisible now. Some of them were physically present in the city, of course, but Bibhupada was no longer in touch with them. This was probably the law of ageing. Bibhupada had not yet crossed fifty, but the world had already created a forest for him to retire into. People don't have to go to the Dooars or to the jungles of Madhya Pradesh in search of forests;

their friends and family themselves turn into trees and mountains and cliffs. Those who can find glades or hermitages amidst those forests can survive; the others have to spend the rest of their lives battling with the beasts in the jungle. Bibhupada had those battles too. He had cliques to fight at the office. Even if you did not want to attack others you had to defend yourself from them. He could not afford everything his family needed; he had to wage a superhuman struggle every day to keep the expenses of feeding, clothing, supporting and educating his wife and children under control. It wasn't as though the engine of the household didn't threaten to break down now and then. But even amidst all this, Bibhupada had still managed to create a small glade, an arbour for himself. The name of that flower-bedecked garden of eternal spring was Sheela Dattagupta. Actually, this flower-bedecked dell was also a creation of Bibhupada's own fancies, desires and dreams—for Sheela was neither beautiful, nor in possession of the unbridled physical exuberance of youth. Her oval face was sweet however. Looking into her large black eyes made Bibhupada think of a sea of dreams. But there was none of the infinite lustre of the young woman in Sheela's underdeveloped, tall, slender frame. Just as she came from a poor family, so too did she lack in physical beauty. Had Sheela been a little prettier, Bibhupada would have enjoyed the vision of her a little more. But since she was not, there was no use rueing it! There was no choice but to accept that, man or woman, no one had any control over their own beauty; everything here was subservient to nature, dependent on it. Nature bestowed attractiveness in abundance on some people; to others she gave but a few drops of it; to yet others not even that. Of course, no one considered it nature's whimsy any more. Biology must have a logical explanation for why a particular young woman is not beautiful. But how would Bibhupada benefit from memorizing this explanation?

After all, he could not use it to transform a homely woman into a beautiful one. He could, however, sit by her side in silence on a bench in the Eden Gardens in the dim, dark evening, or take her hand in his while sitting on the paved ground by the river and gazing at the stars in the sky, the current in the river and the endless necklace of light in the distance, crossing the frontier of death to be transcended into an infinite realm of beauty beyond it.

Bibhupada had similar expectations of this evening. After a cup of tea with Sheela, he would take her out. If a taxi was to be found a taxi it would be, else a phaeton or even a rickshaw would do. Sheela was afraid of riding in a phaeton. Who knew what tales she had heard, but a deep terror about phaetons had been entrenched in her. Apparently, to ride in those carriages was to court extreme danger. The coachman would spirit them away somewhere, extort money from them; who knew, he could rob and plunder them too. Still, Bibhupada had managed to get Sheela into a phaeton on a few occasions. He had no objections to the phaeton. He was content with any manner of transportation except the bullock-cart. As long as he had company, he never bothered about where and how he was travelling. He lost himself completely in his female companion. And it was to lose himself for some time that he sought a companion. The woman was just the pretext. Whether she was beautiful or not was irrelevant; a feminine name was sufficient.

Bibhupada had decided not to insist on anything too strongly today. There was no hope of securing a taxi after five in the evening. If Sheela did not want to get into a phaeton, let her not. If she was embarrassed to take a rickshaw, if she was afraid of being seen by someone she knew, he wouldn't summon a rickshaw. He would walk down to the river with her. They would sit side by side on the steps leading down to the water, gaze at the sky and the water. The sight of ships floating on the water would make them dream of travelling to a distant land. They wouldn't even realize how an hour or two would pass in a flash. Then, on the way back, if they were fortunate enough to find a taxi they would take it; if not, a rickshaw; if that wasn't available either, there was always the foot bus. At Esplanade he would see Sheela off into a bus for Shyambazar and himself take a tram to Kalighat.

Not every day—Bibhupada's routine of the restaurant followed by a promenade with his young girlfriend took place two or three, or at most four, times a month. It did mean some expenses, of course. He compensated for it by being thrifty in other ways. Bibhupada never tired of the taste of mixed fear, apprehension, affection and love secreted in these assignations. In fact, the warmth he gathered from his intimate proximity to a young woman supplied him with energy for the entire week.

Colleagues of his age had an inkling of what was going on. There was much joking and laughter over this weakness of his.

'Well, Majumdar, how is the evening promenade going?' some would ask. 'How do you manage? Doesn't Mrs Majumdar suspect anything? Doesn't she create a scene?'

Bibhupada wouldn't answer clearly. 'What rubbish you people talk,' he would smile.

'This is the real elixir of life,' Sehanobish from accounts would observe. 'Haven't you seen how Majumdar doesn't have a single grey hair even though he's over fifty? How well he has maintained his body—strong, robust and proud. All thanks to those evening promenades. The blessing of the female company he keeps.'

Bibhupada neither admitted nor denied any of this. 'What rubbish,' he protested mildly, embarrassed.

Bibhupada knew that Sheela's company brought him warmth and joy. She had a lovely, melodious voice. He would express his regret that she had not trained to become a singer despite such a beautiful voice.

Making do with sugar in the absence of honey, Bibhupada would cajole her to recite poetry if she wouldn't sing. Sheela seldom complied with his request. 'I simply cannot memorize poetry,' she would say, 'I'm just not up to that kind of thing.'

Still, it was a sweet melody that floated into Bibhupada's ears. Even a discussion on the price of eggs in that voice sounded like poetry. The young woman was bereft of most qualities; the only fortune she possessed was an exquisite voice.

Bibhupada moved away from the magazine-stand and continued to wait. When it turned ten past six, there was no more hope. Sheela wasn't coming this evening. But if she wasn't going to come she could easily have telephoned. The phone was within easy reach. Didn't she remember he was waiting for her? Surely Sheela had no idea how difficult it was to just wait for someone for an hour or more.

Bibhupada walked up to Curzon Park and sat down on a bench. It had another shareholder, who stood up immediately, relinquishing his rights. Bibhupada was pleased at being able to occupy an entire bench all by himself. He would sit here for a while. Not for any other reason, but simply to wait for the trams and buses to become a little less packed. Once the crowd thinned down, Bibhupada would be able to take a tram easily, even find a seat. That would be his only gain today.

The rest of the time had proved a complete loss. Was Bibhupada still young enough to waste his time in expectation of the arrival of a woman? He could have used the time in other ways. If he had behaved like the perfect head of the family instead and bought a whole fish from the market on his way back home, his wife and children would have been pleased. The evening would have passed pleasantly enough over a cup of tea in the company of his near and dear ones. Bibhupada would have been spared this feeling of hopelessness, depression and humiliation.

Really, Bibhupada himself didn't know what attraction had kept him chained, why he had made a rather ordinary young woman an intrinsic part of his life. He had known Sheela for about three years—but had their relationship progressed in this long period anywhere beyond spending some time together, having a cup of tea, chatting, or, rarely, watching a film? Sheela hadn't allowed it to. And Bibhupada had not had the courage to proceed against her will. It wasn't just a lack of courage either. His sensibilities had prevented him. What was the point of forcing himself on her, he had concluded. If it had just been a case of physical desire, there were other ways to attend to it. But Bibhupada did not seek naked fulfilment of his libido. He preferred to keep his desire hidden under a beautiful multicoloured wrapping. He could not possibly throw away his dignity before a woman half his age. It was better to bear the agony of remaining unfulfilled than to lose his prestige before a modern young woman.

'Really, I have never had a friend like you,' Sheela had often told him. 'I don't have even one other well-wisher like you.'

Bibhupada'd had to remain content with such faint praise.

'Believe me,' Sheela had said, 'I cannot go to anyone as freely as I can to you. I don't wander around the city with anyone else, I don't spend hours chatting with anyone else either.'

In other words, Sheela wanted to say that she had given Bibhupada what she had given no other man. But her gifts were rather paltry. Could any man feel glory in receiving so little, could his desire for conquest possibly be satiated this way?

'Don't you have any other men friends?' Bibhupada had asked her occasionally. 'Someone whom you have truly loved? Someone whom you have given not just your friendship but something more?

You can tell me freely, I will not be jealous.'

But Sheela had refused to accept that another man had ever come into her life. Nor was she particularly keen on it. She had little interest in young men. They were garrulous, flighty. She got no pleasure in conversing with those who had no experience whatsoever of life. It was impossible for her to even imagine any of them as her husband. 'But that isn't normal either,' Bibhupada had remarked.

'Then you'd better assume I'm abnormal,' Sheela had responded.

Bibhupada had tried to delve into the reasons behind this young woman's indifference. Hers was a lower middle-class family. She had lost her father when she was sixteen or seventeen. The responsibility of supporting a widowed mother and three younger brothers and sisters had fallen on her. She was a clerk at a post-office. Her salary was not sufficient for all the expenses of the family. She had to give private lessons to make up the deficit. Sheela had told Bibhupada everything. Was it this poverty, this unbearable burden of responsibility and fear that had gradually emptied Sheela's heart of all emotions, turning her into an ascetic in the prime of her life? Sympathy welled up in Bibhupada's heart.

But sometimes Sheela acted rather irrationally, like she had today. Was it right of her to have broken her promise this way? If she wasn't planning to come, couldn't she have telephoned to say so? Considering how she prattled on the phone, couldn't she have at least given him this information? Would he have turned up here had he known beforehand? And wasted so much time? Sheela really did behave stubbornly and unreasonably at times, as though she completely lacked the ability to appreciate other people's difficulties.

◆

The first thing Bibhupada did after signing the attendance register at his office the next morning was to telephone Sheela. There was pique, there were protests. There was a mild scolding too.

Sheela said she hadn't even been to office the day before. She had been cooped up at home all day. Bibhupada would learn the reason later. She was in a bind. She would tell him everything when they met. He should come to Esplanade after work and wait for her in front of the restaurant.

Bibhupada did not have to wait very long today. Sheela arrived in about five minutes.

He took her into a curtained-off cabin as usual. 'What'll you have?' he asked her lovingly.

'Just a cup of tea,' answered Sheela. 'I don't feel like anything else. I'm not hungry at all, believe me.'

'You have conquered all kinds of hunger and thirst,' Bibhupada smiled. 'I'm famished, however.'

'Why don't you eat something then?' Sheela said.

Bibhupada ordered chicken cutlets for both of them. 'What happened yesterday?' he asked. 'I waited for a long time. You didn't come. You could at least have informed me.'

'Didn't I tell you I couldn't even go to the office yesterday?' said Sheela. 'There's no phone nearby in the neighbourhood that I could have used. Besides, my mother was keeping a strict watch on me all day. I had no way to go out.'

'You weren't one to follow rules and regulations all this time,' said Bibhupada. 'What made you a dutiful daughter all of a sudden?'

Sheela was silent for a while. She seemed to be suppressing her laughter. Did anger not suit Bibhupada? Was his rage nothing but a source of mirth for a young woman?

Sheela looked at him after some time. 'If you'd heard the story, you'd have known how impossible it really was for me to have come out yesterday.'

'Why, what happened yesterday?' asked Bibhupada.

'The same old annoyance again,' responded Sheela. 'Bride-spotting. And not just a casual visit, but for the final approval this time. I quarrelled with my mother and younger brother almost all day over this. When I've already said I don't intend to marry, why this nuisance? But who's listening? Ma shouted loud enough for the entire neighbourhood to come running. What a scene! Finally I said, do as you please.'

Bibhupada sank into an abrupt silence. He had not imagined that something like this could have been the reason behind Sheela's absence. Yet how natural it was. This was the law of the world, Bibhupada mused—to meet one, you must part from another. After a bit he said, 'The semi-final must have taken place before the final. You never told me.'

'I certainly would have if it had been worth telling,' said Sheela. 'I had expected to avoid this one too, like before. But eventually I couldn't.'

'Just as well,' Bibhupada told her. 'What's the young man like? Is he handsome?'

'What do you think?' Sheela retorted. 'You could say we're made for each other. He passed his BA exam just the way I did, scraping through on the second or third try. He is the junior-most clerk in his company. His salary is five or ten rupees less, not more, than mine. But he has fewer encumbrances—just the one sister. She's a college student; I used to be her tutor. This is her tribute to her teacher. Reba is actually the matchmaker.'

'That explains it,' said Bibhupada. 'So you knew each other already.'

'It's not what you think,' answered Sheela. 'A familiar face, that was about all.'

'Is that the truth?' Bibhupada smiled.

'I've told you over and over again, romance just isn't in my nature.' Sheela said. 'I'm just a block of wood.'

'But still a wood primrose has bloomed,' said Bibhupada.

'People like you make it bloom,' answered Sheela after a pause.

Her voice was soft and sweet already. Gratitude seemed to make it even tenderer today.

'Do you recall what a trivial incident brought us together?' Sheela continued. 'I used to sell stamps at the post-office; I simply couldn't balance the accounts; I had to pay out of my own pocket to make up the deficit. You gave me an extra rupee by mistake one day. When you came again the next day, I called out to you to return it. That was how we met. It was you who took it all the way into a friendship. Would I ever have dared to?'

Bibhupada was silent. Sheela had never spoken to him this way before. All this time it had only been her voice that was sweet; what she said never held any particular sweetness. Every complaint she had against the universe assumed severe proportions as soon as she met Bibhupada. But still he was reminded of a few memories from monsoon and spring over these past three years—a few golden afternoons and silvery evenings.

But instead of referring to any of these, he suddenly brought up a prosaic subject, asking, 'But how will your mother's household run? I'm told your brother's still studying; your sisters are in school too.'

'That was exactly why I had objected,' Sheela told him. 'Let's wait another two or three years, I'd said. But my family is well-matched by the other side. All of them were adamant. But I have forced an agreement too. Until my brother is able to earn for himself, my entire salary will go to my family.'

'This I admit is a good arrangement,' said Bibhupada. 'But will it last?'

'Of course it will,' averred Sheela. 'Do you think the other agreement will remain if this one's broken?'

The waiter parted the curtains to serve the food. Sheela drew the plate to herself eagerly. Bibhupada smiled to himself. No matter what she might say, she must be starving.

Bibhupada cut a piece of his cutlet with great reluctance and speared it with his fork. Before raising it to his mouth, he said, 'This is the last time then. We won't meet again.'

'What! Why won't we meet again?' asked Sheela.

'You're getting married now,' Bibhupada told her. 'You'll have a new family.'

Sheela looked at Bibhupada, then said with a smile before raising a piece of her cutlet to her mouth, 'So what? If your having a family doesn't prevent anything, why should mine?'

Bibhupada raised his eyes. No, it wasn't sarcasm—the innocent, gentle amusement on her face was indeed making Sheela look lovely today.

Making Out

HINA SIDDIQUI

He was a good kisser.

Slow, soft, smooth—his eyes closed, hers barely open, his tongue running circles within, his breath heating her cheeks, his chest rising against hers—and he even managed to keep his nose out of the way.

They had been acquainted for two years, friends for a little longer, dating since the past half year and making out for the past ten minutes. He had taken his time getting there. Mutual confidants had assured her that he was just that kind of guy. And the way she could feel her body priming told her that the wait had been worth it.

So it came as a complete surprise when he pulled away and left her sitting alone against the cushions just as she had figured out how to undo his shirt without breaking the lip-lock. For a minute her mind couldn't compute—it had had other priorities just a bare minute ago and that combined with the watermelon daiquiris she had quaffed that night, made returning to any sort of logical thinking a little difficult. He was walking away now, towards the balcony, tucking his shirt back in—like that was going to save the evening. His back was towards her which, all things considered, was good, since she could look at him with uninhibited disgust. Seriously, wasn't he a bit too young for this shit?

Heaving a sigh, she too began to straighten her kurta, bringing her bra back in alignment with her breast. She had spent quite some time planning this little escapade. Though he had proved amenable to most aspects of their togetherness—so much so that she had begun to suspect that he was a typical Mr Whatever-you-say-is-right—he had held out on the sexual frontier with almost unbelievable reserve. And now, when the moment was finally upon them… Poof! Her man had pulled away—a dampener if there ever was one. People could go on ranting about liking someone for who they were, but the truth was that if a prospective didn't stand the bed (or in her case, couch) test, no amount of intelligence, sense of humour or charm was going to save them. Turned off, embarrassed and not a little pissed as she was, it was still her house and she had to say something.

'Everything alright?' she asked with careful curiosity.

Predictably, he remained silent.

'Stress at work?'

Subtlety was not her middle name. So be it.

'Err… not really,' he replied, his voice thick with what she could only imagine was serious, red-faced moroseness.

'You want to talk about it?'

Aww hell! It was one of those stupid things that tripped off the tongue. She didn't really want to discuss his issues, but social propriety or gender roles or some such nonsense had forced her to create an opening for something she'd rather avoid. Just as luck would have it, he turned around to face her.

'Do you really want to know?' he asked earnestly.

No! No! NO!

'Yeah sure.'

He took a deep breath, as if unsure of what to say. What could he say? I'm on some kind of medication?

'Do you really want to know?' he asked again. 'I mean, many people say they want to, but they don't really and they're just being polite, and you want to tell them something important, you want them to listen not just hear, but then that's not what happens.'

'Hey, hey...it's me...and it's not that big a deal...seriously.'

She knew he talked nineteen to the dozen when he was nervous—she had been through a similar situation when he had asked her out the first time. She spoke to calm him down—more anxiety at this point would do neither of them any good.

'It's not what you think,' he started off with something that vaguely resembled pride in his voice. 'It's just that...just that...I don't want you to...there are these...err...'

Out with it!

'It's my body, I don't want you to see...' his voice trailed off and he lowered his eyes.

His body? He was conscious of his body? Well, he was no super-model, true—neither was she—but there was nothing so grossly displeasing about him. One didn't have to see someone naked to know that they could use a workout or ten. He looked good, dressed well and despite the hint of a tummy, had quite an attractive physique. So what exactly got his goose?

'I think you're overreacting a bit,' she offered.

'No, it's...when I was a kid, my mother used to punish us, my sister and me...' His mouth opened and closed several times, whatever it was, it was very difficult for him. 'She...she used the iron.'

It was her turn to fish-mouth him.

'T-to burn you?' she asked.

He nodded, still staring at the floor. 'It's left scars and they are not very...I mean, they're...they're ugly and I didn't want you to freak.'

'How many times?'

'I don't remember.'

'Why?' she found her incredulous tongue intoning.

He looked up in momentary defence, not realizing that he was not required to provide an answer to her last question.

'She got angry a lot,' he began awkwardly, 'it started when I tried to tell her that our uncle had tried grabbing my sister, but she wouldn't listen, and then she started punishing us if we ever said things she didn't want to hear. I'm sorry; I don't want to ruin your mood further.'

The maternal bits in her were wailing that she run and embrace him that very instant, but her more practical parts were busy pointing out the pitfalls of the move. Then there was that miniscule iota of perversity that just wanted to look at the scars. The man had been severely abused as a child. She felt disgusted, yes, sorry, definitely—but who wanted the drama? Hug him now and she'd virtually be converting her sex-life into a damn ordeal!

'You're not ruining anything. Tell me.'

Talk a little more, that made sense, didn't it? So she spoke from her place and he stayed where he was.

It was like an eternity before he spoke; all that time, pros and cons converted her head into the expressway on a day with an unusually high rate of fatal accidents, but when he did speak, it was not his voice that took a hold of her.

She watched the way his eyelashes fluttered—though a little long for a guy, she considered them by far his best facial feature. His hands fidgeted, now tracing the circles of his shirt buttons, now running through his hair, now feeling his belt buckle—moving all the time, as if looking for a place to hide. His shoulders held themselves stiff in a distortion of his generally good posture, giving an Atlas-like edge to his persona. That and many more things arrested her—the reddening ears, the shifting gaze, the perspiration running down his neck—their summation clenching her so viscerally that she had to bite her lip to keep from overreacting.

It cost him so much, so bloody much to give her that part of his life which would have been enough to cause nightmares in any sane person forever. She didn't need to hear his story to know how many girls had been abandoned on the couch in an effort to hide the scars of a monster's brutality. His words were irrelevant, all they did was validate the trust he was placing in her. She understood now all those silences he had returned her familial enthusiasm with, all that vagueness when they were exchanging histories. Yet, there was that stuck-up bone of practicality, the ender that always wanted to ascertain a happy conclusion even before the advent of the experience—that bone kept sending up red flags, setting off Big Ben scale alarms all over her brain. 'This is not going to work!' it was caterwauling at the moment. Yet there was that part of her that was secreting steady doses of compassion—the part that couldn't contend with wanton vulnerability, yet didn't want to face up to being unable to help someone after they had just surrendered part of their soul as down-payment.

Would it be so wrong to offer herself to him, to neither romanticize his pain nor victimize his past, to see the scars as part of him and not a past that had to be exorcised? The more she thought, the more incontrovertibly convoluted the situation seemed. And all the time he stood there, silent, unmoving, defeated, until her judgement pronounced him otherwise. That she held such power over him wracked her with overwhelming guilt. The problem with decisions was that you always needed to think about them the most when they had to be made the quickest. She could see him slowly beginning to eye his keys and shoes. A few more seconds of silence and he'd probably walk out of the door, disappointed and doubly wary of the latent explosion his childhood could be. When would he ever build up the courage to reveal again the vitriol his mother nurtured him with, how long till he showed his scars to another, how many more pointless encounters before girls gave up on him or worse, he gave up on himself? Just a few more seconds and the decision would not be hers to make.

Hands outstretched, she walked the few feet that kept him from her. His eyes finally rose when her fingers coiled around his. A smile pasted itself on her lips, radiating sympathy. His eyes shied away, but she smiled wider and gently guided him back to the couch. She made him sit, next to her as before, but the confessional rigidity was still up on him. She sighed, spoke a few words, and made all the right noises. He sat there unreactive as she ran her hands over all the spots, slowly rubbing, gently tickling, consciously titillating, and undoing buttons that he had so scrupulously tied together. He tried to stop her—his need to talk still possessed parts of him—but his breathing grew more laboured even as he tried to hold on to the memories, his mouth fell open, his eyelids dropped, his body rose in response.

'Don't worry about the scars,' she whispered, biting his ears, her hand working downward. 'We'll just put the lights out.'

The last thing he made out before it went completely dark, was the pity in her eyes.

◆

Making Out is the Editor's pick from the shortlisted stories in the Landmark Grey Oak Urban Stories Competition.

In Love with a Stranger

IRA TRIVEDI

How long do aching hearts ache? As I sat before my marriage altar, I could only think of him. I was oblivious of all the happiness that encapsulated me; of my family and friends with their bright faces and festive clothes. They were like drones, and I sat looking at the sacred marriage fire, my eyes cast down in good bridal etiquette. The soft yellow sari that I wore was redolent with my dead Grandma's scent. And then I thought of his scent, of his cardamom-ey taste, and I wondered if I would ever see him again.

It all began on a hot summer day, on 31 May. I remember that day so vividly, so clearly; I guess this is how these days are. He had offered to drop me home after the gym, though we lived in different directions, different parts of town. Half-way home he had asked me if I wanted to come over for a drink. I remember those firework feelings, that tingly excitement that made me glow every time I saw him. That was the day he took me in his arms and kissed me. That was the fortuitous day that it started, and now almost one year later I sat across a sacred fire getting married to another man.

Why do we fall in love? And what defines it? Why was it that I fell for Atul, inappropriate for me in every way? For one he was fifteen years older, and for another, he was a Christian. My strict Marwari family would never accept him. He didn't even look like the boys that I normally liked—tall, dark and handsome. He was short—my height; with fair skin and a dimple on his left cheek, which erupted like a sunburst every time he smiled. His eyes—strangely I can't remember them now, probably because I never understood them—or him for that matter. They say that the eyes are the windows to the soul, but he never let me in. I would never share the experiences that defined him. There was so much of him that I could never understand; there was so much of his life that would never be shared with me. I could tell, even in my naiveté, that he had gone through difficult times—a broken marriage, the shards of which still stung; the deaths of his parents and grandparents. Underneath his flippancy and his distance, I felt the rawness of his pain and the tenderness of his feelings. There was someone innocent and young underneath it all, perhaps someone even younger than me.

My love for him crept up on me. I never expected it to do so. It started off as something casual, and I surprised myself by indulging in it. I would get intermittent SMSes asking me to meet him for a drink, to come over to his place, and I would do it because I was bored, and I somehow enjoyed spending time with him. He was different from anyone I knew and he wasn't connected to my life in any way; he didn't know anyone I knew and I liked it like that. With him I felt as if I was sixteen again; full of gaiety, vigour and an excitement that I didn't know existed within me. Somehow it grew. Maybe it was after I made love to him, when I shared the most precious part of myself with him.

Love affects the mind in inexplicable ways. It becomes your

second skin, suffocating you behind closed doors. It burns a hole in the heart, spilling emotions carelessly. I somehow lost control of myself, and I never knew how I would react to a situation after that. I found myself behaving in inexplicable ways, becoming angry when he distanced himself; afraid and nervous that I would lose him. I don't know why he never allowed me to get close to him; why he never allowed me into his soul.

Happiness eluded me that year. I tried to catch him, but he would never be caught. He remained distant, covered by a heavy armour of sorrow and of pain. I continued to see him, once in two weeks now. I never understood him, and at times I wondered if that is why I loved him. I tried to rationalize with myself; there were constant debates between my head and my heart, and I vowed never to see him again. But when that SMS came, I would jump up and go see him. I couldn't help myself. We would talk—sweet nothings, and then we would go to the bedroom. Physical intimacy was an unguent to the searing pain, but a temporary one, and the day after the pain would return with greater intensity than before.

That was when Siddhartha came into my life—my mother introduced us; she had located him on an online matrimony site. Perhaps he came to me at that time because I needed him the most. In the beginning I didn't pay any attention to him; my heart was elsewhere. Due to my parent's nagging, I spent more and more time with him and I grew to like him. What was best about Siddhartha was that he was real; our relationship was real, as real as it could be. Atul and I continued to meet, and during the two weeks that I wouldn't see him, I wondered what he was doing, who he was with.

In many ways Siddhartha rescued me. I was drowning and he pulled me out. With his sweet words, he soothed my tantrums. With his loving caresses he soothed the pain; with his gentleness he made something hard inside me melt.

A lifetime of happiness was encapsulated in a single word— marriage. All I had to do was marry him, and my life would be exactly what I wanted it to be. He was from a good family, handsome, well-educated, with a good, steady corporate job. Then why did I remember the sadistic pain of last year? Why could I only think of Atul's mocking eyes and his supercilious elegance? Why was it that despite the constant training that I had given my heart, I could only think of him? I loved Siddhartha, I told myself. Loved him for his handsome dignity; for the way he loved me; for the way he cared about me; for the way he looked at me as if I was his... Why was it that I could only think of Atul then? Of our illicit meetings, of his hungry kisses, of his cardamom-ey taste? Why was it that I could only think of the man who gave me nothing but pain when the future was standing in front of me, willing to embrace me with arms wide open?

One day as I lay with Siddhartha, he kissed me gently, 'What are you thinking?' he asked me. 'Tell me, what is running through that Maggi-noodle head of yours?' I smiled. How could I ever tell him the truth? That I was in love with another man who was a stranger? Would I let his memory slowly fade away with time?

I told Atul over lunch. He held me, and I longed for that sweet cardamom-ey kiss, but he wouldn't kiss me because he didn't want to hurt me. Had he not hurt me enough already? What was one kiss going to do at a moment like this? 'No baby, I love you, I won't hurt you.' The first and the last time he would say love. Something luminous passed between us as he held me and we cried silent tears, for different reasons. We both knew it was the end. Some small part of me hoped that he would tell me not to marry Siddhartha. He would tell me that he would come through; that he and I would be together, like we should be. But he didn't, as I knew he wouldn't, and I wondered yet again what was wrong with me that he couldn't.

The day of my marriage was interminably long. I was weary of the smile that was plastered on my face. I felt the weight in my heart helplessly. As the pundits chanted, a paralysing fear wrapped itself tightly around my body and I felt as if I would faint. I sat across from the pyre, Siddhartha's soft loving hand in mine; but only Atul's face flashed in my mind, and I wondered where he was, who he was with, and what he was doing—was he thinking about me? I prayed to the Gods to incinerate my memories of Atul, if that was the only job of this fire. The pundits continued one long complicated chant after another, each second leading me towards my destiny far away from him.

I sit on a beach, the wind like a gloved hand against my skin. Siddhartha, my husband, is napping next to me. A thin watery sun shines over the two of us. I know that I have to let the past go, it is the only way. I have to be at ease, to allow the future to arrive at its own pace, unfurling its secrets. I realize something; if I had married Atul, it wouldn't have been the same. Perhaps this kind of love only happened to me because we could never be together. Atul couldn't give me more than what he had, and I had to accept it or else. Love in marriage is different, I have realized; it is solid, nourishing and soulful. With Atul it was a different kind of love— crazy, passionate, burning. I don't think I could have married that kind of love. I think of Atul with sweetness and some emptiness, and in some way I am glad that Siddhartha's love is different—that his love is a balm. I know I have to accept gracefully the solid, wonderful future that rests next to me.

The Last Look

ROHAN SWAMY

*D*ie endgültige Aussehen…

There are no settings today. Nothing swanky. No big windows, no light, as a matter of fact, no people around either. I am sitting with the Mac book in my attic on an antique bed. The only light in the room is from a small skylight in the roof and from the screen of the laptop. I travel back in time to the previous day, the run of a millennium and to the story of a lifetime. I settle down finally on the old bed which creaks gently and reminds me of the many days that it has endured. With a deep breath and a faint reminder of what could have been if it was different, I begin to write.

The previous day: Morning

I awoke as usual to the sound of the noisy alarm in the room. Kerry King screeched his vocal chords on a song from the album, which I thought was aptly titled *God Hates Us All*. I sat up in bed, not sleepy at all, wondering about the many million things that were going on inside me. I had barely slept for the previous three days. The reasons being fairly obvious—it involved me and more tangentially a girl (as always) and the many complicated things that adult relationships are often based on. As I shut off the noisy alarm, I began to go back in time, in time to a place where I had desperately tried to run away all my life. I began going back in time to myself. I was trying to understand the hollowness of my existence and the simple life that others lived, while I carried out a search for real people. I started to think of her, and about her smile. I looked at the clock half-heartedly, watching it patiently spin around, watching me fight back emotions and fight back time. I was hoping against hope that her train would be delayed, that for one more day she would bring dead flowers back to life. And that for one more day the cowboy would be able to wrap his arms around the angel. But it wasn't meant to be.

Mom called out loudly, as I walked into the dining room. A bag of warm food lay wrapped in a neat bundle, awaiting me to take it for her. Mom couldn't sense my moroseness. Primarily because she did not know what I felt inside and secondly because I did not wait too long for her to deduce it as I quickly took the bag and left the place. In the background I could hear my mom remind me to tell her to have a safe journey back home. My bike did not harass me today. She started on the first go and I plugged the iPod into my ears and raised the pitch so that the noise hurt my eardrums. Noise was good. Silence wasn't. Noise always reasoned, whilst silence only burnt. I raced through the gears and the city traffic; raced all the way to her place. The fresh transfer and the acerbic voice of my boss announcing the same played back minute by minute into my mind, as I dashed towards her house. She had known all along what I had felt. I couldn't hide it because my eyes always gave me away. But I had to fight it all down. Goddamned old feelings. Because I understood what something else in the world meant to her; what someone else in the world meant to her. Even though it was on rocky grounds as of late, I still wanted her to be happy.

No malice, no selfishness, only a thought that reverberated in my mind, which reminded me of how desperately I wanted to see her smile. Of how desperately I loved her.

She opened the door on the third knock. She had been woken abruptly from her sleep by my knocking. She looked like a goddess from an unknown world. She was dressed simply in a black tee and slacks with dishevelled hair and half open eyes; she looked like a million bucks. She smelt like another million and radiated this glow that reminded me how desperately I wanted to be with her. She smiled a sweet welcome and ushered me in. I gave her the bag and she called up my mother and promptly thanked her for it. They spoke for many moments in hushed tones, and I could sense it in her voice, the way it rose and fell, that she wasn't very enthusiastic about going away either. After she got done with the phone she came and sat beside me, held my hands and intertwined her fingers with mine. 'Not this,' I said to myself. The old goddamned feelings fighting their way to come up to the surface, I tried equally hard not to let them come up. More silence. More burning. And after what seemed like aeons, she spoke to me. Spoke honestly, spoke quietly, spoke simply; of her initial days in the city; of our chance meeting; of getting used to the people she had met and of her relationship with a being born of the sea, which was no more to be. I wondered whether she was good at hiding emotions; she wasn't, just as I wasn't. I couldn't hide what I felt for her; she couldn't hide her pain. Her fingers intertwined more tightly and I fought down everything again. She looked at me with dreamy eyes as I looked at the watch on my wrist that patiently signalled that it was time for me to go to work in a new department as a features column writer. I rose from the huge beanbag. My fingers refused to leave hers but they had to. In halting tones she asked me if I would come to the railway station late that evening to see her off.

I replied in the affirmative; she smiled back sweetly; her hair was still dishevelled, her t-shirt and slacks were still black and she still looked a million bucks.

I reached work at around eleven thirty that morning. The slanting rays of the sun told a bleak story. I felt the same too. It was a slow day and there had actually been nothing that was worth being written about. To top it all she was going away. And I couldn't help myself from being so terribly smitten by her that I couldn't even tell her. I was struggling to understand what I was going through. There was a girl whom I liked, fair enough. She had just ended a serious relationship with someone. So what? There was a rational side in me, which said yeah, go hit the iron and get her. This is the time. And then there was my irrational side, which said: is this what you wanted for her? Did you not say that it was important for you to see her happy? Then shouldn't you just help her be happy even if it meant that you were the one who remained screwed up for a long time? And I chose to listen to my irrational side, because I really loved her. Because all I wanted was to see her happy. Because all I wanted was to see her smile. I was lost in these thoughts when my boss came in and said that I had to cover an assignment in the evening. 'That's not fair,' I thought. I had to go to drop her off. And I just wanted to spend some time near her, seeing her and thinking of just how perfect she was for me. As I got lost in my thoughts again, my boss brought me back to reality by asking me (for the second time) to cover the event. I nodded and he left. I spend the rest of the day looking at her pictures that I had taken through the Kodak Viewfinder. There was a different set of words that I used to describe her, 'emotionally beautiful', because that was who she was. She could actually bring back dead flowers to life by just smiling at them. And she portrayed this unknown serenity which made me feel complete, like the lone cowboy searching for the lost angel or the iceman searching for this haunting tune on his violin.

The day progressed slowly. My father came to my office (surprisingly) in the afternoon. He came to drop off some more food that my mom had made for her journey. Sometime later I took it all and ran down to the office of another bespectacled friend who worked downstairs and handed her the parcel, asking her to deliver it in case I couldn't make it to the station. She smiled back, hard, undecipherable and quiet. Evening came and so did 5 p.m. I went to the seminar, which eventually turned out to be a sinfully boring event. But the good part was that I didn't have to go and file it. It was too late for the next day's news so I was at ease. I rushed the bike at top speed to her house, keeping an eye on the gas gauge, which patiently indicated that I had to refuel the bike. I decided to save that for later, I had some hopes of my bike, if not a lot. I reached her place. She was ready but I could sense that she had cried a lot in the washroom. I didn't need a fairy to tell me that. But she looked calm and composed. She came into the room and sat down beside the beanbag chair. Her brother sat opposite us and I sat in the middle on the beanbag. She offered me tea and I drank it. It was after I was halfway done with it that she remembered I didn't drink tea. She apologized for forgetting. I said she didn't have to. The goddamned old country ghosts. The bridges of old Tuesdays, the mystic feelings, and her beautiful smile. It all came back. I looked into her eyes, and time stopped. It was quiet and peaceful when all of a sudden it was torn open by my ringing phone.

It was my boss; he snarled into the phone. Something about coming back to office right then and filing the conference story; something about ruining my world; something about seeing the angel go away; something about just being so terribly in love;

something about not seeing her go. I went to the window by the indoor swing, took a long breath, swallowed blood and wiped off a lone tear from the corner of my eye in silence without her seeing it. And then I went and told her that I had to go back to work, and that I might not make it to see her off at the station. I saw the expressions on her face just as I was leaving. They were classic. Anger, denial and reluctant acceptance. I wanted to be there with her so much. But that didn't look like it was to happen. The time on the clock read 7 p.m., as I started the bike.

It had been exactly fifty minutes when the attendant locked the hose into the fuel jack of the bike. The serpentine queues at the fuel station had ensured that I had wasted a full fifty minutes there. The hands on the Vacheron Constantine strapped to my wrist showed the time in a bright whitish glow as I restarted the bike.

7.55 p.m.
With extremely alarming precision I flew down to the office in fifteen minutes, whereas it normally took me about half an hour. I dashed up the stairs, not waiting for the lift and began frantically typing my ID into the system when my boss called me again.

8.25 p.m.
The meeting lasted a full fifteen minutes. The time on the digital clock by my desk read 8.25 p.m. I fumed; desperately fighting back everything as I furiously wrote the story. The boss wanted 500 words, I gave him 750 hoping that he would let me run to the station, but that was not to be. He asked me to stay back till the copy was sub-edited. And for once I gave up. I called her brother and told him I wouldn't be able to make it to the station. He said he understood. I didn't speak to her. I couldn't meet her voice. Because even if it wasn't meant to be, I was deeply in love with her. And I just had to look at her one last time and drink to my heart's

content. Because I knew I would never meet her again, although I did want to. I knew it was going to be tough and the chances of that happening were very slim. That's why I wanted to see her one last time, and it had all gone away with my boss asking me to stay back.

I went to the sub-editor, I couldn't convince him to let me go, but my eyes did. He told me that in case some queries were to arise about the story, he would call me. I acknowledged what he said. All I was asking for was fifteen minutes. I dashed down to the bike when I saw the time with a sinking feeling that I wasn't going to make it.

8.47 p.m.

Desperately trying to fight the sands of time I flew down to the station. Took a series of wrong turns, lost my way in the process, and even broke signals. But that evening I didn't care. I wanted to just see her one last time before she went; I just wanted to. The big station clock showed 8.51 as I ran past hawkers, irate rickshaw owners and dogs into the station. I ran like Pheidippides, into the station, onto the platform. I ran the other way round when I realized that it was the wrong end. Phone in one hand and duffel on the other shoulder, I ran back the entire length of the train to the other side, to the seat where she was sitting.

I looked at her for a full minute. My throat was parched and my lungs were bursting for want of air but I still looked at her. She smiled back and I realized how it was to be. It was what I had fought to see. That smile. It was precious. I could have walked right over the Grand Canyon to see her smile like that always. As I was lost in these thoughts, the train began to move. She intertwined fingers through the window bars one last time with me. We said a million things without speaking. I desperately prayed for her happiness and at the same time I killed everything that was rising inside me. This time my tears didn't flow. Everything was gone. Everything had been burnt away. I just wanted to see her smile and she did just that as our fingers left each other and the train left the platform.

I went down on my haunches. Through my blurred vision I could see the train moving farther and farther away by the second. My bespectacled friend came and offered me water. In an almost hoarse, inaudible voice, I mouthed Pheidippides's dying line— *Rejoice...we conquer.*

Even though I had never told her what I went through, I got to see her smile—for one last time—and I could live on that. Just on that. My friend sensed what I was through, without even actually having to sense it. I drank a sip and realized how badly I had underestimated my body. How terribly broke it was. And on the spur of the moment I realized what I had given up.

Today:
The light streams in through the attic skylight. It reflects off the tears rolling down my face. I miss her terribly. I cannot even conceive how much; cannot even conceive of having that thought. But I knew it had to be done. I have to give up and pray; just to see her smile; to see her be happy; to never let her know how badly I miss her. As I ponder for a suitable title for this story I strike upon one. Her saved picture on the desktop gives me the name. I call the piece—'Die endgultige Aussehen' or 'The Final Look'. As I save the document and shut down the system, she smiles at me for one last time. The system finally shuts down, and the dam that I have been holding back from the previous night breaks down.

High Time

KAILASH SRINIVASAN

Muralikrishnan Iyer—or Krish to his friends—had turned thirty this morning. He had only just opened his eyes when his mother waltzed into his room with the biggest smile on her face.

'Kanna,' she cooed—an endearment she reserved for moments when there was a favour to be asked, or a touchy subject to be trod upon. 'The good lord should save you from all evil eyes. Happy birthday, Kanna,' she said and cupped his face in her hands, while Krish squirmed uncomfortably.

'What, huh? What? So now that you're thirty, your mother isn't allowed to show any affection?'

'Amma, please, can you just…'

'What? Leave you alone? Okay, fine. Get ready. We're going to Sushila Maami's house.'

'I am not going anywhere. I have plans.'

'Nothing doing. You're coming with us. I have already given my word to Sushila Maami. She has been phoning me day in, day out asking whether I'll bring you along. Also, she wants you to sing for her some of your Sai bhajans when we're there.'

'What nonsense? But how can you promise someone on my behalf? I get one day from work, one day, and I have to do all this socialising with people I don't even care about!' Krish flung the sheets aside and stormed out of the room.

She followed him to the washbasin and spoke as he brushed. 'Well, you might not care about her, but she loves you like her own son.'

'Dad. Dad!' Krish called and went to where his father was reading the newspaper. 'Did you listen to what she just said? Tell her this is not done.'

'What do you do for this house? Do you do dusting? Wash clothes? Buy vegetables? I mean, what do you actually do for this house?' his father asked, his tone unusually dramatic, like that of the characters from those Tamil serials he watched on Sun TV.

'What? Wait, where's this coming from? I'm saying something else and you are talking about something entirely different.'

'We ask you to do one thing and you are creating such a scene. I don't understand why.'

'I… I…What? Never mind.'

'Wear your kurta pyjama, that blue one. Dress decently for once.'

Krish threw up his arms. 'Are you both even listening to what I'm saying? I don't want to go. Period.' He went into his room and slammed the door shut, wondering whether he'd ever have his own place and the much needed privacy.

His mother started off with her usual rant, audible enough for Krish to hear. 'You wouldn't know now. Once I'm gone, then you will realise. You will cry, "I troubled her so much. Aiyo Rama, aiyo Krishna," but it won't bring me back. It's okay, it's okay. I never got the kind of respect a mother should get anyway.'

Unable to take it any longer, Krish opened his door and craned his neck out. His mother gazed at him for a split second, but then crossed her arms and looked away.

'Amma, please, will you just…'

'Will I just what? Shut up? Sure I will. One day, everyone has to shut up for good.' Then, sniffling and drying her watery eyes and nose with the corner of her sari, she said, 'Why did you bother to step out of your room, Sir? I'm there no? Your unpaid servant. I'm getting you your coffee. Please go back and slam the door in my face again. Such a fool I will look in front of Maami. I'll have to lie again, tell her something like, "Oh, he is so busy all the time," or "He went to meet someone from work." Everywhere I go, they ask me, "Where's Muralikrishnan? Where's Muralikrishnan?" And here you are, with no feelings, no sentiments for anyone in this world.'

'Amma, please! Will you put an end to this melodrama? And please stop watching those silly programmes of yours—Kokila and Kolam and Metivoli and what not. This goes for both of you.'

'I should go away to Chennai. I can be of some help to my poor old father. At least he will be appreciative of what I do. Hmph! Why should I suffer here?'

Krish's father, in his white vest and dhoti, looked up from his newspaper, causing his mother to say, 'It's coming, it's coming. Have some patience. The milk has to come to a boil first, no? And then the decoction has to seep through.'

'Why are you getting mad at me? What did I do?' his father asked, followed by an amused cackle.

'You are no less by the way. Demanding this and that. Not even moving a finger. Tch! This is it for me. This is my life—to rot in the kitchen. One thing ends, another begins. After coffee, prepare breakfast. Breakfast over, think of lunch. Lunch ends, make evening snack. Snack over, cook dinner.'

'Arey, how many times have I told you: *Ni daan ellam*. You

are everything.'

'Bullshit. This is all just hollow talk. If I was so important, would my own son treat me like I was some babbling mad woman?'

'Fine! God. I'll come along. But don't think you can blackmail me into doing things your way every time,' Krish said.

'Slam the door slowly this time, the hinges will come loose otherwise,' his mother said earnestly, as Krish walked away with his coffee. 'And wear the blue one.'

◆

Sushila Maami hugged Krish and kissed his cheeks with her thin, chapped lips. Her wet-sock-like breath greeted him and he almost fainted. She made him sit next to her and wrapped her chubby arms around him. Krish shifted uneasily, while his mother beamed with pride at her son being showered with affection by someone other than her.

'You look so nice today, Muralikrishnan,' Maami said.

Krish cringed at the use of his full name. 'Thank you, auntie.'

'I heard you turned thirty today. Happy birthday, ma.' This gave her another opportunity to kiss Krish's face, and this time he held his breath. 'It's high time now, isn't it?'

As Krish wondered what exactly it was high time for, Maami hollered, 'Kamakshi, vaa ma. Look who's here.'

It took Krish a split second to understand what was going on. As he watched in horror, out came Maami's daughter, carrying a tray with bonda, bajji, laddoo and coffee.

'This is Kamakshi,' Sushila Maami said, pointing to the double-chinned woman with an ample distribution of tiny, needle-like hair on her chin, wearing a heavily embroidered yellow silk sari.

Maami made Kamakshi sit opposite Krish. 'She came from

Chicago only yesterday,' she added, pronouncing Chicago with a 'tch' sound. 'Go ahead, Kamakshi, you had questions for Krish, no?'

He quickly glanced at his parents, but they were busy staring in awe at Kamakshi, waiting to hear her speak. They always had this thing for people, especially distant relatives, with accents. It amused them but, at the same time, it was also a matter of pride. 'He doesn't speak Tamil. Only English,' they would say about him or her to others.

Kamakshi took her time. She studied Krish from head to toe—from his curly mop of hair to his cherry-red frames to the way he kept his beard, right down to his brown leather sandals. And despite his annoyance at being dragged into this, Krish found himself fixing his hair and running his palms over the fine wrinkles on his kurta.

'Tell me a bit about yourself? Your hobbies, how you spend your spare time, etc., etc.,' Kamakshi said. It seemed to him that words were raining out of her mouth, like they were trying to escape. There was an unmistakable Tamil lilt to her American accent. That arrogance was there too, which automatically attaches itself to the bodies and minds of immigrants, especially those attempting to be more local than the locals themselves.

Once she was done talking, Krish was certain he heard a muffled squeal from his mother. As he tried to draft a suitable response, his mother piped up.

'He does copywriting, something, umm no, he does communi… cation, yes?' she asked, searching Krish's face for confirmation.

Krish pressed his knuckles to his mouth. 'Uh, I am into communications—PR, content, that sort of thing.'

'Achcha, anyway, he is also an actor. You should see him on stage. My god, the way people applaud for him.' She paused for her revelation to have the desired effect. 'He's also a writer. His book will be published soon. Buy a copy, okay?'

Kamakshi gave him a look that demanded further explanation.

'Well, yeah. It's a collection of short stories.'

'He studied in Australia, you know, for one full year.' She paused again. 'I was so worried. Day and night I thought of him. I only called him, he never did. Expensive, no, calling from there. A nicely paying job he needs now. Education loan has to be repaid, no?'

'Kamakshi has been in Chicago for more than ten years,' Maami offered, drawing a look of adulation from Krish's mother.

'Ohhh. So nice, so nice. So you have any vellakara friends?'

Kamakshi looked perplexed by the word vellakara, but Maami jumped to her rescue.

'No, no. No white friends. Only hi-hello type friends.'

'Oh, good, good. By the way, Krish has always wanted to go to America, no, Kanna?' Krish's mother said addressing him, but her eyes were fixed on Kamakshi.

Krish smiled awkwardly.

'He's also a great singer. He has won so many awards, you know. He tried for *Sa Re Ga Ma Pa* also, that show with Sonu Nigam? But didn't make it. There is so much politics, I tell you. No ear for true talent they have. And look how many terrible singers there are on that show now. Tch! Anyway, Kanna, sing a song for Sushila Maami and Kamakshi. Anything you like, bhajan, ghazal, film song, anything.'

'Uh, no please. I don't feel like it. My throat doesn't feel right.'

'Come on now. Don't act so pricey. Just one song, right Maami?'

'Aama, yes, only one.' Maami winked at Krish's mother, like he wasn't even there.

Finally, after incessant coaxing from the two ladies, he started off with a bhajan. He must have sung two lines, when Kamakshi interrupted. 'Don't you like know a Coldplay or a James Blunt number?'

'Enough with your English songs ma,' Maami interjected. Then, facing Krish's family, she added, 'She's been in America all her life, no. So she listens to all these crazy people. God only knows what they are screaming about. They have no raagam, no melody. Appa, appa!' Maami touched both her cheeks with the tips of her fingers.

'Amma, please. Just because you can't understand them doesn't mean they aren't good,' Kamakshi said.

'Say anything you want, but Carnatic music is Carnatic music. Enna gamakam, what reverence those singers have for their music, what deep meanings the lyrics have, aha, aha. You carry on, Kanna,' Maami said.

And so Krish went ahead with his bhajan while Kamakshi sat through his performance with no interest.

'So, as I said, Krish is a singer, actor and a writer,' his mom said, summarizing his core skills for Kamakshi's benefit.

'*Kamaskhi* can dance like, who's that woman ma? Shakuntala?'

'No Amma, Her name's Shakira. God,' Kamakshi said, blowing out air through the side of her mouth.

'Abadiya? Sooper,' his mother said, as if she knew everything about Shakira.

'Can we go now?' Krish asked.

'Yes, yes. One second. So Kamakshi ma? All okay? You like Krish?'

'Amma, what the hell are you doing?'

'Yeah, he's alright,' Kamakshi said as a favour to her dumbstruck listeners. She could have sworn at them and his parents would've still hung onto her every word.

'Very nice, very nice.'

'If I may, with everyone's due permission, ask a few questions as well?' Krish inquired.

'Yes, yes. You can. Not every day you get to talk to someone from America, right?' Maami said, and with a straight face.

'Gee, thanks,' Krish said. 'Okay Kamakshi, tell us about yourself. What do you do in Chicago?' He deliberately said 'Chicago' with an American twang, prompting a question.

'Were you ever in America?'

'Nope. Made in India, all the way.'

'Ah, okay. Anyway, I'm between jobs at the moment.'

Krish's mother elbowed him.

'She means she isn't working right now.'

'Oh ho. Okay, okay, continue.'

'I like to travel, I listen to alternative rock—well, mostly—and I love Facebook. That's it I guess... I mean, how much time does a person have anyway?'

'Hmm, very true,' Krish said, striking a serious pose. 'Any hobbies?'

'*Daai, rock na, kallaa*? She likes rock?' his mother whispered.

'Tsk! Illamma, it doesn't literally mean a stone—it is a type of music.'

'Oh ho.'

'Umm, no I guess, no hobbies,' Kamakshi said.

'How do you pass your time then?'

'Oh, I love to go to clubs.'

Sushila Maami immediately gave Kamakshi a raised-eyebrow look. 'It's like a large hall with lights and music, more like a marriage reception. They gather there and dance like those Hare Krishna followers,' Maami said, turning clubbing into a holy experience.

'They have those there also?' his mother said with a twinkle in her eyes. 'Tell us more about vellakaras. It will be so useful for Krish.'

'Umm, well, Americans are picky and impatient. They fuss about a lot of things—like their coffee has to be just the right temperature, their meat has to be cooked perfectly. 'Awesome' is their favourite word. They love their beer, they want things to be easy and uncomplicated, they love to file for divorces, they like Indian things—colourful saris, yoga, herbs. They love Indian women, almost worship them. My last boyfriend was…' She started laughing, but then went silent abruptly, realizing she had said too much.

'Boyfriendaa?' Krish's mother's eyes were as wide as saucers.

'Aiyoo, by boyfriend she means a boy who is a friend, right Kamoo?' Maami said. She was smiling, but her eyes spoke of the horrors she was capable of. 'Like Muralikrishnan must be having girls who are friends, so girlfriends, no? Illa Kanna?'

'Nooo! Never!' Krish exclaimed, his face the epitome of innocence.

'Maami, my Krishna has never even looked at any other woman, let alone be friends with her.'

'Kamakshi also same, only a little different. She isn't friends with anyone and everyone. She only befriends those who are innocent, good boys from good families to be married soon.'

The smile on Krish's lips was now slowly starting to touch his ears. It broadened further when he saw the expression on his parents' faces. It reminded him of the time when they had learned that one of his male friends had a boyfriend.

'Okay, okay, forget about all that. I am telling you, so many people want to marry her, you know,' Maami announced proudly. 'I rejected all of them. Why? Because I know only our Muralikrishnan is perfect for her.' She looked at the three of them and nodded for effect. 'So, shall we freeze the dates then?'

'Yes, yes, the earlier the better,' Krish said. 'Isn't it so, Amma? Correct?'

'Heh, children. Shut up, Krishna. How many times have I told you not to talk when elders of the family are talking? What do you know about dates and such? Just give us some time to think, Maami.'

'What's there to think ma? Will you find a better daughter-in-law than Kamakshi?'

'Yeah that is there, but…'

'Not only will our Muralikrishnan be having a wife as talented and as beautiful as Kamakshi, he will also get the green card, no?'

'I agree. Very correct, very correct,' Krish said, his tone laden with mock conviction.

'But we will still need to consult our family astrologer, pick out auspicious dates, and make other arrangements and such. So we will need time,' his father said, speaking for the first time since they had arrived there.

'Do you take me to be that inexperienced? I have already consulted Sundara Shastrigal and, according to him, any date from 23 July to 30 August is auspicious.'

'Okay then, we shall let you know Maami,' his mother said, getting up and pulling Krish along with her. As he got up, Kamakshi suggestively licked her lips in slow motion.

'If you ask me, there's nothing to think about. But if you like, take a day. I will call you tomorrow or, better still, come over to your house with sweets.' Maami giggled like a schoolgirl.

◆

In the car, Krish started, 'Amma, so this Kamakshi is such a nice girl…'

'Shut up Krishna. Just…,' his mother said. There were things on her mind. Maami would be coming over tomorrow.

'Maybe if we lock the doors from inside, turn off the lights and remain very silent, Maami will leave,' Krish's father suggested.

'She's a hound dog ma. She can sniff us from a mile,' his wife said, her voice quavering with panic. 'What if we leave town for a few weeks?'

'No, no, I can't get leave at work.'

'We obviously can't shift houses, no,' she said. 'Or can we?'

Krish sat through this with a look of amusement.

Then while they halted at a signal, she had an epiphany. She said, 'Krishna, that Manikandan fellow has a boyfriend, no?'

'Yes. Why?'

'So, he likes boys, no?' She said with distaste.

Krish nodded. 'Why?'

'No, just like that.'

◆

High Time is the Bookchums pick from the short listed stories in the Landmark Grey Oak Urban Stories Competition.

Beyond Reasonable Doubt

SNEH THAKUR

'Maybe he just doesn't love me anymore.'

The couch was uncomfortable. Parts of it had sunk in, adjusting its grooves to its more regular guests. Mala looked up at Fatima. This was her eighth session but she felt no different.

'Mala, I need you to focus on yourself. Have you tried talking to Dev?'

Mala looked around the now familiar room. Plants sprouted out of colourful pots. A painting of red poppies hung on the wall across. A sheer curtain fluttered in the distance. Everything in this room was bright and vibrant. She had never felt so at odds with a space. She closed her eyes, took a deep breath and counted the days in her head. Six months and fourteen days. The same question had faced her, chased her. Of all the wisdom the world had imparted to her, she felt there was none to help her deal with her new reality.

'No. Not yet. I don't know.'

Fatima smiled at Mala kindly, 'Give yourself time Mala. It seems impossible now. But you will find your way.'

Mala opened her palms and stared at her wedding ring. When Dev and Mala first met two years ago, it was Mala who was instantly drawn to Dev. Dev was an artistic playwright with a relentless passion for the written word. They had shared a table outside a well known theatre and ended up talking about Anton Chekhov's form of writing, unaware of the increasingly intensifying rain and curious mosquitoes. Later, they shared an auto rickshaw and a promise to meet again. Dev was intrigued and did not wait long before calling Mala again. They met at coffee shops and dined at cosy restaurants. On weekends they rode on Dev's motorbike to the latest art exhibitions and plays. Mala loved the theatre and could always be identified by the heartiest laughter in the crowd. Armed with a sunny smile and curly hair that had a life of its own, she would talk animatedly about her life in the city. Dev fell in love with her sundrenched spirit. Innumerable evenings were spent walking through the Mumbai rains discussing their common love for Woody Allen's humour over cups of tea served in kullads. Such was their joy and visible love for each other that it came as no surprise when they decided to marry.

'Thanks, Fatima. I'll see you on Friday.' Mala managed a small smile.

Mala slipped her feet into her white Jodhpuri jutis and picked up her satchel. She wasn't like this earlier. Her nails were always painted cherry red and her eyes always lined with kohl. She had a striking face and though she was well past her thirtieth birthday, her youthful beauty had not faded. But the last six months had taken a toll on her. She now dressed casually, often picking out the first thing she found in her wardrobe, avoiding glancing at the empty shelves on the left side of the cupboard where Dev's clothes once lay stacked.

Mala took the long route home. This was a new ritual after

her sessions with Fatima. She would drive down unfamiliar lanes, absorbing the sights, diverting her thoughts. It was a foreign feeling, this, of trying to avoid home. With Dev, she would rush from work, often stopping by the grocery to pick out exotic ingredients, which they would later harmonise into a meal.

A flower seller knocked on her window, 'Didi, please buy the flowers.'

Mala looked at the bunch of white carnations with their soft white centres and wilted sides. The way the flowers had looked on the evening after her wedding reception. She kept her window rolled up for the rest of her drive home.

In the first year after their wedding, Mala and Dev were deliriously happy. They were in love and united by the bond of friendship. They lived in a small one-bedroom apartment in Bandra. Though the apartment was in a building that could be best described as 'needing renovation', the location provided them easy access to both centres of theatre in the city. Mala spent hours scouring the markets at Colaba and Chor Bazaar for artefacts to beautify corners of their home. Dev took it upon himself to repaint the house and fix everything broken or dripping. They would sometimes argue about the creative choices of the colour of the paint or the location of the sofa, though anyone hearing them would wonder if 'Baby, that is a horrible idea' or 'Miyan, you might not like this couch but I am going get it anyway' were words spoken in anger or jest. In time, wooden Buddha carvings, colourful prayer flags and oil paintings of landscapes had found shelter in the corners and on the walls of their home. Every room mirrored the harmony they felt together.

Dev's writing was going well in the space Mala had created for him; walls fitted with wooden shelves that bore all the greats—Tolstoy, Ibsen, Boris Pasternak and Dostoevsky. He spent hours at his writing table, which overlooked a park with gulmohar trees. A new sensitivity had found its way into his writing. He attributed this to Mala, who often read peeking over his shoulder and gave her opinion on dialogue, enriching scenes by seeing matters from a female point of view. Evenings were spent entertaining friends in their new home. Miles Davis's *My Funny Valentine* played over an old gramophone they had found together on the streets of Chor Bazaar. Wine glasses clinked and were never empty. Looking back, she found it hard to believe that so much had changed. The gramophone now sat silent, a layer of soft dust settled on its surface.

She was called Radhika.

She was Dev's friend with the olive skin and wide smile. It was her big theatre debut as well and she was ecstatic to play the role of Vrinda in Dev's play. She was charming and smiled often and somewhere in the fantasy created on the stage and the reality of their lives in their home, the lines had blurred. The signs had been there: long absences on account of work; the quiet distance that had formed between them; the infrequent proclamations of love; the rare occasions when passion overcame them. When finally Mala, ridden with doubt, had checked Dev's phone, she saw a message from Radhika that crushed her.

The words spoken that evening were etched in her memory. She had just come back from a day at work. A little kohl lay spilled over the rims of her eyes. She asked him what the message meant, knowing what it did. Confused she sat still, uncertain about how to react.

'It's not how you imagine it Mala,' Dev had said softly. 'It was a transient attraction, an emotional lapse of reason. Nothing really happened between us.'

Each time she thought of that moment, she remembered clearly the look on Dev's face as he spoke—a face stricken with remorse. They had not spoken for days after. Two strangers in a room avoiding each other, tip-toeing around what they felt and the new direction their relationship was taking. The breakfast they once shared together squabbling over the crispiest toast was now had in silence. The clink of spoons and forks were like guests at their table. Where once there had been no distances in their embraces or their bed, there lay emptiness. Irritating rituals like the hour where Mala would pester Dev about his opinion on what she should wear for work was lost too. The silence between them had transformed into a living being that filled up the spaces in which they lived and walked. It was as though they bore the burden of a dark cloud containing a thousand raindrops. In the stifled stillness, a million thoughts ran awry colliding, circling but always gathering intensity.

'Mala please, let's put this behind us. I love you. I want to be with you. Radhika was a mistake,' Dev had pleaded.

In the beginning, she thought she could handle it herself. It had been an emotional straying. But the more she thought about the fact that he could have loved another however briefly, the more unsettled she felt. How had this happened? Had he fallen out of love with her? And most importantly, would he betray her again? The questions mounted within her into a cold wall.

Her mother had been generous with advice, 'Patience and compromise are key, beta. All couples go through tough times.' But then Mala had not confided completely in her mother. She had thought the problem too intimate to share with anyone else. She chose instead to absorb herself in her work. Her colleagues saw her working late hours on marketing campaigns, sharpened pencils in hand. What was mistaken as effort towards the race up the corporate ladder was actually confusion in disguise.

Mala's phone rang as she turned in the lane near the house. The number needed no memory, no name. It rang for a while persistently. She imagined the disappointment on Dev's face. He had tried to speak to her in the last few months to no avail. She stepped out of the car, skilfully navigating her red umbrella to avoid getting drenched in the unexpected rain.

'Mala Didi, there is a letter for you. And Dev Saab was here.'

The night watchman, dressed in a blue raincoat fashioned out of a cut-out tarpaulin sheet, rushed over to her and handed her a brown packet. On its cover was her name scribbled in Dev's handwriting. She stared at the familiar curl of the L. As she reached for the packet a few drops of rain met the letters, soaking them into a watery blur. Instinctively, Mala held the packet to her.

'Dev saab came today?' Mala asked surprised.

It had been months since their pact. They had decided to be together only if she could put Radhika behind them. The pain of her silence had been too much for Dev to bear, a constant reminder of the hurt he caused her. Till such time and on Mala's request, Dev had allowed her the space to sort through what she felt. She had not seen him in six months and while he called regularly, this was the first time he had come to visit.

'Haan didi—he said I was to give you this.' The watchman pointed towards the boxy brown packet.

'Thank you,' Mala said and walked up the stairs. She took one step at a time, her fingers feeling the edges of the box.

It felt like stacked papers. 'It must be important; why else would Dev come to visit that late?' she thought. Perhaps he was calling her to check if she was home. He had not waited. As she reached her door a thought struck her and she stopped still. Had Dev given up on her and decided to move on? They had spoken about opting for an amicable divorce if things did not work out. The lawyer had told them flippantly that all it took was two signatures and he could start the process of separation. Was it possible that his patience had run thin? Perhaps she had taken too long, her doubts overriding her faith in their possibilities.

Panicking, she hunted for the keys in her satchel. Her fingers trembled as she opened the door. She reached out for the switch of the floor lamp and sat on the cane chair in the centre of the living room. Mala took a deep breath and placed the brown packet in front of her. Slowly, she broke the string around the box and unwrapped the brown cover. She closed her eyes and took a deep breath and lifted the lid of the box dreading the worst.

Inside sheaves of papers lay resting. Some sheets showed creases as though crumpled and then salvaged from a bin. Black ink splotches lined the sides of the white sheets. Words rethought were scratched out and synonyms were squeezed into the cramped spaces above. Scribbled in Dev's handwriting was the script of his new play. A yellow post-it was stuck to the first page in the box. It read, 'Mala, I wrote this for you.'

Mala sat in the soft yellow light of the room. As she read the six words crafted on a yellow note, she felt a weight lift from her shoulders. Her doubts disappeared as though they were a wispy swirl of air that faded as it lifted. She opened her palms and stared at her wedding ring as the teardrops began to fall. The pain lay splattered on the floor. Like a thousand fragments of broken glass. And she walked on it slowly, carefully, for the last time.

She reached for her phone and dialled his number from memory. Three rings, an impatient wait and then a familiar sleepy voice.

'Hello Dev.'

'Mala...' She could hear the smile in his voice.

Pause, Rewind, Play

SHOMA NARAYANAN

Pause

I leaned back in my chair and looked at Rahul. 'You know, when I decided to join advertising, I thought I'd be shooting award-winning ads in spectacular locations and hobnobbing with glamorous people all day long. And look at me now—I was up till two in the morning yesterday working on a diaper ad, I have bags under my eyes and you are the most glamorous person I'm likely to meet today. Which reminds me, have you decided whether you want to do my ad?'

Rahul grimaced. He was a good-looking chap, and if I didn't hate all client-servicing personnel on principle, I could imagine having the hots for him. I was trying to convince him to model for an underwear ad where we were operating on a very, very tight budget. We often did that—got presentable looking people from the agency to model free of cost—and most people jumped at the idea of some free visibility. Rahul, unfortunately, had issues with modelling semi-nude, and it didn't help that I was two days behind schedule on the diaper ad which I was doing for his star client.

'Can we discuss it later? I really need to get this ad done,' he said, and added with unnecessary nastiness, 'We actually have the money to hire real models for this campaign, so it would help if you took it a little more seriously.'

Stuff like this reminded me how much I disliked Rahul. He had a habit of running off and cribbing to my boss about my missing deadlines, and had got me top billing on her people-to-be-pulled-up list more than once.

I took him through the concept—clutter-breaking stuff, in my opinion, but Rahul didn't think the client would buy it. 'I know The Singh. He'll hate this.' Surinder Singh, the Marketing Head for the client company was a fire-breathing monster who starred in the agency staff's worst nightmares. 'I need to go meet him in two hours. Can you give me another option ASAP?'

I gave him a long look and then pulled out a storyboard that was lying under my desk. It was the ultimate in clichéd advertising, but Rahul glanced at it and brightened up.

'This is good. You're coming along, right?'

'I'm not sure. I was thinking of sending K2.' K. Karthikeyan was the senior-most guy in my team, and he was brilliant. Unfortunately, he also had dreadlocks, halitosis, smelly feet and an utter contempt for clients and the client-servicing fraternity. Client meetings which included him usually ended with us losing the account. Rahul blanched.

'Can't you come?'

I pulled out the sketches for the Rebel briefs ad and leafed through them slowly. Rahul snatched them out of my hand. 'I'll do your damn chaddi ad! Don't you let K2 anywhere near my clients.'

The meeting with The Singh went off surprisingly well, and we had lunch in a little café nearby to celebrate. We were walking towards the cab stand when I stopped to look at a selection of scarves at a pavement shop—Rahul walked a few paces ahead. A couple of bikes roared past. A third followed, the biker taking a turn at tremendous speed and losing control of his bike. He missed me by inches, skidding into a 'No Parking' sign ahead of the stall. The post crumpled under the impact and the circular sign flew off it, spinning through the air before it hit the back of Rahul's head with a sickening crunch.

I screamed and kept screaming for a few seconds before realizing it wasn't doing any good. Rahul was lying on the road, clearly unconscious, but—equally clearly—not dead. I ran across and knelt next to him. There was a lot of blood all over the place, some of it Rahul's and some belonging to the biker who was still conscious but had an ugly gash across one leg. A cow standing by the road gazed calmly at us and then lifted her tail and urinated on the sign which had rolled to a stop next to her. A stream of yellow pee mingled with blood flowed into the gutter.

By the time our cab got to the hospital, Rahul had bled freely all over the seat. He was coming to at intervals, groaning and then lapsing back into unconsciousness. The cabbie pulled up at the emergency entrance and leaped out yelling for a stretcher.

It took an hour to get the wound stitched up—the doctor did a CT scan and a whole bunch of other tests, and decided that Rahul needed to stay in the hospital, under observation for twelve hours. I waited around till he was shifted to a room, though I badly wanted to go home and change. My kurta was grimy and blood-stained—unlike Hindi film heroines who always wear white in such situations for the best dramatic contrast, I was wearing blue and looked a right mess.

'Feeling better?' I asked when I finally got to see him. He nodded. 'Head still hurts. Thanks for getting me here—I guess you saved my life.'

'Umm, I seriously considered leaving you on the road to bleed to death, but…'

He grinned wanly. 'I'm glad you changed your mind!'

We were both silent for a while, and I was thinking of leaving when he said, 'Nitika, can I ask you something?'

I nodded.

'Are you married?'

I stared at him. 'You know I'm not. Why do you ask?'

He looked down and muttered, 'I thought I remembered seeing you—a long time back. In Goa.'

'Which year was this?' I asked.

'I dunno, I think 2003. I'd gone there on a shoot. I was wandering around a beach when a guy stopped me and asked me to take a picture of him and his wife. Her hair was longer than yours—other than that, you look just like her. She was wearing shorts and a t-shirt. She had these huge stacks of bangles on each arm and mehendi all over her hands and feet. It should have looked awful, but it was actually rather cool. The guy had grey eyes…'

'Green eyes,' I said automatically.

Rahul looked up. 'So it was you! I don't know why I never realized it earlier. It suddenly struck me today when…' His voice trailed away and he said uncertainly, 'Did you guys split up?'

'Abhishek went swimming in the sea the evening we met you. The sea looked calm and he was a strong swimmer, but there was a freak current that dragged him under. He drowned.'

Concern and embarrassment warred so obviously on Rahul's face that he looked faintly ludicrous. 'I'm so sorry. I didn't realize. I shouldn't have brought it up.'

'It's okay; it was a long time ago. What made you ask today?'

He looked confused. 'I don't know. It suddenly came back to

me when you walked in at the door now—something about your expression triggered it off. I even thought I saw your husband that night, getting into the train to Mumbai. I guess it couldn't have been him if...' his voice trailed off again.

I left the hospital feeling rather disturbed, though it had been six years since my brief, unconsummated marriage to Abhishek had come to a sudden end. I hadn't been in love with him—it was an arranged marriage—but dealing with his death had been traumatic. It was such a horrible, futile way to die. Like an ant getting flushed down the toilet. His body was never found, though a band of local boys dived in the area for hours looking for him. I hadn't even realized how far he'd swum out—I'd been splashing around in the shallows and got salt water on my contact lenses. I had gone back to the car to wash them out. I was heading back to the beach when a foreign tourist raised the alarm. I remembered trying to decipher the tourist's thick European accent through a wave of rising fear and shook myself. No point thinking about it.

Rahul got back to work a few days later. His face was still a mess—I had to get a model for the underwear shoot after all, and the client wasn't pleased (especially after the model decided to walk off with a dozen unopened packs of chaddis that had been ordered for the shoot).

We were on our way to The Singh's office when the topic of my marriage came up again. Rahul was driving (he'd recently acquired a car), and I was admiring his profile as he hummed to himself. This time he wanted to know if I was still in touch with my in-laws.

'No,' I said. 'And why are you so obsessed with my being married anyway? Even my parents have forgotten about it now.'

He turned a dull red. 'I...I guess I've always had a thing for you. You didn't like me much before the accident, so I never said anything.'

I opened my eyes wide. 'Didn't show it, did you? Looked like you were doing your best to make my life difficult.' He stayed silent.

'I wonder if I'd like you if you were ugly,' I mused aloud after a while. 'But maybe if you were ugly, you'd be less obnoxious, in which case you wouldn't be you.'

The fight we had after that remark resulted in Rahul going into a sulk that promised to last indefinitely.

Rewind

A week or so later I went to Rahul's desk to search for a Cross pen he'd borrowed and conveniently forgotten to return. He was away at a client meeting and his laptop was unlocked. I glanced idly at his mailbox and saw a mail in his inbox from Abhishek Malhotra. Granted it wasn't an uncommon name, but I clicked on it out of sheer curiosity.

Rahul,

The marriage wasn't registered—we were to get it done after we returned from Goa. I'm not sure if Nitika is legally my wife. Maybe you could get a lawyer to check.

Regards,

Abhishek

I took a deep breath to stop myself from hyperventilating. I scanned rapidly through Rahul's inbox and then through his archives. It took me around half an hour to figure out what he'd been up to and I was so upset I felt I couldn't stay in the office a minute longer. I was getting out of the lift downstairs when I spotted Rahul walking into the building. I grabbed his arm and dragged him into a corner.

'When were you planning to tell me about all the detective work you've been doing?'

He gave me a defensive look. 'I don't know what you mean.'

'Like hell you don't! Sneaking around and figuring out that my so-called husband isn't dead after all. He's gay, and he's in the Czech-fucking-Republic with his boyfriend. And that he planned the whole death-by-drowning act! Were you going to tell me ever? Or just get your jollies pretending to be Karamchand, or the Hardy Boys, or or or...'

He handed me a handkerchief as I burst into tears.

'Karamchand?' he asked.

'The guy on TV who ate carrots! I don't know why we're talking about him! When were you planning to tell me about Abhishek?'

'Your dad was going to speak to you.'

'My dad?' I stared at him in disbelief. 'Ok, we need to talk, and now. I don't care what industry-changing campaign you're working on, we're getting out of here right now.'

The explanation didn't take much time. Rahul had been very, very sure that he'd seen Abhishek leaving Goa the night he was supposed to have drowned. A Google search threw up a few dozen random Abhishek Malhotras across the globe, and a reference to Abhishek's death in a blog written by one of his college friends. He did a second search, narrowing it down with the name of the college and found Abhishek's profile on the corporate website of an obscure software company in the Czech Republic.

It was easy getting my father-in-law's number—Rahul persuaded someone in HR to give it to him from my insurance records. Figuring out how to tackle him was a tougher task. He finally called him pretending to be from the Czech embassy, saying he was doing a verification call to confirm that the India address in Abhishek's visa application form was still valid. Instead of a distraught father telling him about his son's death, he got my father-in-law calmly confirming the address.

By then, Rahul was in too deep to back out. Sensibly, he decided to speak to my father rather than to me—he'd anticipated that I would be furious with him for interfering. My parents hotfooted across to confront Abhishek's father. Rahul wasn't part of that meeting, but I could imagine my mom in a Rudra-Kali avatar, forcing the story out of the Malhotras. I could even bring myself to feel sorry for them.

Abhishek had been in the US on a project when he'd met Petr. Till then, he'd carefully suppressed his homosexual tendencies but, away from India and his parents, he quite genuinely fell in love with Petr. They were living together for the year that he was in the US, and the initial plan was that he would come back to India, tell his parents and then relocate to Europe to be with Petr. When he got home, he chickened out. His parents had met me, decided I would make an ideal bahu, and preparations were in full swing for our wedding before he knew what was happening.

Petr was devastated when Abhishek told him. They had several stormy phone conversations and Petr finally came down to India on a tourist visa the day before the wedding. Maybe seeing him again did the trick—it finally sank into Abhishek's thick skull that he was about to do something really, really stupid. By then, it was too late to back out of the wedding without creating an even bigger mess.

The way out struck Petr when Abhishek said despondently that if he hadn't been a good swimmer he'd have considered drowning himself in the sea at Goa. It wasn't a difficult plan to implement. Abhishek struck out to sea once I was safely on the beach. Petr picked him up on a speed boat he had hired for the purpose, dropped him at another beach a mile off and then came back to raise the alarm.

'I met the son of a bitch!' I said when Rahul got to that point. 'He was that tall nerd who got onto the beach and started raising a ruckus!' Rahul nodded, looking relieved that I was finally directing some of my anger in the right direction.

The rest of the story was less complicated. Abhishek left Goa that night with Petr. He got in touch with his parents a couple of days later, and they were so relieved to find him alive that they would have happily agreed to a declaration that he was going to spend the rest of his life having sex with a blue-bottomed baboon. However, the whole 'biradari mein naak kat jayegi' thing was still a concern, and Abhishek left the country without anyone other than his parents and sister getting to know the truth.

Play

'Where do you come into all this?' I asked Rahul quietly, once he'd finished. My initial rage had subsided, leaving me feeling drained and depressed.

He shrugged. 'I don't, actually. I thought you should be told but, strictly speaking, it's none of my business. Your dad was going to come over next week to speak to you. I've been in touch with Abhishek because your dad didn't want to speak to him.'

'I guess I should thank you.'

'You don't need to.'

'My mom must be thrilled with you.'

He smiled. 'She's a nice lady.'

I snorted. 'Nice lady, my foot. She's probably decided you are good next-son-in-law material.'

'That's your decision. I'd be happy to be her next son-in-law if you're okay with it.'

'Is that supposed to be a proposal?'

Rahul nodded.

'No ring?'

'I'll buy you one right away if you say yes.'

His phone rang. He looked at it and then back at me, clearly wanting to take the call, but worried I'd bean him on the head if he did.

'Let me guess—it's your boss.' He nodded. 'Take the call.'

He spent ten minutes trying to convince his boss that he had vanished because I had insisted on discussing a new client brief outside office. He hung up looking harassed.

'Rahul, let's make a deal,' I said. 'I'll marry you if you promise to quit the agency and go work someplace else.'

'Actually, The Singh's offered me a job. Higher salary, company flat. You think I should take it?'

'You should. And quickly, before I change my mind about marrying you. Now please switch off your phone and let's go buy me that ring before the shops close.'

Obviously, it wasn't as simple as it sounds. It took a while to sort out the legal mess that Abhishek's fake death had got my marital status into. Rahul was still as irritating as ever at work, until he left to join The Singh's team. However, he was wonderfully and gloriously straight, and I was the envy of all my female relatives for the 'chikna chhora' I had managed to nab.

We married once my marriage to Abhishek was annulled, and our son is now the star model in The Singh's latest diaper campaign. While I have it on good authority that Rahul irritates his new colleagues just as much as he irritated us at the agency, he has turned out to be surprisingly good husband material. The only problem is that he still refuses to model for any of my ads…

Sahana or Shamim

SANGEETA BANDYOPADHYAY

TRANSLATED BY ARUNAVA SINHA

Even when 9/11 took place, Sahana had bought fish regularly. Also when the Godhra incident had taken place in her own country. Taking advantage of Paramesh's absence, she had bought fish every single time, overcoming her hesitation. So many people were dying every day in Kashmir, America was tearing Iraq to pieces. Militants nurtured by the ISI were taking shelter in Bangladesh, even Kolkata wasn't safe any more. The air was thick with rumours, you felt afraid to step out of your home, being in a crowd was uncomfortable, the cinema-hall made you claustrophobic—but still, skirting all these truths, Sahana had continued buying fish. When she entered the market, she looked around and then casually approached the area where the fish was sold. She bought the fish, put it in her shopping bag and went home. She did all of this with her mouth clamped shut. Cautiously. Even rinsing the fish slices made her hands shake.

It happened every time—from the moment of buying the fish, through bringing it home in her oversized shopping bag, rinsing the slices gingerly, gathering the scales and the other parts to be discarded with an unerring hand, till she had thrown them away from the high-rise she lived into the thicket of fig trees on the grounds of the British bungalow next door. Her hands shook, she found it difficult to breathe, and her head reeled!

And how self-flagellating the act of frying the fish was. Constantly she felt as though Paramesh was standing next to her, crying, 'Flesh, flesh!' She started in alarm every now and then, certain that her fear would lead her to cause an accident. Her own carelessness would make her burn to death. The stench of her burning flesh would mingle with the flavour of fried fish.

But death would not bring deliverance. The forensic report would definitely indicate that she was burnt while frying fish. Paramesh's heart would no longer harbour the detached respect and love that people customarily felt for the dead. If there were any photographs of her in the flat, he would throw them away, damning her as a traitor. And then, he would hate her as long as he lived.

Sahana mused about all of this as she cooked the fish. She usually felt overwhelmed when she was done with the cooking. Unable to control herself, she ate the fish with rice, experiencing an acute sense of satisfaction. But as soon as she had eaten, she began to pant. Fear seized her, weighing her down like a huge slab of stone. She didn't even blink till she had washed and scoured the utensils, the ladles, the table, the oven—the entire kitchen in fact—until they gleamed. She sprayed freshener in every room, poured phenyl into the sink. Picking every single bone with her nails, she put them in a polythene packet and threw them out into the thicket next door. She poured soap on her hands, rinsed her mouth out with mouth-freshener, shampooed her hair—she showered! She showered!

Not a trace of the smell remained. Still she sprayed the freshener once more in every room and sniffed both sides of her palm. Sometimes, unable to handle such anxiety, Sahana pounded garlic into a paste and fried it in oil. All smells were certain to be buried.

But the situation had not been even remotely like this when they had met and exchanged hearts. Fish had not appeared a significant issue during those early days of their romance. In fact, she had never felt as though she were treading a path of sacrifice in the process of linking her life to Paramesh's. She had accepted the whole thing without protesting. Although she realized now that she had indeed wanted to protest—but hadn't been able to.

'I'm vegetarian,' Paramesh had told her. 'You mustn't eat anything non-vegetarian at home.'

'What about elsewhere?' she had asked.

Silent for a couple of seconds, Paramesh had shrugged.

'I don't mind chicken. But as for fish, you'll have to give it up everywhere, at home or elsewhere. I simply cannot tolerate the smell of fish, Sahana. I throw up on the spot. It makes me so sick that I've had to be hospitalized in the past. I hate fish. Moreover, Sahana, I cannot dream of kissing or making love to someone who eats fish. I can't enter someone who, in one way or another, is fishy.'

Holding up the middle finger of his left hand and shaking it, Paramesh had conveyed both meanings of the word fishy to her, 'So you have to give it up.'

By then Sahana had fallen in love with Paramesh. If it had been only love, it might have been different, but she had also become psychologically dependent on him. She had realized that she would have to give up fish if she wanted Paramesh. She had effortlessly uprooted the very desire for fish from her heart. She had trained her sights instead on all the other kinds of food in the world. For two years she had not eaten any fish. Then she was possessed again by its taste.

And she began to eat fish in secret, and she started to fear Paramesh. For she was only too aware that if Paramesh came to know, their relationship would end. Alternatively, a conflict would erupt, the kind of conflict that we are familiar with. The more Sahana began to fear Paramesh, the more she began to loathe him too. Hatred. Or, one could say that the more she became aware of Paramesh's abhorrence for fish and those who ate fish, the more determined she become to retaliate with a proportionate degree of abhorrence for those who did not eat fish. She seemed to feel a certain responsibility to do this. She found her self-awareness offering ammunition for her opposition to, and disillusionment about Paramesh.

'Those who eat fish and those who don't are poles apart, separated by a deep gulf of mutual contempt.' When she grew deeply emotional about fish, she argued with trepidation, 'Why should I be deprived of fish Paramesh, just because you don't enjoy it, just because you cannot stand the smell of fish? Why should you impose your behaviour on mine? I'm not you, I'm a person of my own, I shall remain a distinct person. Isn't this a mistake on your part, Param?'

Paramesh became furious, telling her about total surrender. 'Even if I'm wrong,' he replied, 'I expect unquestioning submission from you in this regard. Remember that there is no alternative if this relationship is to be maintained in its most peaceful possible state. Or else, as you know, terrible things may happen; you'd better not blame me then.'

Sahana's former lover Manish returned to her life at this precise juncture. Because hate spirals upwards and the reasons for the hatred fade while the object of the hatred becomes the most important thing, Sahana entered into an illicit relationship with Manish more or less needlessly, simply out of loathing for Paramesh.

Paramesh came out sharply against eating meat and fish one evening at a small party at a friend's house. 'The most extreme form of enjoying meat is cannibalism,' he declared. 'Human flesh is the most delicious of all!'

Sahana wept buckets that evening, sitting on the toilet in the friend's house. Finally, she ground her teeth—'So it's hatred? So much hatred?' On the way back Paramesh's face appeared to be composed of nothing but a glutinous green substance. The next day she not only cooked some fish, she ate it too in Manish's arms. Then, drawing strength from ultimate hatred for the first time in her life, she let Manish have her. But she could see that this hatred was working in its entirety on her and her alone. Since Paramesh could perceive nothing of it, since he had no inkling of this nightmarish loathing, the only person who had to bear it was Sahana herself. Poor Sahana! Not only was she the one to hate, she was also the one to suffer from its impact. Just like cheating—as long as the person being cheated is not aware of being cheated, they don't have to bear the burden of being cheated, it is borne entirely by the person doing the cheating. And again, the moment the person being cheated gets to know everything, they're no longer being cheated. And yet the person who had done the cheating continues to bear the entire burden, as before! In other words, people can cheat, but people can never be cheated—it really is entirely one-sided.

In the same way Sahana cheated Paramesh, but Paramesh wasn't cheated. Sahana hated, but Paramesh did not feel hated. Sahana remained perpetually drenched in her own loathing. Yet whenever during the day or the night Paramesh wanted to be intimate with her, he smelt strawberry, gulab jamun or mint on her breath. He was able to relax his body completely and kiss her fervently. He could say, 'Don't you love me any more, Sana? Why is your mouth so cold otherwise?'

On the other hand Sahana frequently discovered when trying to cook the fish she had bought that it had rotted. Rotted completely! When having sex with Manish she discovered she did not want him; during intercourse with Paramesh she suffered from guilt, disquiet and fear—and she filled the rest of her hours with hatred. It was an unarticulated, unstated hatred, which progressively crossed the limits of forbidden pleasure to rot just like stale fish. Yet Sahana could not simply separate the scales and bones and throw them away. She could not forget that Paramesh and she were repulsively unlike each other.

Paramesh had been in London on 7/7. Sahana didn't know anything about the explosions till Pubali called her in the afternoon with great anxiety, for she hadn't switched her TV on.

In a frenzy she tried to call Paramesh on his mobile. But a pre-recorded voice kept informing her that 'the subscriber is out of reach at this moment…'

Their friends gathered one by one. Manish, Pubali, Tushar, Vasundhara. Each of them tried in their own way to get some information about Paramesh. But evening stretched into night, there was neither any news of Paramesh, nor any communication from him.

Despite their collective efforts her friends could not calm Sahana. Her behaviour was out of control. Although they could make out her words, none of them could understand what Sahana meant.

'My hatred has killed Paramesh,' Sahana was shrieking, 'my continuous hatred.' In tears, she continued, 'Was it necessary to hate him so much?'

The day passed in a whirl. Paramesh did not return. A week later Sahana took a flight to London, along with her sister and brother-in-law. And returned without Paramesh.

There was no trace of Paramesh anywhere. No sign. It wasn't even obvious whether he was dead.

A couple of months later Manish visited Sahana. She seized his arm. 'I'm converting, Manish,' she told him. 'I'm going to become a Muslim.'

Manish was so astonished he was unable to say anything. He could not grasp how this was related to the grief resulting from Paramesh's disappearance, or whether it was at all related.

'Paramesh used to talk of complete submission, Manish,' Sahana continued.

'We cannot live together until you become me, he would say. I could say that to you too Param, I used to reply angrily.'

'He would shake his head. Ultimate submission means unquestioning surrender, he would say. Where there is no scope for asking questions. Where questions don't even exist.'

'Now that I don't know whether Paramesh will be back, Manish, I have found only one way to offer the ultimate submission he wanted. Only one. In a couple of days a senior Muslim priest will convert me. My name will be Shamim.'

Possibly understanding some of what Sahana was getting at, Manish reached out to move a few strands of hair away from her face. 'Is there no other way, Sahana?' he asked.

'No there isn't Manish. There's no shortcut. No room for bargaining. I cannot become you with anything less than this. All effort will go waste. This is what complete submission means Manish. When Paramesh comes back he will realise that even if it took time, I have been able to accept him with my heart.'

Don't raise any questions about this story, reader. Before you can, I would like to remind you that this is a story of unquestioning surrender.

Measures of Life and Love

ANANT TRIPATHI

To Girish, complexity had never made much sense.

He had seen his share of life, caroused in its flippant joys and wallowed in its shallow sufferings. Like other people, he had been through its circles and come out a smoother man every time.

But in his years, he come to see life in plain relief. There was a simplicity to things: to choices, to relationships and to the way people were. There was right and there was wrong. Was there much else needed for a man to decide?

Apparently there was. There were many complexities to be considered, it seemed; many variables to keep track of. People perceived life and its colours in large measures of relativity. This affected that, and that bore down on this: the intricate web of life.

While Girish did understand such things very well, he could not stand inside such a tangled view himself.

He had seen many sorts of people. They came to him quite often in fact. For, though he did not really know it, he had an uncanny knack for setting them at ease. So it was that he had listened to the many lamentations they were always so ready to share. And having seen them so closely, he could grant them that theirs could be complex lives, at least if they were wont to believe so.

But he could not help seeing his own in a simple light. His ruling was that of conscience. And it was enough to keep him going. Sometimes he thought that, maybe, in his pessimism, he had made life too simple. But then, maybe it really was.

He was thinking of such things while he sat looking at the waves throwing themselves against the rocks. He watched the roar of the breakers every time they crashed into the craggy shore, and he watched their retreat in foam. It was ruthless as slaughter.

The day was disorderly and there were autumn leaves in the thrashing wind. It howled as it swept his hair into his face. The rain could arrive anytime now. The sky was bulging with it. Girish would rather be back inside his damp room at the lodge when it came. But Mira liked the rain—as she liked the sea, and the sun, and summer. So he did not really mind.

She was down among the rocks, collecting shells from the shallow pools. Even as Girish looked at her, she lifted her face and caught him in his observation. Smiling, he waved her over. She walked to him, barefoot over the rocks, with seashells in her cupped hands, hair and stole whipping about her frame in the punishing gale.

He watched her come in silence, his heart clenching in that peculiar manner it had, reminding him of the only part of his life he could not get around, the only complexity: her.

She came and sat beside him—carefully, so that the shells did not fall. He sat looking at her soft hands for a while, thinking of how he would ask her what he meant to.

But she spoke first, breaking his silent struggle. 'How long before you have to leave?' Her brown eyes were dark with confusion as she asked this.

Girish did not make a direct reply. 'I want you to come with me,' he said.

She smiled at him, but it was a solemn smile. 'You know I cannot.'

'But why?'

When she did not say anything, he turned away. The sun was somewhere above the horizon, just behind the swollen clouds, but the light was already thinning. As the silence stretched, Girish felt his urge weakening again.

'You do not have to take money from other men,' he said feebly. It was not said in accusation, but as a plea.

He knew she was not looking at him when she replied. 'You ask the same question every time, Girish. I cannot come with you.' She paused, and he realized that she had bent forward to pick another shell. He could not tell how it had managed to crawl so far up the crags. Still busy with the shells, she continued, 'And you know I have to take the money. A woman has to eat.'

Girish sighed. 'Come with me this time, Mira. Please.'

'Then marry me.' She said it in a way that brought him around. Her expression, he could not really place. He had never seen it before. She looked almost vulnerable. 'Marry me and take me with you, I will come.' Then she smiled, and she was the old Mira again. 'But I know you cannot. You cannot marry me. I cannot come with you. It's okay. Life is complicated and we cannot have all of everything—I have come to accept that. I love you. That is enough for me.'

He did not know what to say to that, so he held his silence and his grief close about himself, not willing to let go.

Mira held him in her gaze for some time, but when Girish did not say anything, she turned back to her shells and gently lay them down. They were like so many dreams, lost and scattered in the sand between them.

After some time, arranging her treasure, she said, 'So, how long before you go back?'

The red of dusk was beginning to deepen into the shades of approaching night. Darkness was falling, and still the waves seemed adamant in their resolve to die against the rocky shore.

Girish decided to give it another try—the last one. It was all the hope he had. 'I want to live with you, Mira. I want to get used to you, and not the just the thought of you. I'm getting old, as are you. How many years before you run out of customers? A woman has to eat, yes, but how long do you think you can sustain this barter? Beauty is good only for so long. And it's no different for me. I am a man of the people. This city and its trappings hold no charm for me. If I ever come here, it is to see you. I am an ageing activist, Mira. I do not have anything in terms of property, or a real livelihood. I work for the villagers, thrash my limbs to see that they get what is rightfully theirs. I am happy with whatever they can give me in faith. It won't be long before I, too, cannot go on. They are my people as I am theirs, but even I cannot hope to live off them after I am too old to be of use to them. There is only so much a man can do for love. I want to settle down Mira. Have a piece of land, rear a buffalo or two. Come, Mira. Please. Don't be so cold to me.'

He paused, struggling to keep his voice calm. The world could crack up and swallow itself a hundred times before he would shed a tear. He was an honest man, and love was not enough to weaken him.

Mira was looking at him, her eyes moist. More than love, it was pity he saw in them and that suddenly enraged him. His tone was still as death when he asked her, 'You won't, then?'

He knew that she had heard the finality in his words, but he had said them. He was a simple man. His meaning could not be simpler.

Her shells were forgotten. She looked at him for some time, a silent question in her manner, and then turned away as if she had made a decision.

When she spoke there was no pity in her voice, only sorrow. 'I understand you cannot marry me Girish. That is the reason I never asked. Even when I did, I was not hoping for an affirmation. Marriage does not stand in agreement with your principles, and I respect that.' She faced him, and in her eyes was such compassion as he had never seen before. 'You are an idealist, Girish. A romantic. You think only by conscience, and that is enough for you to make your choices. But I am a woman Giri! A woman has to be realistic! When she starts dreaming, things find a reason to topple down. I cannot dream Giri.'

He knew there was love deep as the sea in her compassion, but it crashed against his resolve like the breakers in the bay. He lashed out at her, saying, 'Women do not take money for love. Come on Mira. You are no woman. No, you're a whore!' He knew how venomous he sounded. He knew how shattering it must be, coming from him.

But her face did not show the hurt he had thought it would. She just smiled sadly, and for a moment he thought that he had fallen into some self-made trap, done something horrible that she had somehow known he would. The compassion in her smile was like an accusation. Then his rage came rushing back, along with the perceived injustices and all the pent-up hurt.

He got up. His foot scattered the shells that Mira had been trying to put into a pattern. He looked down at her and she was looking up. Many hurtful words came to his mind, each equally vicious, equally punishing. He stood there for a moment, waiting, probably hoping, for a sign. But there was only silence between them. Silence, and seashells, and sorrow, and dreams that could not be woven into their lives.

Then he turned around and left her there, his turban flapping in the wind behind him.

His heart ached with longing at every step he took away from her. It was the most difficult thing to walk away from love, almost like betraying his conscience. He saw life in simple contours, yet love was difficult.

He was a simple man, and his ruling was that of conscience. It was either right or wrong. There was not much needed for him to decide. Yet he felt like a criminal as he walked. Even the world seemed like a mirror to the wretchedness he had just stained his soul with. The sun had gone down some time ago, but he had not noticed its passing. The stars were probably out, but he could not see any. There were dirty clouds in the sky, and they lit up with harsh lightning every now and then. Soon the rains would come. He meant to be back in his damp room at the lodge when they did.

He never looked back.

Strangers

AHMED FAIYAZ

I caught a glimpse of her the very day I got to Chennai. I noticed her going down the elevator while I ran down the stairs and headed out on to the street, looking for a grocery store to buy a bottle of water. Her gaze met mine as she entered the elevator; she looked petite; the most beautiful girl I had seen in a long time.

I had landed in Chennai a few hours ago, having flown in with some reluctance. I had been sent down from my office in Pune to Chennai to manage a project for two months. I hesitated and grumbled a lot before I actually got on the plane and flew down. It was a place I hadn't been to, and a city where I knew very few people. Compusys had arranged for me to stay in a plush service apartment off Khader Nawaz Khan Road, a posh neighbourhood in Chennai; this was one of the perks of holding a management-cadre position in a leading software company. But my life was far from perfect; I had just broken up with my girlfriend of three years.

I saw her again three days later. I was returning from work at five in the morning feeling dog-tired when I saw her come out of 404 in a track suit and walk past me. She gave me a knowing look, and smiled at me as I walked to the door. I was in 403, across the hall from her.

Later that evening, I answered the doorbell expecting Surya, the caretaker, at the door with milk and bread. Instead, I saw her standing before me with a smile on her face.

'Hi; I'm Kavita, your neighbour. Can I come in?' She smiled at me cheerily, as I gestured sleepily, inviting her to sit down in the living room.

'I'm Abhay,' I said not too loudly, as she looked around the room with interest. 'I've just moved here from Pune to manage a project. I'm with Compusys.'

'I see,' she said, before sitting down. She wore a simple white and blue salwar suit; her long hair tumbled over a shoulder and moth-kissed lips spread in an engaging smile as she looked at me.

'I don't do much; at least not at the moment.' I felt compelled to say into the silence. I figured that possibly she had got married recently and moved to the city. She certainly didn't look as if she was from these parts and had a mysterious air about her.

'Anyway, I don't mean to intrude on your time; you must be busy. Why don't you drop by for a cup of coffee tomorrow evening?' she asked.

'Sure…'

'Great; it's nice to meet someone my age. This building is mostly inhabited by families with kids.'

'Sure; it was great meeting you, Kavita. Thanks for coming by,' I said, as she walked out of the apartment. She turned around and smiled at me with a twinkle in her eyes.

'Welcome to the neighbourhood, I'll see you tomorrow…' she said shyly, as she walked across the hall. I watched her walk across the hall thinking, 'Wow!' I certainly hadn't expected this kind of a reception in Chennai.

The next day, I managed to sleep a little during the day, thinking about my appointment for coffee with Kavita. At half-past four, I wore my crispest shirt, a clean pair of jeans and after spraying Davidoff Cool Water rather excessively on my hairy chest, I walked across the hall and rang the bell.

Kavita, wearing an apron and with her long tresses tied in a bun, opened the door waving me in. She smiled at me with a look of confusion, possibly wondering if it was a good idea inviting home a complete stranger. I handed her the box of chocolates I had picked up at a store in IT Park late last night.

'Thanks; you didn't have to!' she exclaimed. 'Why don't you sit down and make yourself comfortable? I'm just frying some pakoras for us.'

I sat down on a cane chair, looking at the sparse furniture in the apartment. There was a small sofa, a dining table and a few cane chairs. There were unopened boxes lying in a corner. She joined me after a few minutes with a plate of onion pakoras and two cups of filter coffee.

'You're not from around here, are you?' I asked. I didn't see any family pictures on the walls, a common sight in Indian homes.

'No; I'm basically from Indore. I moved here after my marriage to Vijay ten months ago. He's a doctor, based in the US at the moment. He moved there a little while after our marriage…'

'So do you plan to join him soon? It must be difficult living alone, that too in your first year of marriage.' She looked hurt, but composed herself.

'It's been eight months; it's not so bad. I hope the coffee is okay. And are the pakoras fine? I'm not much of a cook really…' she said.

'No; they're really good, thanks. You shouldn't have taken so much trouble.'

'It's not much; it kept me busy. I have nothing much to do

really. That's why I don't have a maid. I keep myself busy looking after this apartment.'

'You don't get out much?'

'Not really. I used to work with my Dad back in Indore. He runs a textile mill. I even have a degree in business management. But I haven't really looked out for a job here. Anyway...tell me about you. How do you like the city?'

'Not too bad actually, it's better than I expected.' Thanks to you, I thought, noticing her look at me with her button-like light brown eyes. 'The weather is a bit too humid for my liking, but it's a nice, laid-back environment at work. The people, once they get past the fact that you do not understand or speak Tamil, are quite friendly, and I do enjoy the vegetarian food.'

'Ha ha yes. It isn't too bad. I didn't like it initially, but now I'm okay.' We chatted for a while, and she spoke about her parents and her brother back home. She didn't say much about her husband, and I didn't probe.

An hour later, I walked over to my apartment, wishing I had spent more time with her.

The next morning, I met her in the corridor. 'Hi, how was your day at work?' she asked, removing her iPod earplugs.

'Not bad...' I said, smiling. This definitely made up for sitting up all night and checking codes my staff had written.

'Do you want to come by this evening? We could chat over a coffee and play a game of chess.'

'Sure. Give me your number. I'll call you when I wake up and confirm a time.'

'I don't really use a mobile phone, I don't need one. Come by anytime; I have nothing much to do anyway,' she quipped.

'Okay, sounds good—see you later,' I said, before waving her off.

I went back for a cup of coffee that evening, and for many evenings that followed. She was more than glad to have me over. We often played a game of chess, listened to U2 or Jagjit Singh's ghazals or watched a movie on television. Sometimes we played Pictionary and solved puzzles together. I enjoyed spending time with her and we grew to become close friends. I spoke to her openly about my past relationships, to which she listened intently and said very little. She always had an innocent look about her and she seemed naive at times. She declined my offer to take her out for dinner or for a movie.

'I don't know what people in this building might say. People talk, you know? I would rather chill with you at home. I hope you understand.' She gazed at me with a look of despondency.

'Sure I do. I don't want anyone saying something inappropriate about you.'

'Thanks,' she said, before leaning in and kissing me softly on my cheek.

I went over frequently and spent every other evening at her place, listening to music, watching a film or playing board games. Surya gave me knowing smiles as I wandered in and out of my own house. He noticed that I was always out and came home late in a good mood. I still wonder what he thought.

One afternoon I rang her bell, anticipating spending some time with her. She opened the door after a while and invited me in with a smile. Her hair was wet and she wore a long bathrobe.

'I was in the shower,' she said. She looked at me with a flirtatious smile. We had grown pretty close to each other and often flirted harmlessly.

'Happy Independence Day,' I said, before giving her a potted plant I had picked up for her.

'Wishing you the same, come and sit down. I'll make a cup

of coffee for you,' she said, before disappearing into the kitchen.

She was back with two cups of coffee, wearing track pants and a sleeveless grey top. She sat next to me on the couch while we sipped cups of coffee and ginger tea and watched an old rerun of *Maine Pyar Kiya*, the Bollywood romance of the decade which ushered in the era of Salman Khan, and heralded the beginning of his reign over Bollywood.

At some time during the second half of the movie she disappeared for a minute and came back wearing a sexy knee length nightdress. She walked towards me with a seductive smile; I drew her towards me and kissed her slowly. Her pale cheeks were filled with colour. She sat on my lap, facing me, and ran her fingers through my hair, nibbling on my ear playfully.

I unhooked the strap on her nightdress and ran my fingers all over her bare back, to which she responded by taking my hand and placing it on her supple breast. We made love with a sense of urgency and with hungry passion; and then again, slowly, on the couch with her legs wrapped around mine, and with our arms wrapped around each other. She moaned with delight and responded with ecstasy to moves I didn't know I had. We lay there for a long while afterwards, listening to the rustling wind and the sound of falling rain. It poured steadily for a long while, an unusual occurrence in Chennai in the month of August. I squeezed her close, unwilling to let go. I realized that I was falling in love with her. I trailed my fingers over her lips and her cheek while she lay on top of me with her eyes closed.

'Why don't you leave him? Does he know about me?'

'He doesn't; why should he? It isn't that easy! You don't understand,' she cried out, turning pale.

'I'm not sure I understand this fully; you clearly don't seem to love him. You won't even talk about him.'

'Vijay is my husband; we're married,' she said, abruptly sitting up and pulling her crumpled nightdress from under the sofa. 'I don't know how much longer I'll stay here,' she said turning away, while I looked at her with intense eyes.

'Today was good,' I said reaching out to hold her, 'For weeks I've wanted to hold you in my arms and kiss you…' I said trying to lift her spirits a little.

'I did too,' she smiled warmly. 'I think you should leave; it's quite late.'

'Why can't I sleep over with you? It'll keep me warm,' I said making no move to pick up my clothes from the floor.

'Ha ha, don't be a badmaash! Enough for one night, don't you think?' she tossed my boxers to me.

'Well as long as we can get together tomorrow night and make love again.' She blushed, looking me in the eye. We locked lips again and kissed for a long while, before I reluctantly said goodnight. I went back to my apartment with a grin on my face, my shirt half tucked in and my hair all ruffled. Surya greeted me with a jealous smile; he realized I was getting it, thankfully he didn't know from whom. I slapped him on the back like a brother.

The next evening I went to her place straight after work. I got her a bunch of roses and a bottle of red wine. I had hoped on seducing her again and sweet-talking her into leaving her so-called husband. I rang her doorbell twice, to which there was no response. I waited for ten minutes and rang again. No luck.

I went home, my tail between my legs, all hopes of having mind-blowing sex blown to dust. This had happened a few times before. She had later said that she was asleep or had gone out grocery shopping. I went back the next day and rang the bell hopefully. There was no response again. I began to get agitated and impatient. I had just another week in Chennai and I was losing sleep over why she wasn't opening the door for me. I spent waking hours mulling over our last conversation and wondered if I had said anything I shouldn't have.

I went back every day. I hoped that she would forgive me and open the door. Two days before I was to leave, I stood at my usual spot tapping on her door when Surya came out of our apartment.

'What happened saar?' he asked. He had a look of confusion in his eyes. I wondered if he knew where I was spending a lot of time.

'Nothing man. I'm just checking to see if my friend is at home.'

'Inge? But nobody lives here sir....' he said looking exasperated.

'You must be mistaken, I have a family friend living in this apartment,' I said in a matter-of-fact way.

'No saar. My boss is the owner of this apartment; I have the keys. Wait here one minute...' He came back with a set of keys and opened the apartment.

What I saw was nothing like the apartment I had been visiting. There were a few chairs, the sofa-set was covered with an old white cloth and the apartment was covered by a layer of dust. It had a musty smell, as if no one had lived here in a long time.

'Patiya saar! They shut this apartment after the problem sometime back saar,' he said, sizing me up with a suspicious look in his eyes. He possibly thought I was hallucinating.

He walked back to our apartment while I stood frozen; I was too stunned to move. Everything that had happened in the apartment where I stood was real. I had gone back there every other day for eleven weeks, and spent time with a woman I was now desperately in love with. I couldn't comprehend what was happening.

I looked around the living room that was filled with dusty old boxes, clothes hangers lying on the floor. I also noticed something strange and walked over to pick it up. It was a collar button from the shirt I'd worn the day Kavita and I made love on the couch. It must have come off when we undressed in a hurry. So it wasn't a dream. I had been in the apartment before. Surya came back with an old newspaper and asked me to read a paragraph on the third page. It was an edition of *The Hindu* dated 24 March 2009.

'See saar, look at this,' he pointed out.

'Suicide at Sundaram Heights' the title screamed. I read on:

Last evening, Kavita Saxena took her life by jumping off the balcony of her fourth floor service apartment residence. Kavita was from Indore and had recently married a cardiologist based in Houston— Vijay Kumar. The couple flew into Chennai yesterday morning and were supposed to fly out to Malaysia for their honeymoon last night. From a letter found in the apartment, Vijay Kumar had left her there and slipped out of the apartment on the pretext of making some travel arrangements and taken a flight to the US in the afternoon. In the note he apologized for the situation he had put her in; he had been forced by his family to marry her. He was apparently in love with an intern who worked with him back in Texas Memorial Hospital. Vijay, in the letter, said that he couldn't get himself to accept the marriage and go ahead with it. He stated that a copy of the letter had been sent to her parents and that he would be wiring them a reimbursement for their expenses on the wedding. He admonished his family in the letter and urged her to return to Indore. The last line of the letter said—'I wish I didn't have to put you through this. I don't have a choice but to do what I'm doing.' The police also found a copy of Kavita's passport and their tickets to Malaysia on the table.

The deceased appears to have taken her life, grieved by the deception she faced from her husband and the embarrassment from the situation for herself and her family. The shocked mother and father of the deceased along with their relatives arrived in Chennai late last night. Reportedly, the mother was 'inconsolable' and the family was in deep shock and grieved by her untimely death and her decision to take her life. 'Kavita was a quiet and reticent child, it must have affected her very badly. This guy needs to be arrested,' her angry cousin, Akhil, told reporters. 'Beautiful and simple' is how her childhood friend, a teary-eyed Neha Mohan described her. The police say they are investigating the matter, and Vijay Kumar's family is to fly in from Bhopal this afternoon. Residents of the neighbourhood are shaken by the incident. Mrs Iyer, who saw Vijay and Kavita come in to the building with their bags, said that the couple appeared cheerful and described the suicide as a sad loss and an unfortunate incident for Kavita and her family. 'This does not appear to be a case of homicide, as the caretaker Surya saw Vijay leave the apartment at 14:00 hours, while Kavita jumped from the balcony at 19:30. We are investigating the matter and trying to track Vijay Kumar down,' Inspector Sundaresh of Nungambakkam Police Station said in a press release to the media. Ramanand Subramaniam, Crime Reporter.

A picture of the balcony from outside the building was also shown above the article. Surya stared at me wide-eyed as I read the article.

'Patiya, do you see this? Because of the scandal, this apartment is locked saar. Everyone knows about it; your friend must be in some other apartment,' he said.

'Yes....I guess I was mistaken,' I mumbled as I tried to gather my wits. I walked back to my apartment and lay flat on the bed wondering what the hell had gone on for the past few weeks. I was completely shaken up.

Later that night, when I went down for a walk to clear my head, I saw Surya chatting with the watchman in Tamil. From the little that I could gather, I heard my name and 404 being mentioned. The watchman looked spooked and stared at me in disbelief, as if I was some mad man. I walked past the gate ignoring them. Tears welled up in my eyes thinking about her and her decision to end her life. I could picture her sitting alone in the apartment and reading the letter her husband had left her. She certainly deserved to live; she deserved someone who loved her.

The next day, all packed and ready to leave, I walked down the corridor to the elevator and called for it by pressing a button. It went down before my eyes, without stopping on the fourth floor. She stood in the elevator giving me a knowing smile, while I gaped at her as if I had seen a ghost.

The Girl Who Was Too Loud

GAYATRI HINGORANI

Finally, she had to be gagged.

It was the summer of 2010. They had started dating around six months ago. Neither was serious about the relationship at the outset—it was just one of the many things you plunged into and got out of when the peak was achieved. He had first met her at a friend's house—one of the many Saturday evening dos he had learnt to frequent after he came to the city. It was the best way to feel the pulse of the city, meet like-minded people and, more importantly, guzzle spirits of good repute and share a few Marlboros for free. She was standing alone in the balcony in a little black dress and mismatched chappals, amusing herself with smoke rings spewing out of her rounded mouth into the still and warm evening of March. They were introduced by a common friend and talked for a bit about the changing role of the media, the latest Bollywood flick and their common fondness for Salman Rushdie. He dropped her home along with a bunch of other girls and promised to add her on Facebook.

It didn't take much to ask her out: coffee, a few whiskeys

and three long puffs of a shared cigarette, at the end of which he slipped in the proposal. By the time the ciggy burnt out and turned into ash under his feet, she confirmed that she was available and willing to give it a shot. That was it: simple, smooth and official. He had already got the essentials in the first few dates—small town girl wanting to fulfil starry dreams, living footloose, fancy-free, no strings attached. He didn't need to know more at this stage. His side of the story was similar and the commonality was enough to move ahead.

With her, he had hit the stage of physical intimacy faster than others. Their first kiss came naturally after a long walk ending at her apartment. They didn't talk about anything in particular, but a goodbye kiss seemed like the obvious thing to do and he was glad that she expected it too. Soon they were canoodling and slurpily kissing. They made use of every opportunity—a dark cinema hall, an empty kitchen in a loud get-together, a rickshaw cruising on the highway. She didn't hesitate to make the first move in these encounters. He liked that—it cut short the will-she-won't-she syndrome in such situations, when one's blood was all but moving upwards.

It didn't even take long to get her into bed. It was a hot sweaty night at the far end of May when they made love for the first time. It happened at her house, after a long evening of drinking with knowns and unknowns. Her roommates were away, and he was the only man Friday left to help clean up the after-party mess. It was fated, that night, and magical too. He led her into bed—and she was willing—calmly, smoothly, longingly. They were done soon, but he enjoyed it immensely; possibly the best he'd had in his string of short-lived affairs. She was aggressive, but in a non-dominating sort of way, and hinted at a wild side that the women he had dated hadn't cared to explore. As morning came, he craved for it again.

He turned towards her and she was awake—her dark brown eyes deeper than ever and a naughty smile hovering around her lips. He tried and she relented easily. It was heady.

The next week he subsisted during the day and sprung out like a jack-in-the-box at night. Every tryst was an experience that would fill up hours of daydreaming. And every day he had more fodder than before. They mostly made use of her rented apartment—her roommates were accommodating and gave them time and space. And sometimes, when they were in his side of the city, he managed to sneak her into his hostel. All he needed to do was send a quick text message to his roommate of two years to scoot to the adjacent room before he came in with his girlfriend of two months. By the end of it, he was consumed. She was desirable, giving and passionate—why couldn't he have her forever? A tingling sensation made him feel all warm inside. He believed in cut-and-dried relationships, but now he saw pink balloons and red roses at traffic signals. He called her every spare minute and yearned for her the rest of the time. She reciprocated with as much fervour.

Nothing was amiss until his roommate pointed out, 'Dude, that woman is loud!'

'Huh?'

He let it pass at first, but the remark stung him for hours. He went through denial (obviously his roommate had made it up to avenge the discomfort he was put through), then anger (maybe he should confront his roommate for having dared to say it), but later, when it settled down in his mind as a possibility, he flushed with embarrassment. He now had to hear her himself.

And he finally did that night. It was in his room, way past midnight when the dogs were barking themselves crazy that his girlfriend rose to all her glory and he fell flat just as quickly. He imagined his roommate on the other side of the wall, possibly covering his ears with a pillow, or plugging in his iPod to mask out the opera on the other side of the wall—or, perhaps, even pleasing himself in bed! He couldn't tolerate the thought.

He told her. She dismissed it with a laugh. He couldn't, and resolved not to make love in his hostel room again.

By the time winter set in, their relationship was as strong as the cool wind blowing outside the balcony in their apartment. They had moved in together now. He was the one who had suggested it about a month earlier. He had recently got a pay hike in his job at a media company and could afford the full rent himself. She was willing, as always, and it also proved economical for a freelance writer like her. She packed up her bags within a day and set up home with him. She had become better for him with time, like wine in a cellar. Their lovemaking had also caught a whiff of aggression. She was good as always and he delivered as promised. But the intensity waned as her voice rose. He had realized that a private haven was the best way out of the situation. At least he didn't have to worry about people hearing her now—he just had to deal with his own awkwardness.

The first few weeks had gone by like a charm. If he liked to read the sports section, she liked Bollywood gossip—they nicely separated without causing much havoc in the newspaper. She came back home and yelled for a cheesy pizza just when he was rummaging through the menu cards for Domino's. She was obsessive about cleaning, which suited his lazy self well. They were compatible in every way, almost like a couple perfectly matched in heaven.

Until he let the Devil enter his mind. Like the time when he was running late to work and decided to drop her, en route, to one of those book launches she frequented. They went down the elevator along with the neighbour and her two teenaged children.

The young girl first let out a suppressed giggle, and then her older brother let out a bolder and louder one, encouraging the start of a volley that ended only when the mother pinched both of them. He found that strange, but moved on.

The old fart of a building watchman gave him reason to worry though. She had gone up to him one evening, when they'd got back from their shopping trip for home supplies, to enquire about the absence of the housemaid. Standing there in the corner, oblivious to the eyes of passers-by, he saw the watchman press his unmentionables awkwardly, just as she spoke to him like a child trying to find her lost toy. He heard her again that night, loud as ever against the regular beating of the stick by the pervert watchman on guard.

And then he saw the notice at the building entrance, right there along with others regarding building repairs and the upcoming Holi party. It was to do with curbing noise in the building as it was affecting the elderly and the schoolchildren preparing for their annual exams. He hadn't seen that one before and, somehow, though it seemed ridiculous to his own left brain, he felt that his bedroom was being targeted.

He told her again that day. She laughed nervously, but didn't let it pass.

The next morning she was thoughtful, but by evening her face cleared up. The agenda for the night was evident. Before they got into bed, she told him to cover her mouth if it got too loud. It started out well but wavered into edgy ground. The only way to salvage it was to release the simmering tension. And she did—loud as ever.

He did as he was told. She bit him so hard it hurt for days and left a mark forever.

A Simple Question

NAMAN SARAIYA

'I'm asking you a simple question, Anhad! When was the last time you felt that?'

◆

He struggled, night after night, to complete the final chapter of the book everyone seemed to be waiting for. Being inept was not his cup of tea and neither was wasting time. But he was young (or so he thought), fearless and had taken the plunge—he was way ahead of the game and a lot of expectations were at stake. This would be a good time to quit he thought; and then floated away into a dreamland before snapping back to reality. Anhad Sharma, thirty-four, had been signed on by the biggest publishing house in the country for a debut novel he was mulling over. Disaster, he said to himself; pulling those strings had done him in. He was better at being a corporate slave, damned impulse!

The entire novel situation had made him a nervous, emotional wreck and it seemed like doomsday was fast approaching. There was no doomsday, except for the one in a recent trashy movie and there was no one else but Anhad who would have to string the words together. Time was running out; patience had long run out too. There was uneasiness in the approach to work—his desk, the keyboard and the screen, all felt alien. His computer was his worst enemy now. Withdrawals of varied kinds, disarraying thoughts and merciless dismissal of any kind of hope—this was his life for now. Anhad Sharma, the once successful corporate honcho, winner of several awards and now, this. It was all a little too strange to believe, but the truth could not be bettered or changed for that matter. There was far too much monotony in the given situation, far too much.

Trips to hill stations had been made, inspirational music was heard and all the other rules of the author-cliché textbook had been considered, executed and failed. There were times when the ridiculous thought of getting married occurred to him too. He drank a bit then and laughed at the stupidity of his own thoughts—the marriage one in particular. He never had a problem bringing women home, did he? The only problem, his mother said, was they would leave the next morning and not visit her nearby. Like every self-respecting Indian mother, Anhad's mother wished to see her son married and dropped in a gentle reminder every now and then, hoping he wouldn't react violently.

'Ma, writing! Writing is my true love. No woman can ever live with that!'

So be it, said the mother, so be it, knowing his radical thoughts on marriage. Earlier, she had let his idiosyncrasies pass as a phase that every teenager faced, despite his girlfriend and her well-known existence and importance in Anhad's life. But, when he turned thirty, she began to worry a bit—after having given herself some more time. She had prodded him that day, a little over twelve years ago, about how he had to get married soon (if he wished to, of course). That resulted in an outraged response from him, a kind she had never seen. He spoke of how he needed time to get over Manya after she left him. He had used the word stranded here. It was a difficult time and his mother had known that but she also thought he was punishing himself a little too much for that. It had been seven years since they separated, seven years. Maybe time didn't heal all wounds; maybe time was not the healer.

◆

An artist in her own right, Manya Bhardwaj had made a name for herself in the growing and somewhat surfacing independent music scene in India as one of the few leading ladies of a popular jazz-fusion-rock band in Bombay. Spotting her was not a task—a walk down Hill Road, Bandra or maybe the pubs of Lower Parel and you would often see her with a few friends, having a good time. If you got to know her a bit, a sense of pain in her laughter, a hesitation in her smile could be spotted. But not everyone saw this—they were just friends from the 'scene', fans-turned-friends, other musicians, photographers and publicity people—not real friends either. Of course, her band-mates knew her music was about someone they had never met and someone she would never talk about. But that was all they knew or would ever know.

She was surprised she never saw him at any concert. She knew he would never turn up at any of her band's performances, but his absence bothered her. She never spoke of it. If the thought did occur, it would be successfully whiffed away with a little marijuana. The yearning was obstinate, but she did pretty much okay except on the occasional rough trips. Love, she believed, was a puritan concept and she had known that only with Anhad—the only other thing that came close to it was, for her, her music—when she was on stage, lost in transition between the real and the surreal experiences of feeling divine. Sometimes, she wished she could combine the two, but the reality biting into the thought made it even more unpleasant than it already was. There had to be a way to get over this, she thought. It had to be quick, real bloody quick. Seven years, quick.

Earlier, she had ignored his calls. As the world was ushered into a technologically advanced space, she ignored everything else too—texts, social networking requests and emails. But she knew how to keep a tab on him; he had done the same. And over the last couple of years he had stopped calling or communicating. She knew he had moved on; she knew they could be civil to each other if they wanted to be; she knew it all—but it didn't help one bit. He knew all of it too. But they both feared a relapse, feared what they thought would never happen to happen once again. The pain would be unbearable this time around; yes, it would. She had music and some men she had passed by knowingly, willingly. Finding Anhad in each one of them wasn't the answer. It clearly wasn't.

'Manya, it's time you let go. It's been so long, I don't even remember what he looks like!'

Her father—her best friend, parent and support system— insisted, every time.

'I have, okay? I have! But, I'm not interested in anything. Music, that's it.'

She screamed, voice quivering and cutlery clanking. That was all.

And then they would resume dinner. Of course, this was a six-monthly spat, which was followed by about a week of silence and then the usual apologies. Her father often made it simple for her to live life on her own rules, doing what she wished to do—but they lived together. It was almost inevitable to see the other everyday, knowing things were okay. But the father's only concern was to not see his daughter walk out on her past, like her mother had. He wanted her to be with Anhad. Both sides were ideologically balanced that way—at least from the parental perspective. It was bound to be that way. That was all there was to it. No contact, no communication, only gentle reminders.

◆

Anhad, unlike other authors, had not shared his book with anyone before it was launched. Of course, he would've shared it with Manya—had she still been around—but she wasn't, and no one came close to her, no one understood him the way she had. Maybe there were several who did, but the walls he had built around himself restricted any kind of emotional connection building with anyone else. However, Paromita—the editor of his book—understood him. Line after line, chapter after chapter as the novel progressed, bit-by-bit. She had waited upon the final chapter for over a month now. Her feedback was minimal; she kept going back to Anhad with a broad smile, ruffling his hair and thanking him for writing so effortlessly. It made her work easy, she said. He smiled, but his eyes didn't emote anything. Nothing.

'I can't do this Paromita. I can't. There's no drive to conclude. I'm clueless.'

And then he turned around, away from her, facing the window in front of his desk.

'Give it time, Anhad. It's fantastic, till now. It'll just pop up some day—hopefully, soon.'

She looked down at her toes, sitting on the couch in his room. And sighed.

'This can't be happening. Did I tell you I got thoughts of scrapping it?'

His position remained unchanged; he was still staring out of the window.

'Okay, we've had enough drama. Quit the view. It's only a slum. Get to work!'

She patted his head and left the room. He heard the door shut, silence fell everywhere.

Manya was sitting in the balcony of her house in one of the bylanes of Bandra. Her father had acquired it from an Anglo-Indian family about three decades ago and changed the interiors completely, retaining only the fireplace and the pots hanging outside. A fireplace in Bombay was an oddity, but it worked well with the wooden flooring of the house. The first-floor balcony helped her father greet people and she often sat there on gloomy evenings. All of a sudden, she spat a little bit of her chai—stood up in an instant and then turned away, all in a flash. Anhad was standing there, looking up, like he always did in the past. Those seven years of denial disappeared in an instant and it was almost like she was staring down at her future, the way she had imagined it to be—Anhad, under their balcony, as romantic as ever.

She turned around, after a minute—gathering the courage to look at him, but he was gone. She ran down the wooden, blunted staircase—but she was a little too late. Manya stood by the gate of the little house and found a large brown envelope there, placed carefully and strategically while she was looking away—away in denial; away in the fear of acceptance of what could have been; away from the cause of her happiness. She picked up the envelope, opened it and found a couple of pages stapled together and a little note clipped to it. She instantly recognised Anhad's hand. She was too scared to read it, and kept looking around for some support. Then she stepped inside the front yard, sat down by the door and tore open the envelope.

Manya,

I'm writing a novel. It's my debut and the biggest publishing house in India has signed me on. I'm lucky, to say the least. Paromita, my friend from college, is editing it. These pages are the final chapter of my book and she hasn't read them yet. I need your approval.

I dropped by your house and disappeared in an instant— all for a reason. I didn't want to see you. But, if by chance I were to see you—I wanted to be prepared. If I did see you, I'd be glad I did and when you read the final chapter, you will know why I say that. In all possibility I will be glad if I do see you or bump into you and that should be reason enough for me to believe that I have done a fairly good job. The final chapter of my book answers a simple question you had once asked me before we went our separate ways.

But I believe we never really did go on our own ways. We just walked on the same path, hoping the other would join in—but seven years is a long time. We've grown old now. But I'm sure we're not far away. The years don't matter. Okay, maybe I should stop. I think the final chapter will tell you all that I've always wanted to over the years.

Hoping you understand me—this one last time.

Anhad

As Anhad walked back home, he knew he had written the perfect last chapter and now would just wait for Manya to say it was okay, so he could send it in to Paromita. He called Paromita and said he had finally written it but would send it to her in a couple of days. She didn't question him; she just agreed and hung up. The letter was essential; the reaction even more so. Secretly he had hoped to catch a glimpse of her so he would know the answer to her question—the question that always made him feel he had not loved her enough; maybe never told her how much he did. As he watched the sun set that evening, sitting at his desk, glancing through the last pages of his debut novel, Anhad smiled genuinely for the first time in ages—despite images of their separation flashing before his eyes.

◆

It was a gloomy day in July when Anhad was waiting in the dingy living room of the apartment he had recently rented out. Manya had wished to talk to him about several things for a while and asked him to take the day off which he did. As she walked in, water dripping from the jacket because of the slight drizzle that ensued, she kept everything aside and sat next to him. There was an eerie feeling in the air and Anhad was not particularly keen on breaking the silence between them. Manya took the first step and laid out her problems, ambitions, desires and anxieties—Anhad sat there listening, holding her hands, and feeling numb. This was not what he had been expecting. The sofa felt as if it were sinking, the weather suddenly cold and the strange feeling in his throat—a lump, a big one.

Her complaint: she loved him but wanted time for other things. Another complaint: he didn't love her enough but was just used to her being around. After airing several such issues, she had him feeling ridiculous, stupid and dejected—but that was all. He asked her if she wished to move on; she said yes. He asked her if she wished to remain in any form of contact; she said no. He asked her if there was anything else she wanted to say; she said that was all. He remained seated, lit a cigarette and said, 'Okay then, I have nothing to say.'

No melodrama, no excessive explanations. Anhad was calm and Manya possibly misunderstood his silence and the lack of reaction. Author-to-be, singer-to-be divided by a wall of silence and misunderstanding. That was the end of them, then.

◆

'...she asked him, trying to hide any sign of a tear.'

He finished reading this line as the doorbell rang. He wasn't expecting Manya to be there and had been prepared to wait for a couple of days. But he froze. Pages fell to the floor.

'I'm asking you a simple question, Anhad! When was the last time you felt that?'

Manya asked him, standing at his door.

'Felt what?' he countered.

'That feeling in the pit of your stomach, Anhad?'

He picked up the pages from the floor, ruffled them—still looking at her, and read...

'Right now, as I look at you, from the pit of my stomach to the tips of my fingers. Right now.'

Twisted

LIPI MEHTA

I still haven't understood why I agreed to go for my office party that evening. I think office parties are the most overrated thing in Pune's corporate world—apart from birthdays, of course. Even so, I went. Maybe I was really bored that evening, or maybe I was just destined to meet Stephen. As soon as I entered, my eyes started looking around for Riya, who I thought was the only sensible person in my department.

My department? Marking incorrect punctuation with a red pen! In the publishing house where I worked, this was supposed to be one of the most important jobs they had.

Important? Yes.

Interesting? No.

Well, the money wasn't so bad after all, and they were giving me a chance to write my own book. Writing came naturally to me and the prospect of having my work published was worth the hours spent in front of dozens of hopeless manuscripts.

At the party, I finally found Riya who seemed strangely excited to introduce me to one of her friends who had come to Pune 'all the way from New York'.

'Stephen!' she called out to him, as we walked towards the bar.

Dressed in a black t-shirt and rather shabby jeans, I could see that this guy did not give a damn about the party-shirt-wearing, excitedly-talking people around him.

As I walked towards him, he looked up and flashed a huge grin at me.

Weird foreigners, I thought.

'This is Stephen. We went to college together,' said Riya as Stephen and I shook hands and smiled at each other. (Nice to meet you too!)

'I have to work late tomorrow. Can you please show Stephen around the city in the evening?' Riya asked me in such a way that saying 'no' wasn't even an option.

'Of course,' I said, as Stephen smiled at me. (So nice of you!)

The next evening, I went over to Riya's house where Stephen was staying and waited at the doorstep. I started the car when I saw him walk towards me.

'Aren't we walking?' he asked.

'Sure!' I said, wondering when was the last time I had actually walked on the streets of Pune. As we walked through Koregaon Park, I started telling him a little bit about everything we saw on our way. I wondered if he was even listening because he kept taking pictures and never once looked at me when I was saying something. Soon we reached M.G. Road and I took him to one of the city's oldest and finest joints, Marz-O-Rin. I could see that he was impressed by how the food was so tasty in spite of being so cheap. While sitting at one of tables overlooking the road below, Stephen decided to finally start talking.

He spoke about the work he had to do in Pune and asked me if I was happy with the work I was doing. As a photographer, he was required to travel to remote places in Maharashtra over the weekends. He said he was really looking forward to that. I had a really good time with Stephen that evening. The best part about talking to strangers is that no question seems wrong and no accusation seems right. I realized that, as I found myself asking him questions that I wouldn't even have asked Riya.

After that evening, meeting Stephen became almost a daily routine. Riya didn't complain—she had her long hours of work to crib about. Sometimes Stephen would surprise me with Chinese takeaway during my lunch hour at the office.

I don't even remember when I started liking him in a way that meeting him became more a necessity than just a casual outing. The day he asked me out was the day I made the easiest decision of my life. I started liking him more than I had imagined I would—and the fact that he was so good in bed was only one of the reasons! I realized that I could have endless conversations with him about things that mattered and things that didn't. Hell, this guy could even make a conversation about streetlights seem significant!

I would ask him questions about life and longing, about love and loss, about this and that. He would answer them all, patiently, effortlessly.

'What is your favourite ice-cream flavour?' I would ask.

'Vanilla,' he would say.

'Who is your role model?' I would ask.

'Spiderman,' he would say.

'What keeps you going?' I would ask.

'Change,' he would say.

We were clearly opposites. I could never think straight and always prioritized the wrong things. He made sure I left my phone behind at home on weekends. Your phone, he would say, is your biggest enemy. The fact that I was so much darker than him ensured that people threw second glances at us as we walked past them. Somehow, that never mattered to Stephen. But it was so evident that it distracted me even when we were in bed.

Sometimes black on white.

Sometimes white on black.

The fear of losing Stephen forced me to think in ways I wouldn't have otherwise. Strangely, I succumbed to that force because it gave me a sense of security. He urged me to make my own decisions all the time. I felt like a kid in front of him. The feeling was strange, considering how I had thought of myself as one of the most mature among my group of friends.

When he called me to see him that day, I skipped work to make sure I reached there on time. From across the road I could see Stephen in the distance, sitting alone. He looked towards me and smiled. I cursed the traffic as car after car rushed past me. As I waited for the traffic to part, I craned my neck to steal a glance at him. His eyes urged me to come fast. I couldn't wait either. We had hardly been able to meet in the last few days.

Suddenly I heard a loud noise, and a split-second later, German Bakery was in flames. I screamed as I was thrown off-balance by the chaos that had suddenly erupted. I called out to Stephen but there was no sign of him. There was no table at the corner and there was no Stephen. I could not understand what had just happened in front of me. I was pushed thoughtlessly by the tremendous crowd that had gathered. Strangely, I couldn't feel a thing. Here I was, standing just a few feet away from where Stephen was and yet, I was away from it all. The noise was deafening—like the explosion of a series of bombs, like the shattering of a million dreams. All that I remember of that day now is the smoke—black as an evil heart.

◆

Two years and countless sleepless nights later, I still can't believe that Stephen is not in my life anymore. Sometimes, I suddenly wake up in the night with Stephen's voice in my ears. 'Nothing is certain,' he says.

There is no one whom I can talk to the way I talked to Stephen. Maybe that is why I still write to him, thinking that the space in my dressing drawer is enough compensation for everything. I stop thinking about Stephen for a while and think of what Sneha might be doing at home. Sneha is patient with me—she hardly asks any questions and she hardly ever complains. Sometimes I feel I am being unfair to her, but I can't help it. I glance at my watch almost five times before reaching home. I hate making Sneha wait for me each day. As I enter my house, I see her reading a piece of paper that I had carelessly left on my table that morning.

Dear Stephen,

I don't feel like working in the publishing house anymore. Everything in my life seems as if it has been decided in advance. I hardly take chances nowadays. Life has become stagnant with the fixed routine I follow now, after my marriage to Sneha. She's a wonderful person but I can never feel for her the way she does for me. I miss you telling me that everything will fall into place. Maybe it was supposed to be this way. Maybe society would never have accepted our relationship the way you and I did. Life is different without you Stephen, but I can't say that I am unhappy.

Love,
Avinash

Sneha, my wife of two years, sees me entering the house with a pensive look on my face. She wipes the tears from her eyes as she turns to look at me, holding that single piece of paper which I had hoped she would never find.

'Avi, is this really yours?' she asks.

◆

32 B

VARSHA SUMAN

'...and a red bra. I think I'm going to take it off now.'

'Stop doing this Tanya, you're driving me insane.'

Good. Serves you right for calling me unsexy. Need to get a new detergent packet—this one's about to get over.

'It's you who are making me go crazy!' I fake a laugh—sexily, I hope. I drain the bucket of dirty water, dropping it by mistake.

'What's that noise?' he asks.

'I'm so drunk, I'm banging into things,' I slur.

'Umm... Are you in the bathroom by any chance?'

I tuck the phone in the crook of my neck, transfer the washed clothes into another bucket and say, 'Yeah. I'm checking out how cold the water is. I feel like taking a shower. If you were here you could have joined me.' I deserve a pat on my back for that.

'What's your flat number?'

'32 B.'

'32 B?' he repeats blankly.

'I said 2 B,' I giggle.

He seems really confused now. This is so much fun! Guys get

manipulated so easily. He thinks he is so cool with his 'ruggedness' and 'arrogant charm' and it took me just fifteen minutes to get him to believe that he was hot for me. I love this!

'I'm coming home in half an hour.'

Wait, did I hear that right? I laugh nervously. 'Stop giving me false hope. You're in another part of the city right now.'

'I'm actually very close to your house. I had some work in the neighbourhood.' He says that as if he expects me to be overjoyed about it. Stupid, arrogant bastard. Like everybody's dying to get into your pants. Concentrate! If you don't think quickly, he's going to find you in a few minutes, washing clothes wearing ugly pyjamas. My heart is pounding. This can't be happening. He can't come. I'm not wearing a red bra, I'm not drunk and I'm not… What else did I tell him anyway?

I try hard to persuade him not to come, but before I can even finish my little speech he cuts in saying, 'Twenty minutes,' and hangs up.

I hate this! Oh fuck! I can't lose face now. Me and my stupid ego. Let's take it one step at a time.

I look at the pile of clothes still waiting to be washed. They will have to wait till tomorrow. I rack my brain, trying to remember all the crap I'd told this guy. Red bra! Red bra! Red bra! I don't own a stupid red bra! I am supposed to be wearing some really short black skirt and a white top. I look down at the pile of dirty clothes and there it is—my stupid black skirt. I pick it up with two fingers. Ego before hygiene. I quickly change into that disgusting skirt and go in search of a white top. My roommate's top will have to do for now. It's some expensive shit which she's been saving for some special occasion. Too bad. I'll try not to stink it up—not too hard, but still. What she doesn't know can't hurt her.

What next? Hairy legs, hairier arm pits, oily hair, oilier face, ugly spectacles, uglier face. And ten minutes left. I quickly lose the specs. Good! I can't see his disgusting face now. Wash face. Shave, shave, shave. Ouch, that hurt. Great! I quickly wipe the blood off that ugly cut. It's going to leave its mark. Switch off the lights and switch on the bed lamp. You can still see the cut. Like he's even going to notice or care.

I go and dump my head into a bucket full of water. I realize a little too late that I'd washed my clothes in that bucket. I think of using the sink—better late than never. Quickly wash my hair in the sink. No time for shampoo and conditioner. Blow dry, straighten. Kajal. Compact. Lip gloss. Wow! That took less than eight minutes, probably a new record. Thank God for my helpful roommate's absence and her stuff.

All done. He'll never get to see my bra (fingers crossed), so that shouldn't matter. Ding dong. Right on time. Wait, I'm supposed to be drunk. I search through all the cabinets. Where's the booze when you need it? There is a bottle of Old Monk next to the dustbin. It still has some rum left from two weeks back. Eww, no way! Ding dong. Ding dong. Stale rum it is. I gargle with it a few times. That should smell bad enough. I'm going to puke now. I hold it in—I'll need it later. I open the door, trip and bump my head against the wall. My face turns red. Oh God!

'You're really drunk!' he says, stopping me from falling flat on my face. For once, my clumsiness has worked in my favour. I give him a big grin and sway a little to add to the act. It works. He looks really alarmed now.

'Akarsh! You came!' I exclaim and start blabbering nonsense. I never knew it was so hard to talk drunken crap. He is totally buying my act, though. He takes me to the bed, makes me sit and is now giving me his full attention. Why is he looking at me so intensely? Creep. Keep talking crap. Now he's humouring me. Aww! He's being a good guy and taking care of the poor little drunk girl. Isn't that sweet? Stupid piece of shit.

'Yeah, even I have had bad experiences standing in line for tatkal tickets,' he says.

Are we actually having a conversation about the Indian Railways at one in the morning? How jobless is he? Okay, I have to get this guy out of my house. I have a very important assignment which I have to finish tonight. I can't let my Sunday go to waste just so that he can be the good guy who didn't take advantage of the poor little drunk slut and sat up talking all night.

I spoke too soon—he is leaning in. 'I'm going to puke now!' Did I say that out loud?

'Are you okay? Let me take you to the bathroom. Puke it out. You'll feel better.'

I slap my hand on my mouth and nod enthusiastically. He leads me to the washroom. I lock the door, open the tap and make weird, puking noises. I count the number of tiles for a few minutes and open the door. He is standing outside with a bottle of water. Is this guy for real?

I drink up half the bottle. I need it—my mouth feels so dry.

'How are you feeling now?' He is a little too close for comfort. Physical proximity makes me very uncomfortable. And I don't even like this guy much. He is just a guy I know who called me unsexy. I never should have picked up that phone of mine. Stupid me.

I let him lead me to the bed. Thank God. Five more minutes and he'll be out of here. Hello, why is he lying down next to me? My heart's pounding. I'm stuck now because I already started pretending I'm asleep. He's getting too close. I do not like this. Stop holding me by the waist! I pretend to kick around in my sleep. He is just holding me closer. Maybe I should try staying still, then. Is he actually stroking my hair? Why am I taking all this crap anyway? I can get up and ask him to fuck off. No, I can't! Then he'll know that I was pretending all this while, and I'm going to look like such a loser. I hate boys! Even more than before.

He is talking on the phone. Make it an emergency, make him leave immediately. Why is he whispering? I can barely hear him.

'I can't now. She's really drunk. I think I'm going to stay here for the night and make sure she doesn't choke on her own vomit or something.' He's saying more things but I quit listening after that sentence. I am supposed to be touched and all—he is being so sweet. Well, try as I might, I am just annoyed. Unsexy and a bitch! I fall more in love with myself each passing day.

I count up to 477 before he falls asleep. I slowly open my eyes. He is out. This calls for assignments! I slowly disengage myself from him and pick up my books. Time for work. He's stirring. He seems to be feeling the bed for something… Oh, me! Okay, he has stopped. He's out again. I run to the hall, switch on the reading lamp and get to work.

The next few hours are a blur. Before I know it, daylight is creeping in through the windows. The stupid nib of my pen seems to have broken. The ink's all over my hands, but I'm nearly done. I need a smoke. Excellent, the pack's finished. Now what? I neatly staple the pages and go around looking for a cigarette. The shops aren't going to open till eight. I am going to go mad if I do not find a smoke right now. Maybe I've hidden one in my cupboard?

This bastard's still here—I'd nearly forgotten about him. I hate him. What do I see? There is a pack of Gold Flakes in his pocket. I love him. I slowly inch my hand towards it. I try to extricate it from his pocket.

'What a pleasant way to wake up,' he says in a husky voice.

God save me, he is up and thinking God knows what. My hand seems to be in a very weird place right now. Shit! He's noticed the pack in my hands. My hands are smeared with ink, the assignment's lying next to him—there is no way out. He knows. I can see it in his eyes. He has figured everything out. All my efforts have gone to waste.

'Nice bra,' he says, getting up. I did not realize that I was bending over him. I quickly straighten up. I look down at the white, frayed bra. Nope, it hasn't magically turned red overnight. He takes a smoke from his pack and lights it. I could kill for that smoke right now. Hell, I could even kiss the bastard for a smoke right now. And that is a big deal for me. After all, he is a bastard. I can't seem to get a single word out of my mouth, even though a million things are running through my head right now. I just sit and stare at him smoke, with a mortified expression on my face.

He flips through my assignment and finishes his smoke, all the while staring at me as if saying, 'Look at what you can't have.'

He walks to the door, looks back and says, 'I could have sworn you looked better last night.'

Think of something witty. Nope. Think of something bitchy. Nope. Just think of something.

'Can I have a smoke?' That comes out in a pleading voice. Nice. Very nice. If you couldn't have thought of something less pathetic, maybe you should have kept your mouth shut. It's too late now.

He tosses the whole pack at me and says, 'Keep it.' At least something came out of it. 'See you around,' he says, winking, and leaves. That does it. Fuck, that was hot! Now I want him.

Two more pages to write and one more bucket of clothes to wash and then I'll go get him. Actually, fuck all that—I want him now!

I run for the door.

◆

32 B is The Tossed Salad pick from the short listed stories in the Landmark Grey Oak Urban Stories Competition.

Coffee?

AHMED FAIYAZ

Suryaraman's tuition class is a popular hangout in Bangalore where the boys from St Wades's College get the opportunity to meet the girls from St Theresa's College. The other hangouts are Mickey's Juice Parlour near St Theresa's and Lucky Stripes Burgers and Shakes outside St Wades's College where students spend more time than they do in class.

Suryaraman took classes in a ramshackle outhouse in an old bungalow, a ten-minute walk from Brigade Road, where the cafés, pubs, restaurants and cinemas are, and a fifteen-minute drive from both colleges. He, however, made sure the girls and guys came in separate batches. Girls had two slots—three to four in the afternoon and four to five thereafter; followed by two for the guys from five to six in the evening and six to seven. Those like me, who managed to join the five to six batch, were among the lucky few. There was high demand for a slot in this batch—we were packed with twenty students and an atmosphere that was much like a classroom.

I spoke to Sania for the first time at Suryaraman's tuition classes. I had seen her a few times before, at inter-collegiate events where

I performed with my band and she played the piano in a solo performance. I thought she was gorgeous, an ethereal beauty. We knew each other by sight but we hadn't been introduced. Nor could I muster enough courage to walk up to her and say 'Hi', although Bangalore is a small world and it was quite common for St Theresa girls to hang out with the boys from St Wades's.

On one occasion when Suryaraman cancelled tuitions for our batch, which he often did for reasons like a cricket match on television, we decided to go for an ice-cream at Corner House. Karthik, who was well known among the girls as he went to school with a couple of them, convinced them to join us. Niharika, Pooja, Susan and Sania joined Arun, Tanmay, Deepak, Karthik and me after making a bit of fuss about deadlines at home. Yes, Sania was to join us as well! The nine of us decided to walk it up to Corner House.

There was a nip in the air and Sania, who also happened to be Karthik's school friend, and I fell back as the rest walked ahead. She was petite and had delicate features. Her innocent smile added to the effect of making her seem more like a schoolgirl than the typical Theresaite. Some of her other friends, like the big-lipped Niharika and the seductress Susan, clearly fit right into the image of the St Theresa type, unlike Sania. It appeared to me that she was feeling cold.

'Are you alright? It doesn't seem as if you want to have any ice cream,' I ventured.

'I really don't! I would much rather prefer a hot cup of coffee,' she said softly with a shy smile. She pushed her dark brown tresses behind her ears and turned her gaze towards me.

'Well, we could stop and pick up a takeaway from Coffee Planet; it is right here. Let these guys go ahead we'll join them in a while,' I said, turning towards the stairs of the cafe. I stood waiting for her to walk up the stairs with me.

'You don't have to...' she said, but followed me up the stairs quickly. I ordered two cappuccinos for us and her gaze met mine for a moment.

'You strum the guitar really well. I watched you play when you guys performed 'Summer of '69' at our campus festival last month.'

'Thanks, I really liked your performance too. It was very soulful and sincere in my opinion,' I said trying not to sound like I was flattering her.

'Well, you should have been the judge. I finished fourth among the six contestants; I guess I wasn't so good after all!'

'Of course you were. Maybe the judges couldn't understand your music! It's all about perspective really and I think you did very well in holding your own.'

'Thanks! So where do you stay?' She looked at me with genuine interest and a sweet smile.

'Not too far, Richmond Town. What about you?' I picked up the two cups of coffee and gave her one.

'Thanks. I stay in Indiranagar, very close to Niharika's place. I'm lucky that way, I manage to hitch a ride to college and to tuitions and back in her car. So Karthik and you are pretty close, huh?'

'You can say that. He was with you in school but I got to know him only a few months back in college. He's a nice chap, down to earth and easy to get along with,' I said before taking a sip from my cup. She smiled in approval while sipping her coffee. Karthik had an eye for Susan and the two of them had begun spending a lot of time together.

'Susan and he make a nice couple, don't they?' I looked at her, noticing the childlike glee in her countenance.

'Well, it's easier when you have parents like hers. My folks are not that open-minded, they would frown even if I went and had a cup of coffee with a guy,' she said looking downcast.

'I guess that's how it is for most girls.' We walked into Corner House towards where the rest of them seemed engrossed in conversation.

'I know, but it's changing,' she said with a glimmer of hope before we sat down next to each other and tried to join in the conversation.

I couldn't take my eyes off her and as her gaze met mine, she blushed and looked away. I was clearly smitten by her and realized how beautiful she looked in her grey pullover and dark blue jeans. She took my notebook, turned to the last page and taking her pen out from her pocket, began scribbling something. For a moment, I turned my attention to Deepak and laughed at his imitation of Suryaraman and his nasal baritone. She discreetly pushed the open notebook towards me and smiled innocently at the rest. *I feel tomorrow is going to be chillier than today... thanks for this cup of coffee though!*

I took her pen from where it lay on the table and scribbled under her writing—*How about two cups of coffee tomorrow then?*

Maybe... she scribbled. Her cheeks were flushed and she lowered her eyes and smiled while the others were busy having a go at Tanmay who was everyone's punching bag. The guys seemed to be pulling his leg with a vengeance to impress and entertain the ladies in their midst.

Deepak turned towards Sania and tried to make polite conversation with her. I noticed her replying to him in her soft voice and smiling at him innocently and I began to feel jealous.

I interrupted the conversation and asked him whether we had tuition the next day, to which he replied saying he didn't know and shrugged his shoulders looking irritated as I had interrupted his attempt to make conversation with Sania. I took the book and wrote in it again—*Can I have your number?*

She looked at what I had written and gazed at me intently looking confused. I feared I had asked her number too quickly and she was possibly offended by what I had written. I saw her put her hand on her chin for a moment and ponder a bit. She tore the piece of paper on which we had our little exchange.

Meanwhile I turned away and made conversation with Pooja who possibly weighed twice as much as Sania and sat on my other side. She seemed to be eyeing both of us suspiciously. On our way out after a few minutes, she pushed a rolled-up note into my hand and walked away with the girls saying a cordial goodbye to all of us. I quickly pushed the crumpled note into the front pocket of my jeans and walked back with the boys to the place where our cars and bikes were at Suryaraman's place. I took my bike out of the parking lot and zipped through the peak-hour traffic in a rush to get home and read what she had written.

I walked into my room and shut the door behind me before I carefully opened the crumpled note. *Call me at 55867XXX. Please call before 8 p.m. and hang up if anyone else picks up the phone.* It was 7.45 p.m. I quickly dialled her number and heard her voice at the other end after two rings.

'Hi, I was waiting for you to call. I really had a nice time today,' she said in a sweet voice.

'Meet me for coffee at 5, same place,' I said in a persuasive tone.

'I don't know…I get home with Niharika every day. What can I tell the girls? They will be suspicious,' she said after a moment of silence.

'Make up something.'

'Ok, I'll see you at 5, but just for thirty minutes. I've got to be home at 6.'

'Forty-five minutes.'

'OK…' she said giggling at the other end.

I stayed up all night thinking about her. I remembered the fragrance she wore, the touch of her skin when I handed her the cup of coffee, her sweet voice and the innocent smile. I could see desire in her eyes for me. I sensed that I was falling in love for the first time and more importantly, someone else was falling in love with me.

The next day I landed up in a new pair of jeans and a sweatshirt at Coffee Planet at 4.30 and took a nice table at the far end of the cafe where no one could see us. I saw her walk in looking like a million bucks in a white Benetton sweatshirt and a pair of worn grey jeans. She seemed shy and I put her at ease telling her about my day at college and asking her how her day had been.

After two cups of coffee and sharing a chocolate brownie, I placed my palm on her hand which rested on the table and gazed into her eyes with passion. 'You're the most beautiful woman I've had coffee with,' I said with sincerity, feeling self-conscious. I had been out with girls before but this was the first time I felt strongly about anyone.

'This is the first time I've been out for coffee alone with a boy,' she gushed with a smile. We spoke merrily about my school days and hers. We talked about the music we loved and our influences before she got up to leave.

'Tomorrow at 4, you missed tuition today and tomorrow I'll bunk. That way we can spend time together till 5.30,' she spoke with a mischievous grin.

We met every day for a cup of coffee; on some days she missed tuition and on some days I did. I also bunked classes in college and went by to hang out with her at Lemon Tree, which was a little more exclusive and thus quieter. On a few occasions I took my Dad's car and picked Sania up from college. We went out on long drives to a nice dhaba and for movies. She preferred not being seen on my bike, fearing her parents or her older brother would see her and she would end up being grounded for life.

We managed to get mobile phones with free calling from my number to hers and vice versa and would spend long hours late at night whispering sweet nothings to each other. I still remember the blue top she wore when I first kissed her at the cinema. It was four months after we had begun dating. I had brought her to see the new Austin Powers movie, *The Spy Who Shagged Me*, which we ended up seeing very little of anyway. We had grown very possessive of each other and we tried squeezing in all the time we got outside of college at coffee or a movie or chatting on the phone for long hours. She managed to join our batch at Suryaraman's, saying that her music practice was from four to five every day. At home, she mentioned that her batch had changed to a 5 p.m. slot. This helped as we could skip tuitions together as opposed to her missing a session on one day and me on another day. We skipped the afternoon lectures in college and spent the time from lunch till the 5 p.m. tuition at Coffee Planet or at the cinema.

At times it was difficult for me, given that we had to pretend like nothing was on and had to sneak around, while I wanted the whole world to know that Sania and I were together. I sometimes got irritated with her apprehensions of who'd see us, but her sweet smile and the way she looked at me more than made up for it.

◆

Last month Karthik threw a party on his terrace and thanks to Susan's help, Sania walked in with her hand in mine. Susan had convinced Sania's parents to allow her to come over and spend the weekend at her place and she brought her to the party on this pretext. We spent most of the time together on the dance floor and after a while we decided to go and spend the night at Arun's place since his parents were away in London. Meantime, we couldn't get enough of each other and made out for a while in Karthik's bedroom before we left for Arun's place.

We spent the night at his apartment while he stayed over at Karthik's. We couldn't get enough of each other that night. I undressed her slowly and got into bed with her. For a while we lay down quietly, enjoying the intimacy of being wrapped in each other's arms. Sania was afraid but gradually got into it when I began kissing her lips, her back and the nape of her neck. We made love with passion and longing in Arun's tiny bed, where she moaned softly and wrapped her legs around me. I told her that nothing would ever separate us which made her dig her nails into my back. I loved her to bits and she realized that.

◆

A week back, eighteen months since we began dating, she seemed aloof and irritable over coffee. She refused to get into it saying her parents were looking out for suitors and discussing alliances for her. I didn't worry too much.

Three days ago, I couldn't get through her number, the message said—*This number is switched off.* Yesterday morning I called Susan to check if everything was OK with Sania and whether they had met in college. Susan mentioned to me that Sania hadn't come to college for the last couple of days and had sent a message saying she was unwell. She was surprised that Sania hadn't spoken to me but did say that she didn't sound too good and it seemed like she had a bad cold.

I couldn't pay attention at tuitions or in class at college. I got out every hour and called her mobile number only to hear—*The number you are trying has been temporarily disconnected.* I panicked, wondering what had possibly happened to her and all kinds of scenarios started building up in my head. I feared her parents had found out about us and they had curbed her independence. I tried her landline but her Dad seemed to pick up each time. I spent most of yesterday hanging around near the bakery by her home waiting to catch a glimpse of her. There was no sign of her leaving the house which made me think that she really was unwell and couldn't come to the phone.

I slept very little last night and walked in for tuitions with a glimmer of hope that she would show up. Show up she did, in a black and white salwar dress sans make up, looking like a ghost of her past self.

'Sania, where have you been?' Suryaraman asked.

'I...I am getting married next month, sir. I won't be coming for tuitions, but I will write my exams and finish the final year of college by correspondence next year. My fiancé, Abid, is waiting outside. I wanted to give you your fees and these invitation cards for everyone. Please do come!' she said mustering a sad smile, sounding nothing like the Sania I knew. I sat there almost paralysed by this revelation. She avoided my gaze, left our cards on the table next to Arun, and walked away.

'That's a surprise,' Deepak said, flashing a wicked smirk watching me turn pale. He grudged the fact that she was dating me and that his sad attempts at trying to flirt with her had come to nothing.

I ignored his comment and turned my gaze to my notebook. I struggled to sit through the rest of the class and walked out with relief when it was over. I walked over to Juice Junction and sat there trying to calm myself down and understand what just happened.

I ripped open the invitation cover which said—*Sania weds Abid.* Inside the envelope of my invitation card I found a note—*Please don't call me anymore. Sorry. I wish I had the strength to make it work.* The ink had smudged with her tears.

It couldn't end this way! I tried calling her—*This is not a valid number* ... I shook my head feeling distressed and helpless, while the waiter stood before me, asking if I would like to drink something.

A Good Day

RICHA S. CHATTERJEE

'Leave me alone.'

Those had been the last words I'd said to her this morning. Just like that, unthinkingly, I had snapped at her—and for no fault of hers.

I was worried about three simultaneous deadlines at work and the late nights I'd been keeping for a while. I had ended up spending only one evening a week with her for the past couple of months and, when she gently brought it up last night, I picked a fight. We slept facing opposite walls.

In the morning she walked out after her bath and pulled my ear in conciliation. I was still seething and snapped. She banged the door on her way out and the noise echoed in my head for a long time thereafter. She had muttered a 'good day' under her breath as the door shut behind her, and this was turning out to be anything but. I had taken the day off and forgotten all about it until I saw her walk out of the door. And now there was no one to spend it with.

I cooked myself some eggs and had a late breakfast at ten-thirty.

Not knowing what else to do, I ventured to the bookstore in an overcrowded shopping mall nearby. I tried not to think about my stupidity but didn't succeed a great deal. I finally called her around lunch time only to be met by a curt, 'I'm in a con-call. Will talk to you later.' I sighed and headed to the cafeteria section of the store, hoping that three years of marriage could definitely weather a stupid mood swing on my part.

Hemingway occupied most of my afternoon and, before I knew it, the 3.30 reminder on my cell phone—to pick up some groceries she had mentioned two days ago—went off. As I headed towards the fancy super-mart where she loved to shop, I tried remembering the brand of detergent we used at home. Just two days ago, she had instructed me with her trademark million dollar smile in place, 'Darling, buy only this detergent. It doesn't harm the clothes.'

Ok, never mind. Maybe I'll have better luck with the coffee. Then again, maybe not. Was it Bru or Nescafe? It suddenly dawned upon me that she made my life so much simpler, that she knew just what to say and when to say it, and that I was a total jerk who probably didn't deserve her affection. I let that thought soak through my otherwise cluttered mind—past office troubles and credit card bills, past coffee brand names, past wishful plans for the upcoming weekend and how I would make up for my behaviour. And as it finally settled in my brain and my being, like fine wine, the aftertaste was most pleasurable. It made me rediscover and remember that, despite the mundane city life of a working couple in a busy city, I truly and deeply loved her. And it was time to make sure she knew that. So, after picking up the groceries, I dialled her again. The first time, the call was dropped. The second time, the network was busy. There were no payphones around. I thought of borrowing someone's cell phone, and then the phone suddenly rang. Thinking it was her, I retired to a quieter, secluded bench in a corner of the mall's huge atrium and sat down to profess my love all over again. But as I looked down, I realized it wasn't her. It was my mother calling from Hyderabad.

'Abhi, you're alright no? I was getting so worried.' She sounded frantic.

'Of course Ma, I'm fine. What happened?'

'Is Aditi okay? Thank God you both took the day off.'

'But what's wrong, Ma? What happened?' I asked.

'Arey Abhi, there have been serial blasts all over. It's all over the news—those bloody images of people crying out. But I'm so relieved. I couldn't get through earlier. I've been trying your number for over half an hour.'

I sighed and thought—not again. 'Where has it happened Ma? Calm down.'

'Next to Aditi's office, Abhi. In the Maylord Towers.'

I went numb. My whole body reacted with a shiver and, in the middle of the crowded mall, everything went eerily silent—silent enough for me to be able to hear my own heart beating. My throat suddenly felt parched.

I looked down at my phone and suddenly remembered that Ma was on the line.

'I'll call you back,' I almost barked into the phone, before cutting it and dialling Aditi's number again.

The call did not complete. All around me, the crowd of people doing their afternoon shopping was thinning rapidly. The news was spreading. I decided to head to her office directly. On most days, it was an hour-long drive, but my reckless driving on the now empty roads got me there in under thirty-five minutes. All the way, I thought of my words to her this morning. Leave me alone. God forbid if…

I heard the tearing wail of sirens before I saw the buildings.

Traffic had been stopped a kilometre away from the scene and I got out and rushed towards the building. Maylord Towers's top five floors were on fire and the falling debris had crashed into her building. There were injured people being carried away—people with broken limbs, blood streaming down their faces which still retained an expression of utter shock and disbelief. I gulped and hoped she would walk out any minute, although I had no idea how long it had been since this mayhem had begun.

The fire-fighters tried in vain to bring in reinforcements to put out the flames at Maylord, even as I searched around for someone from the police who could know something. Finally, I located a burly, moustached policeman who seemed to have an idea of what was going on as he directed some of his men towards the building.

I ran to him. 'Sir, Sir! I'm looking for my wife. Her name is Aditi. Aditi Thappar. She works in that building,' I said, pointing to her office.

He followed my finger and, without so much as a blink, asked, 'Which floor?'

'Second.'

'It's not that badly hit. She should have been able to get out. In any case, you may want to look for her at the police station at S.V. Nagar where all the rescued people have been taken. How would she be travelling home normally?'

'By train.'

'Well, all trains are shut, so my guess is she should be at the station.'

I didn't move as he started to rush in the direction of the cloud of smoke where his men had disappeared. He must have read the expression on my face and, perhaps used to dealing with such situations, he answered my look without a trace of emotion in his voice, 'The injured and the dead are at Gandhi Hospital.'

My voice caught in my throat and as I opened my mouth to speak, no sound came out.

'Let's hope you don't find your wife there,' he added and, after giving me a pat on my back, he was gone.

I wanted to cry, to move, to save her from whatever she could be facing. But no thoughts would come to me. I stood there for a couple of minutes, trying to erect a solid barrier against the thoughts that were running in to flood my being. One after the other, they hopped, skipped and jumped over that feeble wall, and I felt myself struggling to stay afloat in that ocean of desolation. Was she hurt? Did she get out? Where is she? Why doesn't her goddamned phone work? Is she okay? What has happened? Why was I so stupid? How do I get to her now? What will I do without her? She can't be gone, she can't... I have to grow old with her. She must be at the police station, wondering what to do, how to contact me... She can't be at the hospital. She didn't work on those floors. But what if she got stuck? No, only the injured are being rescued now, so she must have got out. Is she hurt? Why didn't I tell her to take the day off? Why am I such a conceited, foolish man? Where the hell is she? I want to see her smile again. Oh please, God! Please help me... Please let this be over... Please get me to her... Please...

The ambulance braked barely a foot away from me, and only then did I realize that I had wasted two precious minutes just standing there. I saw the inspector disappear into the smoke and, as the ambulance driver screamed for me to get out of the way, I started to run to the car. I dialled her number again.

'*All phone lines on this route are busy.*'

Damn!

I fumbled with the keys as they slipped out of my sweaty palms and finally got into the car. No one stopped me as I sped down the wrong side of the road, and I soon figured out why. There was a dead end, a big blockade that had been erected to stop all traffic flowing towards the blast site. I cursed my luck and reversed the car, not bothering to brake on the turn and just about missed the next ambulance approaching ground zero. There would be helpline numbers which they would be flashing on TV. I decided against calling our parents. I tried dialling a couple of friends, but got the same message again. It was like I had plunged into a world of darkness, cut off from everyone, and I kept falling deeper and deeper into that infinite abyss.

She has to be at the station, she just has to be, I kept telling myself as I raced towards the police station hidden in the narrow lanes of S.V. Nagar. Life here seemed unaffected, still carrying on its routine mechanically. The hawkers still cried out their wares, the half-naked children still ran out with their mothers chasing after them, the few foreigners who stopped in the flea market continued haggling with the hawkers. But all I was aware of was her stole in the backseat, the hair brush that she had forgotten in the car and spent two weeks searching for, the smell of her perfume which had lingered in the stale air, and the memory of her smile. Time seemed to stand still inside the car, but outside it seemed to enjoy itself in the normalcy of everyday life.

I finally worked my way through the crowded back streets, only to be greeted by more chaos some five hundred meters from where the station should have been. I finally parked the car in an alley and sprinted to the station. There were so many people gathered around the gate that I had to climb over the wall. The thought that it could be wrong was far from my mind by then. Her number was still unreachable. Finally inside the door of the station, I saw more civilians than policemen. As I sifted through the noisy crowd, someone tugged at my sleeve and I turned to see a ghastly pale woman, aged perhaps sixty, pleading with her eyes, asking me,

'Have you seen my son? Have you?' Behind her, a balding old man stooped with age gently took her arm and led her away, trying to console her as they headed towards the hospital. She kept turning in search of a reprieve, which I hoped she would find.

The crowd of worried, anxious loved ones was becoming thicker and louder every minute, and I pushed and shoved my way to the only policeman I could find in that chaos. He was sitting at a table at the far end of the dimly lit room, trying to answer six people at the same time, looking down into his valuable register of who was where with a look that was a mixture of pity and resignation. I looked around to see foreheads creased with lines, faces with tears streaming down their cheeks, mouths frantically trying to speak into phones that didn't work, and hearts trying to stay hopeful. I dreaded what was to happen and, for a minute, I stopped to wonder if I had the strength to find out and face what he would say. Did he even realize how many futures he was altering as he sat there on his spartan chair, sifting through the register of life and death? But the relentless crowd pushed me on and I found myself at his table finally.

I blurted, 'Aditi Thappar?'

He pointed towards his ear and I shouted out her name again, over the confused madness all around. And then I stopped hearing everything around me, as I waited for his lips to say her name and tell me my fate. Three others were clamouring beside his table, hoping for him to announce their salvation as well, and he heard them all patiently. I offered a hundred rupee note to make him hurry, but he smiled a tired smile and said loudly, 'They all want to hear the same good news, Sahib.'

He found two of the other three names in the 'rescued' list while the third one was in the 'injured' list. Relieved, the other three fell back and I fought to remain composed. He could not find her name, he said. I urged him to look again and he did so tirelessly and thoroughly. He eventually found it, scribbled in pencil on the side of the 'rescued' list and smiled at me. Gasping for breath, I managed to ask, 'Where are the rescued people?' To that, he shrugged his shoulders and said, 'Around.' And then I was swallowed by the crowd once more and, finally, five minutes later, soaked in sweat, I found myself outside the police station gate. I didn't feel a thing. I should have been elated but I was not. I wanted to see her face, wanted to be sure that they had not scribbled her name in the wrong column of that tattered register.

I dialled her again frantically, but this time the irritating voice said *switched off*. I started to walk away, trying to think positive, wondering where she could have gone from here. I didn't have to go far to find out. The crowd at the pay phone was larger than the one at the police station and, as I scanned that crowd of wide-eyed strangers searching for that one familiar face, I kept thinking about the disconsolate old lady looking for her son and I kept whispering to myself, 'God, please... Please...'

A police jeep drove up the road and the crowd of people parted. I gasped.

Next to the payphone counter, fighting the crowd around with all her might, was the answer to all my prayers.

I screamed out in joy and exasperation, 'Aditi, Aditi,' as I flung myself into that faithless crowd. She heard me before she saw me and, as she quit arguing, the people around her forced their way into the phone booth so that she suddenly found herself on the edge of that swarming mass. And then she saw me and burst into tears.

As I scrambled across to her, she cried, 'I thought you would never come,' and hugged me so tight that I felt breathless. I lifted her up and kissed her again and again. God, how close I had come.

I held her even closer, never wanting to let her go.

She had a few bruises, but seemed fine otherwise. I ushered her into the car and she collapsed into the passenger seat, exhausted beyond measure. Neither of us spoke for the time it took to get home. She just sat there with her eyes closed, breathing deeply. I was just thankful for having her next to me—alive and well, even if she wasn't smiling just then. How many others had not been as lucky as me? How many were still offering prayers to their various gods, asking for mercy and hope? How many of them would return empty-handed, their worlds altered forever by the end of the day? I looked at her again and again, making sure that she really was there, touching her arm, asking if she needed something.

Finally, when we reached our apartment building, our watchman—who had newly learnt to speak English—opened the gate and said loudly, 'Good day, Sir,' as we drove past.

I nodded solemnly and sighed, knowing that it was indeed a good day. At least for me.

Closure

RAJNI GUPTA

A Pacific-blue, leheriya-printed silk swaying in the gentle breeze in front of a store catches my attention, and I wonder if that colour would have been better than the onion-pink I'd bought earlier to give to the tailor. I chide myself for being indecisive.

The two Tibetan women near the park are making fresh momos. My mouth waters and I stop at their stall. The smell of the hot sauce and the steaming momos fills my nose as one of the women hands me the plate. The clanging of the metal ladle against the steel pot as the chaat wala across the lane stirs his pani makes me wish I had ordered the pani puri instead.

After the sadistic pleasure of burning my mouth with the chilli sauce, I toss the paper plate in the garbage can, pick up my shopping bag and walk toward the dyers. I can see the steam rising from their cauldrons even before I reach them.

Although I don't hear the ringtone, I can feel my phone vibrating through my handbag. It's an unknown number. Shifting the bag from my palm to my wrist, I flip open the phone.

'Hello,' I say, almost screaming to be heard over the din of the market.

'Hi, this is Arvind.'

'Arvind?' We hadn't spoken in three months, since the day he'd cut short my phone call saying he would call back. I waited but he never did and so I deleted his number thinking we had broken up. I guess we hadn't after all.

'Where are you?' he asks, probably hearing the honking and the screeching of cars.

'Lajpat Nagar Market,' I shout, covering my other ear to block out the loud fluttering of a dupatta being yanked up and down by the dyers to dry.

'Listen,' he clears his throat, 'I was just... Would you like to catch up over the weekend?'

'You mean tomorrow?' I ask, even as a small voice in my head says, 'No.'

'Sure, let's do tomorrow.' Then he adds, 'How about Select City Mall, food court?' It sounds more like a statement than a question.

'Ok. What time?' I ask, against my better judgment.

'12.30.'

'P.M.?' I ask stupidly and hear him laughing at the other end.

'Bye.'

'Bye,' I say, feeling a nervous excitement in my stomach.

'Bhaiyya,' I say, turning to the dyer, 'Could you dye this dupatta onion pink?' I hand him both the white chiffon and the colour swatch.

'Bees minute lagega, madam.' He passes the plastic bag to his buddy and gives me a receipt.

I pay and walk back into the interior of the marketplace. A recent Bollywood number is playing somewhere. It's funny I didn't notice it before. I try on beaded jutis at a small store. A mother is haggling with the shopkeeper while her daughter stands aloof in the corner. The smell of henna from the mother's hair nauseates me and I leave. I am allergic to most smells.

I see a sign for a beauty parlour and walk in. I tell the lady who greets me to remove the blackheads from my face.

'Do you want to steam your face first?' she asks, seating me in a chair.

'How much time will it take?' I ask, thinking of the meeting I have later, with the other designer at work.

'An hour,' she says, examining my face closely.

'No, just remove the blackheads,' I say.

I scream as she begins extracting them.

'I told you to open the pores with steam first,' she says with a smug expression. I grip the arms of the chair and purse my lips as she continues ruthlessly.

◆

Standing next to the token counter, I check the time on my cell phone. He is twenty minutes late already. What if he doesn't show up? I feel a knot in the pit of my stomach. It took me several weeks to recover from the heartbreak when he didn't call me back. I check my appearance in the mirror of my compact. There is a lipstick spot on the neckline of my white smock top. I try to wipe it with my thumb.

I don't see him approaching. It's only when he taps my shoulder that I look at him. He is wearing a black graphic t-shirt and boot-cut jeans. There is a little stubble on his face and he reeks faintly of alcohol and cologne. He shakes my hand and buys some tokens.

'So what's up?' he asks when we sit down.

'I am fine.'

Laughing, he surveys the occupants of the next table.

'I mean, nothing much,' I say, stroking the tips of my nails with my thumb.

'Did you cut your hair?' he asks, leaning forward.

'Yes.'

My vanity is slightly hurt when I do not receive a compliment. I turn my attention to the crowded food court. A bunch of guys laugh at one of the tables. There is a big line at the South Indian food stall and I make a note to try it the next time. I put some hot sauce over my fried rice. Arvind is busy eating his noodles and chicken stir-fry. I smile as I remember that he waits until he has almost finished his food to have a conversation.

'The Chinese food here is good,' I say, savouring my fried rice.

'Mmm.' There is a twinkle in his eyes. That same boyish twinkle I fell for.

'Nice watch,' I say, noticing that he is not wearing the one I'd given him.

'I…I need to get the other one repaired,' he says, shrugging.

'So, how is work?' I ask, my mouth salivating from the sourness of the kimchi.

'Well, I changed my job,' he says, pushing a couple of noodles hanging from his mouth with his fork.

'Oh, good. I remember you were not very happy with your old one.' I pick up the bottle of water, wiping the wet circle it leaves on the table with my other hand. 'Where do you work now?'

'It's a small company you probably haven't even heard of.' His eyes flit to the girl on the next table and linger there.

I choke on the water and begin coughing.

'Are you alright?' he asks.

'Yes,' I say. 'You haven't changed at all.' What I really wanted to say was, 'You are a real dyed-in-the-wool.' From the corner of my eyes, I can see the girl's pearl-drop earrings sway as she talks to the guy sitting with her.

Arvind lifts a piece of Manchurian from my plate with his fork and pops it into his mouth.

'Why did you want to see me?' I ask.

'Well,' he says, 'can't a guy meet his friend?'

'You're just lonely, aren't you?' I refrain from saying.

'But you un-friended me on Facebook,' he says, feigning anguish.

'You were the one…' A loud Lady Gaga ringtone breaks the chain of my thoughts.

He lifts a finger towards me and flips open his phone. I don't know why I think of the Black Eyed Peas ringtone he had earlier.

'No, no, not really,' he says into the phone. 'What time? Sure. I'll see you soon.' He snaps the phone shut.

'Who was that?' I ask, wiping my mouth with the napkin.

'A friend,' he says, the smile from the conversation still lingering.

'Listen, I think I should be going,' I say, throwing the crumpled napkin on my messy plate. Then, pulling the hem of my skinny jeans from under my heel, I stand up.

'Well, even I have to be somewhere,' he says, rising. 'Let's do this again.' He gives me a half hug.

'I will call you,' I say, picking up my bag. The whiff of his cologne along with all the hot sauce I just had makes me sick.

'Can I drop you somewhere?'

'No thanks.' I hurry down the escalators to the main level and walk out of the mall. The air, although warm, is fresh. I delete his number as I wait for an auto-rickshaw.

My Familiar

ROHINI KEJRIWAL

It's just one of those feelings that you can't ignore, much as you try to do so. When you feel it, you want to scream it out in the middle of your college cafeteria and not care about who might have heard you. When someone asks you to define it, you just look at them, smile and shrug your shoulders. You hope, in your heart of hearts, that they get to feel it sometime in their life as well and then perhaps, be able to define it for you. A candle lit in the hallway brings back memories; a familiar smell makes you stop and find out if it is the same perfume being used; hearing a certain song never fails to makes you cry. In more ways than one, love can change you and there's nothing you can do to prevent it from hitting you.

We want explanations for everything—the cause and effect of rising Naxalism in India; the answers at the back of the Mathematics text book; and a valid reason why Rahul did not marry Anjali in his college days and chose Tina instead. But some things in life just can't be explained. And when you realize how much they can affect you, you don't even need an explanation.

We sat there in a cafe in a city that could not be called home by either of us. Conversation kept flowing because neither of us wanted the other to stop. He even sang a song just to make me laugh. We just kept sipping our drinks and stealing glances, intermingled with an occasional blush from me which I could not explain. Finally we had to leave, and the anticipated hug just did it for me. I knew I did not want to let go, but I did. We walked away in opposite directions and unlike the filmy way of turning around and checking if the person is watching you walk away, I just smiled to myself till I reached home and finally slept.

That had only been our first meeting but he assured me that there would be another very soon. We were in two completely different parts of the same country, but phone calls and text messages kept whatever it was that had sparked up in our first meeting alive. He made a plan and actually made it happen—he showed up in my city. I spent the full day with him and the dream-like ride that we were on was forced to end before I had even fully realized that it had begun. We had probably passed through more than half of the city over a few hours, using all the available means of local transport to travel—buses, autos, taxis, and even the ferry! It had not been a particularly romantic day or anything of the sort but was just what it was—mere time spent in each other's company, which had beautifully slipped away from our hands that never touched. He could have held my hand but it was only our second meeting and we were both too shy and too unsure. It was all so real that it felt unreal.

The final goodbye was said in a more idealized setting—under orange streetlights outside a joggers' park where we had been sitting for our last hour together talking about our individual pasts and the simplicity of living life now knowing that each of us had the other. I embarrassed myself when I stopped a football (there were kids playing in the park) from going onto the main road with my foot and tripped while trying to kick it back to them. I embarrassed myself even further when I told him that I did that on purpose to try and amuse him so that the tension of our parting would be diluted. The words that had to be said were spoken and we parted. The last thing he said to me was 'It had to be you.' It was the title of the song by Frank Sinatra, his favourite artist, and it became the soundtrack of our relationship after that.

With all your faults, I love you still
It had to be you, wonderful you…

Whatever it was that we shared lasted almost a year. There were the occasional visits made by him, which was much needed in a relationship like ours—slightly unstable because of the distance, but just the best thing that was happening in my life because we seemed to understand each other. We had even reached the stage that we could complete each other's sentences on the phone. Indeed, there was a magical element in my life that just could not be rubbed off, and I am glad that it was what it was.

On one of his visits, we woke up in the morning and almost in role-play of a married couple or one in preparation of what was to come, he demanded that I go make him some coffee while he sat and read the newspaper. (One would usually expect tea to be asked for when they wake up, but I'd rather write coffee in this story because I prefer it to tea.) I did complain and I did stick my tongue out at him at such a preposterous demand to be made first thing in the morning of me, an independent woman living in a society where men at least knew how to make coffee. But I smiled inwardly and obliged and returned with two cups of coffee on a tray held with shaking hands. We sat beside each other reading the morning newspaper together, sipping our individual cups of coffee. It was sweet enough but decently strong…The coffee, that is!

I saw it going downhill somewhere around the seventh month. I could not fathom living without him in my life. He was my feel-good factor after a bad day at college; he was my drinking partner when no one around me would understand that I needed a glass of whiskey; he was my coach right before my big basketball game when I was the last one picked on the team.

It would not be easy to end something that had become such a habit in my life. It would not be easy to let go of all the memories made over the last few months. It would not even be possible to converse as easily with any other living soul. Or, perhaps that's what I wanted to believe. I was in love and wounded in love. I tried listening to some good ol' numbers by Dylan to make myself accept the most obvious truth in front of me—'I Shall Be Released' "Don't think Twice It's All Right'; the answer was, however, 'Blowing in the Wind.'

I tried my hand at love poetry and the words just wouldn't flow. I tried to speak to him as openly as before, but both of us could feel the drift. I even went so far as to land up in his city to surprise him with the help of common friends, but all I felt then was a hollowness instead of love and joy.

I will never know for certain whether he actually cheated on me physically with someone else or not. But I do believe that the distance made him open his options to local offers as well. One night, when we were talking on the phone, he received a text and I waited while he read it while I was on the line. It was a text from one of his first few lovers and contained a vivid description of acts she wanted to perform with him, most being rather explicitly sexual in nature. He told me about it and I pretended not to care because I wanted to believe that I had nothing to worry about. He tried to convince me that he was not in touch with her at all and that the message was completely out of the blue. He even went so far as to send me the message, which made me just want to throw up on reading it. I don't quite know what that incident did to me or to us but I can safely say that it was the first sign of mistrust in what we shared.

We ignored the text message incident after that but my mind had started to wander too. Unlike him, it wasn't on other potential lovers I could take but instead, on college and extra-curricular work. Prior to the incident, I would forego a lot of my work to make time for him because I thought our mutual feelings were that strong. I started to believe that I was holding myself back from a lot of things because I had him in my life. And one day, I decided not to take any of that anymore and live for myself first, and then for us.

I can't say I regret the decision in the least. At the end of the last trip he made to meet me, we were sitting on the terrace sipping beers and talking about whatever came to mind. He wasn't as responsive as he used to be. He didn't seem as happy around me as he was when we met in the past few months. He even mentioned his ex often. The funny part was that this wasn't even the ex whom he had received the dirty text from a few months back. It was another one whom he broke up with on bad terms because of his own stupidity. I knew in my mind that it was over when in one reference to her, he said, 'You should know…. She'll always be the one that got away.' Luckily for me, I did too. A few months later, I went back to the café where it had all begun. The place was not the same. The feeling was not the same. The names of the items on the menu would be the same, but the taste would never be the same. I sat there at the same table, quietly sipping the same drink I'd had with him—gin and tonic. I sipped, slowly absorbing the music of the space, absorbing the excitement that had once bubbled up within me sitting at that very spot. The drink was soon over. The dues were paid and as I was leaving, I stepped into the ladies' restroom and caught a glimpse of myself in the mirror. It had been a while since I had properly looked at myself. I had changed more than I could ever remember. Perhaps it was the alcohol. Perhaps it was not.

Reality Bytes

ANITHA MURTHY

Quit deluding yourself—you're not Rachel in *Friends*. Go out there and get a life!

Radhika fumed as she re-read the comment on her blog. Just who the heck did this guy think he was? This...GuyInBed? Eeks! What a lousy, lame handle.

Her fingers hovered over the keyboard, itching to type in a remark so acerbic that it would cut him right down to size. Sadly nothing materialized and, all too aware of the ticking clock, she snapped her laptop shut. She had barely ten minutes to get herself ready for the office bus.

The first thing Radhika did on reaching her office was to return to her blog, Girl in Town.

Quit deluding yourself—you're no Ross. Ditto @ get a life!

She typed the message and quickly posted it before she changed her mind. But the comment still rankled.

So what's new? All alone yet again, lounging in my pyjamas, digging into a tub of ice-cream, watching TV. Roomie's out again with a new BF. My love life, on the other hand, never takes off.

Living in the city may seem glamorous to my folks back home, but there's only one dress hanging in my closet: loneliness.

That's all she had written. She hadn't even mentioned that she had, indeed, been watching *Friends*!

His reply appeared shortly.

I wasn't applying for the role of Ross. My point is that if you're even half as smart as your blog makes you out to be, you'd be out there enjoying life—not posting inane stuff like this.

Radhika did not hesitate this time. In fact, she had a brilliant acronym for his stupid GuyInBed handle, which reflected exactly what she thought of his comments: Mr G.I.Be, shortened to Mr Gibe. Perfect!

Mr Gibe, this is my blog and I can write what I want, even if it's inane by your lofty standards. In fact, I'm wondering why you bother to read it at all, considering it's so lowbrow. You've had your say, and I am choosing not to respond this time. Or ever.

PS: Thanks for the compliment, even if you didn't mean it. As you can see, I am smart!

That shut him up, nice and proper.

◆

Radhika stood in front of the mirror, fidgeting. There was nothing more she could do. Her hair fell neatly about her shoulders, her face was lightly made up with just kohl and a touch of gloss, her silky white blouse on faded jeans looked just right for a night out. She sighed as she turned away, for she knew what was wrong— she looked exactly like all the others she would meet during the evening. She was a goddamn clone.

A car honked below.

'Ready?'

Her roomie Noni teetered into the room on sky-high heels. She was from Mumbai and she found Bengaluru rather slow. Her real name was Mriganayanee, but no one knew that. She had persuaded Radhika to come along for a double-date. Her BF was rather boring when drunk, she said.

'Yup, I'm ready.' Radhika hoisted her purse on her shoulder. She was so not looking forward to this outing.

The evening was predictable and forgettable. Inane chatter, much alcohol, embarrassed dancing, and driving around late at night looking for a place to eat. Radhika's date seemed as relieved as her when they were dropped home. Noni crashed immediately, but Radhika cooked herself an omelette. She was ravenous. She had just picked at the greasy food in the shady restaurant earlier.

As she munched, she began checking her mail. One jumped to her notice:

Hi GIT!

Yes, it's me, Mr Gibe.

Life's too short to be mad, so sorry if I've offended you. But honestly, I meant what I said. You seem to be so smart, I can't understand why you're reducing your life to being a husband-seeker. Just read your earlier posts and you'll see what I mean.

Get a life! (And I mean this in the most positive way :D)

Mr Gibe

Radhika marched up to the sink and began scrubbing her plate furiously. This was too much! Reducing her life to being a husband-seeker? God dammit! Just who did he think he was? Some sort of messiah, spreading 'The Word' around? And what was this 'get a life'? Did he even know what she was going through? How much she had struggled to adjust to life in the big city after having lived in a protected environment her whole life, in Teerthapur, AP? How much she had to unlearn and learn? How her blog had been her only refuge, her anonymous outpourings her only relief? If she had turned husband-seeker at the age of twenty-five, was it wrong? Didn't everyone want a little bit of companionship, a shoulder to cry on, and a warm embrace to return to?

By the time she returned to her laptop, Radhika was calmer. She didn't need to respond to him. Unlike the other readers of her blog who were so supportive, he was a newcomer, a troll who just wanted her attention. And that she would not give. She deleted his mail. She was ready to sleep now.

◆

Mr Gibe, unfortunately, did not take the hint. He continued to send her an email every day, quoting snippets from her own posts and signing off with 'Get a life!' every time.

I'm going to buy a box of paints and a couple of canvases this weekend. The scenes, the scenes… There's a little girl who sells flowers at my bus stop, and I want to capture that cheeky yet innocent face before it fades! The old cobbler at the corner is a character as tough and wizened as the leather he works with. What a portrait he'd make! The colourful, busy streets of Malleswaram—it would be worth capturing that atmosphere on canvas. I can almost picture how my painting will look! There's so much to do, I'm all excited. Look out for my sketches, I'll be posting them online shortly.

…Got myself a new Canon this weekend. Look out world, here I come!…

I've promised myself that I will try out one new thing every week. There's so much to do, so much to learn, the sky's the limit! First on the list—pottery. I know, coming from a village, it sounds silly to get excited about it, but hey, I never did do much back home except study or read books. Oh, the books! They were so fascinating, a whole new world opening up every time I opened a new book. What adventures I went on! Anyway, that will probably be a whole new post, so I'll let you know how my first pot turns out. Wish me luck!

Radhika rolled her eyes. She had been so naïve, so gushing, so totally... stupid! She made a mental note to delete her older posts. They were truly cringe-worthy.

But something intrigued her more. Finally, she sent out the mail that had been lying in her Drafts folder for over a week.

Hello Mr Gibe,

First of all, I'd really like you to stop sending me these emails. I find them irritating and, honestly, can't stand reading my older posts.

But before that, I'd like you to answer one question. Why are you doing this? Why me? Do you harass all girls like this or is it just me?

Here's looking forward to NO MORE mails from you,

GIT

The response came almost immediately, as if he had been waiting online for her mail. It was just an infuriating one-liner:

Finally, GIT!

Radhika stared at the message. Was she actually feeling disappointed? What had she expected?

Just then, a chat box popped up.

GIT?

Radhika's heart began to beat just a little faster. She hesitated for what seemed like ages before she typed in with trembling fingers:

Mr Gibe, I presume?

◆

By the end of the first month, Radhika and Mr Gibe had chatted up a storm. She spent every moment looking forward to 9 p.m. She mined the day for anecdotes and lugged the gems home, revelling in their content during her chats with him. They never got personal, they didn't even know each other's names—they didn't care. All she knew about him was that he was a freelance software consultant working from home, where he lived with his mother.

One night, she threw caution to the winds. She typed in the chat box:

Isn't it time we got to know each other better? For starters, my real name is Radhika. And if you tell me yours, there's a reward—I'll send you my picture!

His reply took a long time in coming.

Do you really want to get into that?

Sudden tears stinging her eyes, Radhika disconnected immediately. How silly she was to think that this meant anything more than... What was it anyway?

The next day, however, she could not resist checking her mail. And there it was: his message.

Hey, don't be mad. My name is Arjun—now where's my reward?

Radhika's mood lifted all of a sudden. She browsed through her pictures: too dark, not flattering enough, looked too fat, face was not clear, too come-hither, too disinterested, smiling too much, too glum... She finally selected a photo that had been taken atop Nandi Hills. Her hair was ruffled by the breeze, but her smile was just right.

She uploaded it and sent it off, and spent the next few hours enjoying the little quivers of excitement that ran through her every now and then. She couldn't be falling for Arjun, could she? Every ten seconds she refreshed her screen, till she gave herself a restraining order and promised not to look till 9 p.m. She broke her promise a couple of times, but it bore no fruit. There was no mail the whole day, no chat at 9 p.m. either and, after a sleepless night, the next morning too saw nothing in her inbox. Nothing. She double-checked the photo she had sent. Had she scared him away?

◆

A message from Arjun popped up in the chat box four days later, when she was just about to log off.

Hey, have been busy. And you?

Radhika sat looking for a long time at the message. What was the meaning of this? How could he just pick up where he left off, without even offering an apology? What did 'busy' really mean? For someone of his background, could he really have been so busy as to not even have access to a computer to drop her a line?

She decided to play him at his own game. She didn't respond for two days. When she did, she laboured for a breezy, non-committal tone.

Yeah, long time, I know. Me busy too. Lots of stuff going on.

The response was immediate.

Really?

There! He had done it again. Infuriating her with his sarcastic one-liners. Before she could decide what she would reply, a mail appeared with an attachment.

And here's my pic. Hope you like it!

Her fingers shook as she clicked more than required on the attachment. The photo took its time loading, and she spent at least thirty seconds looking at the top of a white gate that seemed very familiar. Where had she seen this gate before?

The guy in the photo was clean-shaven, with a mop of unruly hair and a congenial grin. He wore a beige t-shirt with jeans and appeared to be leaning against a bike. Radhika sighed with relief—he was cute!

Where was this picture taken? The white gate seems very familiar.

In front of my house. Wait… Don't tell me you live somewhere down my street?

Nope. Just seems so damn familiar… Can't place it though. Where do you stay?

And have you come knocking at my door? No thanks!

Radhika drew back, a bit hurt. Honestly, she hadn't meant to pry. But it felt like a slap in the face. She had always assumed they would meet somewhere down the line. Wasn't that normal? She typed her answer rapidly.

Me, at your door? Ha ha! Dream on!

Something was not quite right. Later that night, as she tossed and turned on her narrow bed (Noni was out late again), she tried to figure out exactly what it was that troubled her. Was it something Arjun had said?

Or was it something he was not saying?

He hadn't mentioned why he had been so busy. He hadn't commented on her photo. He didn't want to meet her. Perhaps she was reading too much into everything. Perhaps he just wasn't interested. That was the only answer that made sense. She pummelled her pillow in frustration—it was so not fair, dammit! She wiped the tears that were threatening to dampen the bed. She was not going mushy over some obnoxious guy if she could help it.

◆

Radhika and Arjun slipped right back into their 9 p.m. chat routine, but her heart wasn't quite in it. The joking, the harmless ribbing and the juicy office anecdotes—they all seemed so fake now. Arjun too seemed to sense the change in the equation, for his appearances online became less reliable. Some nights he'd show up and everything would feel almost normal. But his absences became more frequent, his silences between mails longer.

Perhaps it was all for the best. Maybe Arjun was married with kids. Maybe he was the fat guy sitting next to her at the coffee shop. Maybe, maybe… Her mind played endless tricks on her. It was, she decided, time to move on.

It was while returning from an office lunch party that Radhika spotted the white gate. It was the corner house on the street parallel to where their office was located. No wonder she had found it so familiar!

Back at the office, she stared at her laptop. A nervous energy had begun uncoiling within, sending warning tremors. She could just walk down the road, open the gate and ring the bell. Would he open the door? 'No thanks'—that's what he'd said.

A sudden thought struck her. Did he know who she was? Was he some sort of perverted stalker? Maybe it wasn't his house at all. Maybe it was just a ploy, a hint to let her know that he knew where she worked. And she had been so dumb! But then, why had he suddenly stopped corresponding with her? It made no sense. And for some strange reason, it was becoming urgent that she find out exactly what he was up to.

A reckless idea entered her mind and took root. It filled her mind till there was no room for doubt, for second-guessing, or for stepping back.

That evening, instead of boarding the office bus that stood outside, Radhika walked down the street, adrenaline pumping at every step. When she reached the white gate and unclasped it, her hand was not trembling. She walked towards the door as if in a dream and pressed the doorbell firmly. She waited. And waited. Her resolution wavering, she hit the bell tentatively again. This, she had not reckoned with. That the door would not open, that no one would be there—the thought had never crossed her mind.

Her shoulders drooped in defeat as she walked back slowly to the gate and out onto the street. What had she been thinking? Had she been crazy enough to contemplate confrontation? For what? Tears pricked her eyes and she felt more alone than she had ever felt in the past five years away from home.

As she turned the corner, an auto came by. A hand was pointing to the house she had just left. Curious, she waited. The auto stopped outside the white gate and an old lady disembarked with some difficulty. She spent a few minutes bending over the meter reading and fishing out change from her unwieldy handbag. Then she reached in, as if to assist someone. A thin arm and leg appeared first, followed by an emaciated body.

The person turned slowly, his face visible to Radhika, and she reeled in shock. There was no doubt: it was Arjun. He looked totally worn out, dark shadows under his eyes, a thin green surgical mask across his face, and his head unmistakably bald.

The two of them shuffled past the familiar white gate which swung shut slowly behind them.

Tall Order

MALATHI JAIKUMAR

Chitra did not believe in love—neither at first sight nor after knowing someone for years. She relied on logic and common sense. Romance was for young day-dreaming damsels, not for her who had her feet firmly on terra firma. Besides, she was far too busy with her job as a librarian and her other activities that included dedicating her spare time to an old-age home near her place of work.

But being an Indian woman in India she had to listen patiently to parents, grandparents, aunts and uncles who kept bringing up proposals and 'informal' meetings with 'suitable boys'. Most of these were disastrous and as she crept closer to forty, her parents reluctantly acknowledged that their daughter was 'different'.

Preparing to leave for work, she grimaced at the mirror. A statuesque five feet eleven; clean scrubbed face without make up; large, rather disconcertingly candid, brown eyes; a mouth that smiled far too easily and a very frank and cynical attitude. Most men were rather awed by her size though some did find her quite attractive—until she opened her mouth. Within a few minutes they would squirm, baffled by her candid gaze and blunt manner. She had to admit she also liked to shock people and at times she was deliberately outrageous.

Oh well. She was quite happy with her place in the world. For the next ten minutes she was a whirlwind of activity. By the time she stepped out with two bags hanging from her shoulder and a few files cradled in her arms, she was running late.

She pressed the lift button with her elbow, and then ran out of the lift towards the entrance. Transferring the weight of the files on to her left hand she reached out to push the entrance door when it opened by itself and she went lurching out to slam into what seemed like concrete. Still a bit disoriented by the collision she heard a nice, deep voice say, 'Whew. I did not know they had human cannon balls here'.

She let her head rest against the concrete, confused by the collision and the feel of hard muscles beneath the cotton t-shirt and a refreshing cologne.

Just as suddenly she stepped back, annoyed with herself for her involuntary gesture. She was just about to make a retort when he knelt down to pick up her files. She gave up the idea of talking to the top of his head (a rather well-shaped head of wavy black hair) which would rob the sting out of her reply and went down on her knees as well trying to pick up some sheets of paper when he looked up—his eyes were the colour of bronze autumn leaves with specks of sunlight.

'I have come to spend a month with my uncle on the fourth floor—4C.'

'I am in 4B,' she replied and then cursed herself for volunteering information without being asked. This was most unlike her.

'Gosh. Is that your mom who never stops talking? Whenever I pass by I hear her voice and wonder if she talks in her sleep as well. Sorry. I did not mean to be rude, but I am really amazed at her flow of words.'

Chitra's initial annoyance melted in the face of his cheerfully contrite voice and disarming smile that created two longish dimples on his cheeks. But she suppressed her smile and said in a rather severe tone: 'If you did not mean to be rude why did you say that? She does have a house and family to run, you know. I am sure your mother is no better.'

The smile vanished as he said, 'I would not know. I do not have one.'

Shit. He expects sympathy now, she thought. So like men. She shrugged her shoulders and turned to leave.

'Hope to see you around,' he said.

'I don't think I will survive another collision,' she said over her shoulder and stepped out briskly, leaving him looking after her in a slightly puzzled way.

The next three days went by without another encounter. She did occasionally look out for him and his eyes did seem to haunt her now and then. When she did meet him next, it was during a heavy thundershower. She was drenched, her umbrella a miserable picture of a chalice held aloft collecting the rain. He stopped his car. She mustered as much dignity as she could, very conscious of wet hair and the small pool of water at her feet while he looked dry and elegant.

'I thought you might bite my head off. Do you always try to frighten away people?' he said with a smile.

'People who get frightened are not worth knowing anyway. Time is too precious to be wasted on polite conversation that gets you nowhere.'

'How about a rude conversation? My grandfather is a crotchety old man. But for all his grizzly exterior, he is a real softie,' he said unfazed by her candid manner.

The next twenty minutes of the drive were not as painful as she thought they would be. Her cynicism only provoked a hint of a smile and a twinkle in his eye which she found frustrating but refreshingly different from other men. He was easy to talk to and gradually she let herself relax and stopped thinking of repartees. They found they had some interests in common. He was seven years younger than her, was in between jobs, looked like a model or movie star but was actually a scientist and author.

He dropped her outside the block and went on to park his car without a word about meeting again. Sadly lacks social graces, she thought. He should have parked the car and used his umbrella to see her into the building and not left her standing bedraggled outside. She felt vaguely irritated and confused.

She pretended not to look out for him, but within two days she was trying to catch a glimpse of him and felt a bit let down when she could not. It was a bit like wanting to look at the last page when halfway through a book but resisting the urge to do so.

The next week she was sitting at a Barista coffee shop immersed in a book, when a shadow fell upon her and she glanced up to find him looking down at her quizzically.

'Hi. Can I join you?'

She dropped her book, hastily picked it up, smiled her consent and buried her nose in the book again, very conscious of his eyes on her. She found the silence and his gaze most disconcerting and was just about to speak when he asked, 'Do you always read with the book held upside down?'

She hurriedly turned it over as she replied 'Only when people scare me and then sit and stare at me.' They laughed together. Conversation flowed quite smoothly. They ordered another cup of coffee, some cookies and then more coffee. All of a sudden she looked at her watch and jumped up in alarm. They had been chatting for an hour and a half and it felt like fifteen minutes. She saw her surprise reflected in his eyes as they got up to leave.

Their acquaintance developed into a comfortable friendship. Occasional walks, an impromptu lunch and chance meetings that always ended up lasting longer than planned. He paid her no compliments, never made a pass at her but the moment she looked into his eyes she could see the joy they had in each other's company. At a film show, she became very conscious of his arm brushing against hers and his breath as he whispered in her ear. Her heart beat faster and her mouth went dry. It was quite ridiculous at her age and positively not logical. After the movie, going down the stairs, she missed the last step and stumbled. He quickly held her hand and led her to the car. Arriving home, he took the brunt of her mother's prattle almost from the moment the door opened. He looked in the next day very briefly but just as suddenly vanished from the horizon for the next week.

Chitra fretted and fumed, angry with herself for feeling lost and lonely. She threw herself into her work but it did not help much. Some odd phrase, a chance remark and she would be back to square one. She never realized she could miss someone so much.

One day she felt an urge to get out into the open, close to nature. She went to the beach and sat looking out at the sea when she saw him sitting some distance away. There was a girl with him and even as she tried to get a better look at them, they stood up. Clad in a pair of bright shorts and a brief top that accentuated her curves, the petite girl leaned against him as he put a protective arm around her waist. Chitra felt a moment of intense pain, as if someone had just dealt her a body blow.

She cursed herself. There had been nothing to suggest anything more than a friendship so why should she feel hurt? But all the logic and common sense did not seem to help now. Her heart seemed to be deaf to reason. She began to avoid him and twice when they came face to face she rushed away murmuring some inane excuse.

It was at the coffee shop again that he cornered her. She tried to keep up some small talk but the old spark was missing and every word felt stilted.

'I have been trying to talk to you for the past so many days. I have just landed a good job in Bangalore. I have to leave next week.'

'Congratulations,' she said, faking cheerfulness. 'At least now I will have some peace and quiet.'

'No you won't—not for one more week. You see, I have got used to your rudeness. In fact, I missed it. But right now I need your help. You see, I love this girl very much but am not sure about her feelings. I want to settle down. But I am so scared. What if she turns me down?'

Her heart plummeted even further. So he really was in love with the girl on the beach. And how insensitive could he get? Asking for her advice on his love affairs.

'Well I do not think she will turn you down,' she said. 'She seemed extremely affectionate at the beach.'

'The beach?'

'Yes. I saw you both together the other day. You looked good together,' she said twisting the knife in her heart.

'You idiot. Why didn't you come and meet us. I have wanted you to meet her. If I had seen you, I would have brought her up to you.'

She could not stand it anymore. Sudden, sharp tears welled up and she looked down hastily. She heard a snort of laughter and the next moment he tilted her chin up and gazed into her tear-filled eyes. 'What an utter nincompoop you are. That girl is my cousin. We are very close and she always turns to me for everything. She is not the girl I was talking about.'

Still a bit miffed at his insensitivity at asking her for advice she said, 'Why don't you just ask that girl whoever she is? No point asking me.'

He reached out and took her hand. 'Okay. Here goes. Will you come and settle down in Bangalore with me?'

Stunned she looked at him, her eyes widening in disbelief and surprise.

'Wow.' he said. 'This must be the first time you have been at a loss for words. Well is it yes or no?'

Still unable to speak, she just nodded her head.

'I need to hear it loud and clear. Tell me, are you prepared to spend the rest of your life with me?'

'Only if you promise you will never bore me to death,' she whispered.

'I am very good at thinking of new ways to keep your interest alive,' he said as he held her hands tighter. 'Come. Let's go tell your mom. After I get myself some ear plugs,' he added, laughing at her mock anger.

The Coffee Shop

NIMMY CHACKO

'Coffee?' A lifted eyebrow.

'Coffee.' A curt nod.

We smile automatically. The same smile. Mirror images, in fact. Close-lipped and twinkle-less. Locked tightly inside our individual sighs. And brief, of course.

Her tired hand reaches out and pushes open the glass door. We step in quietly, shutting out the noise.

◆

Earlier in the day...

'Why are you in such a bad mood?' Concerned eyes peer curiously at me.

I bite back a retort, but the frown's already settled on my face, all nice and snug as you please. Thankfully, the second bell rings and I don't have to go through the trouble of making up an answer. I doubt she would understand the many vagaries of my mood.

For the next ten minutes, the class is absorbed, rapt. Everyone—well, almost everyone—is paying complete attention to what's going on. Then the teacher closes the register. The attendance has been taken. In other words, the class is over.

Some heads drop immediately. It's important to complete your sleep, you know. One or two are still wide awake though. The strange ones. Their heads bob enthusiastically until their necks protest, while furious notes are scribbled down in their neatly ruled notebooks. Occasionally, they ask questions that get increasingly unnecessary in nature. I stare at them distractedly for a few minutes.

'Psst. Let's play something. I'm bored.' An annoying nudge.

'Shush. I want to listen.' Not really. But I don't want to play tic-tac-toe either.

'Oh come on. It's Keats!'

'I'm not in the mood.'

'Uff. You and your moods.'

'Whatever.'

One of the strange ones turns and shoots us a venomous look. I decide to take notes.

Spirals. Flowers. Some with sepals. Blissful stars, fiendish crescent moons. Spiked suns, and all that galactic nonsense. Meticulously doodled on white paper. One whole page devoted exclusively to these little masterpieces. A mini art gallery in my fancy five-subject notebook. Why can't they be words? Why am I perpetually stuck with writer's block?

I sigh deeply, allowing my pen to rest and decide to sneak a look. Well, at him. Who else? Bad idea. I know that. The warning signs blink frantically in my head. Don't stare at him, don't stare at him, don't stare… I peek at him from beneath my eye lashes. No… No looking at him! I squeeze my eyes shut. Where is my will-power when I need it? It automatically ceases to exist, I suppose.

'Maya, I hate to break your reverie, but could you please read *Ode to a Nightingale* for us?'

The class waits, in deafening silence. And he catches my eye. I think.

I swallow. Well, this was going to be tough. Did I even have my book?

The images on the next page are frenzied and riotous—painted in mutinous dark-blue ink.

♦

The smell of roasted coffee beans is overpowering, sense-tingling. I absorb it greedily. What is it about this place? What is it?

We edge towards our favourite couch, but it's already occupied. We settle for a small table with puny chairs nearby, ready to move the moment the irritating couple leaves.

I can see her hunched up shoulders beginning to relax, her tangled brows loosening. Behind the counter, I feel the coffee brewing. It's ready. I breathe deeply. Cinnamon, whipped cream and a sprinkling of chocolate. Bittersweet glory.

She sips hers, the glimmer of a cardamom smile on her face.

'So how's your love life going?' A playful smile on her lips.

I let her question swirl inside my mug and reply, 'The same. I stared at him some more today. And I think he may have looked in my direction once during English.'

'Ah. That's progress. He is getting more responsive.' A serious smile spreads like butter on her sarcasm.

'His eyes go all crinkly when he smiles.'

'Yeah?'

My turn. I ask, 'What about your love life?'

She laughs loudly. And doesn't stop. After some time, I laugh with her.

◆

Earlier...

I can't bear it any longer. I can't sulk in the darkness forever. I need to confront my fears. Tackle, fight, punch. Run?

Gulp.

Gingerly, I lift the curtain. And immediately creep back to my safe little corner, shaking.

Footsteps. Oh no!

I sink deeper into the shadows, wrapping the darkness around me.

An impatient tap. 'It's time. The group song's over. Your turn now.'

I walk numbly.

'First solo, huh?' he asks, noticing how unusually white I've become for a brown-skinned girl. 'Don't worry, it'll be fine.'

I nod, still petrified. Stage fright is normal. Right?

◆

'You were so good today.'

'Yeah?'

She nods her head vigorously. I wonder if I should go for a second cup. Maybe a Kaapi Crema? She is just being a friend. I open my notebook and write.

Haiku perched on pen
Ink-coloured and fancy-flecked
Paper nets ensnare

There are words now. Yay! I'm relieved. There are words, there are words. Even if they are nonsense.

She reads upside down. 'Mmm... nice.'

◆

Earlier...

No college today. I should be happy. I need to make a Sunday morning. Ingredients:

1. A fried egg, sunny side up.
2. Two slices of bread, strawberry jammed.
3. Tea in a dark green coffee mug. Milky and watery, if you must know.
4. A bed waiting to be made.
5. Ten games of Pacman, lost miserably.
6. An empty inbox filled with Facebook messages.
7. Miffed newspapers.
8. Imaginary morning rain.
9. Sugary music.

Method? Hmm.

I suddenly can't wait for Monday. I wonder how he spends his Sundays. I don't think I'll ever find out. Will I?

No.

How to make a Sunday evening. Ingredients:

1. Me.
2. Thoughts of him.

Method: Write.

◆

Later...

'Do you want my raincoat?'

'What?'

'My raincoat... You should wear it. It's pouring.'

'Don't you want it?'

'I don't mind the rain.' He grins his grin and I fall into a rain-splashed mood.

We are standing outside a mall. The roads are soaked to the skin. Umbrellas smile and glisten, nudging each other, throwing knowing glances. Stray dogs laugh as people scurry for cover, grumbling under their breath. Clouds emanate silver strings that drop to the earth while the wind strums them in graceful, rhythmic movements.

Rain music is strangely uplifting. You feel like you're part of the harmony. Even though you're just an intent listener.

We carefully step over puddles of water, even though we secretly want to jump straight into them.

I want the rain to freeze. Along with that moment. Everyone knows that rain-splashed moods don't last long. They trickle away too soon. And then the sun comes and pats the earth dry.

◆

'Your hair's still wet.'

'I know.' I smile to myself, and wrap my icy hands around my warm coffee cup.

'You are not telling me something.' A pouty accusation.

'You haven't even ordered your coffee yet,' I tease. I love exasperating her.

◆

Earlier...

    'You hang up.'

    'No, you hang up!'

    'No! You!'

    'No.'

    'Oh my god, we're one those couples!'

    'Haha, yeah. But I'm not hanging up.'

    'Fine, I'll do it then.'

    'Good.'

    'You still there?'

    'Yes!'

    'By the way, I wrote something for you.'

    'Really? Show me!'

    'Check your email.'

    'Is it something dirty?'

    'You'll see.'

◆

'It's 4.15. We can't issue books now.'

    'It's 4.10 by my watch.'

    'It's 4.15 by mine.'

    'I had class till 4. And I have class till 4 every day of the week. This is the only time I can come.'

    'That's not my problem.'

    'It's 4.10.'

    'It's 4.15.'

    'I just want a book!'

    'Then you should have come earlier.'

    'I told you, I had a class.'

    'If you have a problem with the library, go speak to Father.'

'Look, I'll just take two minutes.'

'No.'

'I ...'

'No.'

◆

'The couch is empty now. Let's move there.'

'Hmm.'

'Trouble with the librarian today?'

'Of course.'

◆

I survey myself in the mirror. It's startling how much I can see. Tired eyes that have been smudged with kohl in a desperate attempt to hide the pallor. The cynical eyebrow. The dry throat. The cracked heels. The faltering pace. The controlled rage. And the fear of looking into a mirror.

It's lonely outside. The wind howls in anguish. Searching, looking for things to lift, throw, catch and destroy. I like its strength. I like how it pushes open the shut windows, blows up the curtains into baby-pink balloons, and reaches out to touch my face. Teasingly, it tickles me.

The walls look brown in the dark. It's just afternoon. How did the darkness creep in so soon? I wonder if a storm is brewing.

◆

We talk, she and I. Of things relevant and irrelevant. A little bit of this and a little bit of that. Crushes, lost loves, stage fright and writer's block. Shoes and ships and sealing-wax. Poetry enveloped in mocha mist.

We indulge till it's time to leave. I silently thank her for our silent conversations and our conversational silences. Closing the door, we promise to return. For the funeral of the next day's joys and sorrows. Over coffee.

A Girl Can Dream

AYEESHA KHANNA

She vividly remembered the day she had first met him. She was a week away from her fifth birthday. Her mother had told her that they were expecting visitors for lunch, so she was cleaning up the mess in her room.

'Be good, you! I'll take some time. So stay safe and look pretty, okay?' she said to her Barbie doll, as she placed her upright on her bed.

Mother then dressed her in her favourite pink dress, with pink buckled shoes. Once she was ready, her mother would always do the same thing, like a ritual: she'd hold her face delicately, kiss her on her nose, and tell her she was the most beautiful princess in the world. 'I'm not a princess,' she'd argue.

'But you are mine,' Ma would say.

The doorbell rang and her mother rushed down to answer it. She heard greetings and exclamations as her little feet carried her down the staircase. She looked at the guests—a couple, about Ma and Pa's age, a big girl and a small boy. Hmm. Ma's friends were always more fun. Pa's friends would come wearing boring office clothes and without kids. They'd glance at her once, say she was adorable, and then start discussing the news.

As Ma kept bringing in the snacks, the big girl kept gobbling them down.

'Runi, enough with the cashews already! You'll get a stomach ache!' her mother kept telling her. 'Look how quietly the little girl is sitting. Learn something from her! Aunty must be thinking I keep you hungry at home!'

Aunty was actually thinking why the little boy looked so lost. 'Rian? Would you like to go and play in the playroom? We'll serve lunch in about an hour. You can play with Zoya till then.'

Zoya looked up. What? She hated boys! Absolutely detested them. They were rough and loud and they hated her back.

'Okay,' he said and walked up to Zoya. 'Where is it?'

Ugh. Now the playroom would be a mess in five minutes and Ma would ask her to clean up when they left. He entered, plopped himself on the blue plastic chair and began staring around. Zoya noticed something. His eyes were like Sushmita. Sushmita, her favourite Barbie doll.

Zoya sat in her pink chair and looked at Rian. He was so lost. Thank God he was lazy. No cleaning up. Phew. He just sat in a corner and hummed to himself, staring into nothing.

'You're so boring,' she blurted out. Oops. But hey, in her defence, it had been ten minutes and he hadn't said a thing.

'You're too pink to talk to.'

'Huh? What is that supposed to mean?'

'I hate pink. Blue is my favourite colour.'

Wow! He was boring, he was lazy and he hated pink. Perfect company.

'Do you want to play with cars or something? I don't like you, so I'm going back to Ma.'

Yes, it started early, her habit of saying just about anything and everything she felt. She didn't know how much it would cost her someday.

'You're pretty pretty.'

'What?'

'You're pretty pretty.'

Oh. He was being nice now. She ought to, too.

'You have eyes like my favourite Barbie doll.'

And they smiled at each other.

That night, Zoya climbed into bed between Ma and Pa and did what she always did before sleeping. She'd close her eyes and think of everything she wanted to dream about. She closed her eyes and decided to dream about her birthday dress. They were going to buy it the next day. It would have frills and lace and matching socks. And a ribbon around the middle. And puffy sleeves. And it would be pink.

When she'd finally fall asleep, what she'd been thinking of would often get altered a little. Mountains would become beaches, Ma would be wearing something different and Sushmita would become life-size.

The dress became blue.

◆

It was her first job. And she was losing it. It all looked so easy when Pa did it. It looked like he just sat in the plush leather easy-chair all day and talked to people on his computer. Now she knew: too many wooden chairs would have to be worn out by her to reach the leather.

'Come on! Just one beer. I'll drop you home then.'

'Just get in the car, Moti!'

Shai and Kos, her best friends from college, had spent their college days joking about how Zoya had spent about an hour of her life single since puberty. Till sometime around the middle of college. Then she got un-boyfriendable.

'Fine, one drink. And your arse is Moti.'

She got into the car with them.

Four vodka shots down, she stared at Shai, jealous of her for being able to stand straight.

'I knew I'd regret this.'

'Oh, come on.'

Bone-crushing hug.

'Get out there Zoya, go do your thing, grab an eyeball or two. You're like the opposite of Maybelline.'

'That's a compliment?'

'Yeah baby, you're born with it.'

'That's been your best tonight, missy,' said Kos, appearing out of nowhere.

'And in vain. I'm tired and I'm working tomorrow. Drop me back now, Shai.'

'But it's Sunday tomorrow!'

'I know. I've been talking about that 25th June event for a year now. Get your arse up.'

'Oh…yeah. Twenty-fifth. June is a funny name, don't you think? Joooo…'

'Shai!'

'Isn't it like someone's birthday today?'

Silence.

Kos hiccupped.

Zoya dropped her empty shot glass, opened her bag and started searching for her phone. Oh, good. Unlock. Calendar. June. Twenty-fourth.

'Oh,' she whispered.

Shai snatched the phone from her.

'Ooh! I remember him! Are you guys still in touch?'

'No. Give me my phone.'

'Then why's his birthday saved on the calendar of a phone you bought two months ago?'

'I don't know, mom. I like remembering birthdays I guess.'

'Zoya. Really? It's been six years, dude. Get a life already.'

'Why aren't we getting into the car?'

'Shut up, Kos.'

'Woookey.'

'She's right. We should go. Give me that phone.'

'Call him.'

'What? No!'

'What's the point of remembering birthdays if you don't wish these people? Call him!'

'Dude. No.'

'Aye man, come on! You guys just might have an incomplete story. It might end like a happy Taylor Swift song.'

'It ended. And like the only thing worse than a happy Taylor Swift song. A sad Taylor Swift song.'

'I've got to pee, man.'

'Fine Kos, we're leaving. I'm driving. Get out.'

◆

She could've sworn she'd lost around ten pounds a month just carrying those files up and down. For Christ's sake, why didn't they just use soft copies? Stupid backward banks. Her head was splitting from the hangover. She needed a cool wet towel. And really strong coffee. And an extra hand. Or two.

'One mochaccino, please.'

'Thet will be fifty-fore ma'am.'

Zoya smiled. She didn't know the name of the little coffee girl, but noticed she'd talk in English only to her, and that she loved being corrected.

'Four. Like for. Not fore.'

The little coffee girl smiled back. Her phone rang.

'God, I'm coming. Can you guys stop calling every five milliseconds?'

She was almost done with the coffee. Her phone rang again. She shuffled her files to the other hand as she tried to answer the phone while crossing the busy street.

'Goddamn you. One bloody minute! I'm coming!'

'Umm… Is that Zoya?'

That voice. Oh dear God, that voice.

'Yeah, who's speaking?'

'Hey, Rian here.'

A million emotions, all at once. She wasn't quite sure. Did she want to reach out through the phone and hug him? Or slap him really hard? Or maybe just play coy, say 'Hi'? Nah, maybe she'd try and act cool. Indifferent. Like she'd forgotten the sound of his voice, the way he spoke, the fact that he hadn't called her for six years and that she'd never really stopped loving him. That she'd never really wanted to stop loving him.

'I'm sorry, I didn't catch that.'

'Yeah right. What's up? I know you're up to your neck in work, so how about I pick you up at four o'clock?'

'Uh…'

'Right, I meant fore o'clock,' he teased. They'd fought too much over pronunciations of words in college for him to ever forget it.

And it was like nothing had changed.

◆

His hair was getting grey. Sort of. He seemed taller. He still spoke the same way. Beautifully. His eyes still sparkled. He still seemed lost.

Not one thing was different. Except that, now he was sure he loved her.

He'd walked out on her six years ago when she'd said she wanted to end up with him. Her habit of saying anything and everything she felt. Not wise though, for he'd been scared of expectations, commitment and responsibilities. So he'd walked out on the best thing that had ever happened to him.

'Never again, Zo. Never.'

That night, she closed her eyes and thought of what she wanted to dream about. She never slept with jewellery on, but even if somebody offered her a million dollars, she wouldn't take off that ring.

She pictured her wedding sari. It was crepe. Translucent. With silver work on it. The blouse was a steely grey. The sari was pink.

She fell asleep with a smile on her face.

And the sari turned blue.

Love Is Blind

VIBHA BATRA

A brand new house means so many things to so many people—a new beginning, a sure-fire investment or a dream come true. But to Jignesh and Rishika, it was proving to be a huge source of annoyance.

You may be a trifle surprised. You may say, 'Some people are never happy with anything. Selfish wretches—they finally get a roof over their heads and they are annoyed?' Well, they were a reasonable couple and they had a valid reason for feeling the way they did. When they bought the beautiful house, which was part of an exclusive gated community, one of the twelve breathtaking mini–villas, they couldn't believe their luck. The place was too good to be true. And shortly thereafter, they realized it was. The reason being Sweety, their neighbour.

She owned the villa right next door. As anyone living in normal society will tell you, it is far easier to love your boss than your neighbour. And like most people, Jignesh and Rishika hated their bosses passionately but even those passions seemed tame when compared to what Sweety unleashed in them.

The first time they met her, she seemed innocuous enough. She was wearing a flaming red top two sizes too small for her portly frame. She had teamed it up with a mercifully long skirt which did nothing for her. Except make her look bigger than she was. Jignesh and Rishika had been enjoying a drink after a hard day's work when she materialized without warning. She flopped on to an empty chair next to Jignesh, fixed herself a (stiff) drink and helped herself to some of their food. They were too polite to shoo her away. In any case she was no fly who could be swatted away. She was a grown woman and a big one at that.

'Hello; myself Sweety,' she said by way of introduction. 'My actual name is Satvinder but everyone calls me Sweety. So sweet, na? And yourself?'

Before giving the couple a chance to introduce themselves, she rattled on. 'New here? Where from? You like this place? How long you married? Any kids?'

That's when Jiggy and Rishika made a grave mistake. They answered her questions. After that, there was no looking back. She showed up unannounced at their doorstep every day, without fail. And that too, at a time when all they wanted to do was relax. She would usually pour herself a whiskey or rum (depending on her mood) and reminisce about her past, when she wasn't asking them pointed personal questions, of course.

'I come from a big family in Punjab....'

'I can believe that,' muttered Rishika under her breath.

Sweety continued, unaffected. '....My great-great-grandfather was a very big man. In my whole family no one has ever worked.'

'Now that's something to be proud of,' shot Rishika sarcastically.

'That's what I say. I am working, but not because I need to.'

'You work?' Rishika's eyebrows shot up. She couldn't imagine Sweety doing anything else but eat and drink.

'Yes, I do a bit of kattering.'

'Kattering?' parroted Rishika before realizing she meant 'catering'.

'I don't work from this house. You see, I come here for a few days to relax and run away from my work. Very hectic. I work with a big company. So many mouths to feed. I do have many people making food under me. But as you know an employee is only an employee. They can't be as good as the master.'

'So you come here only once in a while,' Rishika let out a sigh of relief.

'Yes, yes. I get my maid along. She takes care of this house. And the other house too.'

'What other house?' The words were out of Rishika's mouth before she could stop herself. The last thing she wanted was to know Sweety's life story.

Sweety needed no other encouragement and launched into a long drawn out description of her life. 'Myself and my husband not getting along. So better like this. Anyway, he lives in Delhi most of the time. I live in his house back in the city. When our kids come down from Amreeka, all of us spend some quality time together.'

'So why did you buy this house?'

Sweety had a dreamy look in her eyes. 'This is actually my love nest.'

Rishika nearly choked on her coffee.

'You see I am going around with a very sweet fellow. He is my sweety,' cloyed Sweety, sounding very much love-struck.

Rishika couldn't believe her ears. Sweety must be fifty, if she was a day. Was this middle-aged woman telling her that she had a lover boy? She thought such things happened only to people in the film industry or some equally glamorous field—modelling, advertising or sports. But to a plain dowdy housewife in kattering!

'Rahul is in the merchant navy. So he comes down every year for only one month. But that one month is the most beautiful month in my life. He will come down in March. I will give you an introduction with him.'

Rishika could hardly wait.

'What's he like, this Rahul of yours?' she asked her.

'He is tall, dark, handsome. He loves me a lot. Sends me letters. Beautiful ones. Every week. Sometimes not every week but very regular. He tells me all about his life on the sea. I wish he could take me with him on his journeys…' she trailed off with a faraway look in her eyes.

Rishika lost no time in confiding to Jignesh.

Much to her annoyance, Jignesh had a hearty laugh at Rishika's expense. 'Gawd, you are gullible!'

'Oh, you are such a…man. It's so sweet.'

'Love story of a cougar and her toy boy, sweet?'

'What's age got to do with it?'

'Nonsense! This Rahul is a figment of her imagination. Wait a minute! Isn't SRK called Rahul in most of his soppy movies? Really, Rishika, you are so naïve. You believe anything and everything.'

Rishika gave up trying to convince him, but her curiosity was piqued. A romantic at heart, she believed that everyone had a soulmate. So what if he was fifteen years younger or thirty pounds thinner. It's the meeting of the minds that's important. She would wait for March.

Sure enough, at the end of February, Sweety showed up, maid in tow. She got the house cleaned as if it was Diwali. Every nook and corner was inspected. Furniture was polished. The mattresses were sunned. Sweety looked as if she'd burst from all the excitement.

March came. Rahul didn't. It was hard to say if Rishika waited for him more or Sweety. One day she trooped across to Sweety's and found her in tears. 'His parents are forcing him to see girls. For marriage purpose, of course. He can't tell them about me...' she sobbed as she packed her suitcase.

Rishika could almost feel Sweety's pain, her loss. How could Rahul be so callow? Why did Sweety have to fall in love with him? Why couldn't she see that he was using her? He would dump her for a young girl, the way people dumped an old car for a new model.

Jignesh of course was convinced there was no Rahul. 'He will not come because he doesn't exist. Simple. Think about it, Rishika. It sounds like the ramblings of an old maid. She probably tells a different story to every neighbour.'

Rishika was on reasonably friendly terms with another neighbour (she wasn't anything like Sweety, thank god). She decided to check with her. Madhumita told her the very same thing. No one had ever seen a young chap with her. She had dropped in on Sweety once. She hadn't seen any pictures of a young man there or even faint signs to suggest that a young man occasionally inhabited the space.

But it made no difference to Rishika. As far as she was concerned, one didn't need to flaunt a lover to have a lover. And that was that. She would just take Sweety's word for it.

Jignesh was exasperated by her stubbornness. 'Your head is full of this romantic nonsense. Read silly Mills and Boons. You watch those corny SRK movies.'

'Jignesh, we had a love marriage. How can you not believe in love?'

'We were both twenty-three when we met. We were young...'

'So looks and age are everything. Well, I have news for you, mister. Love is blind.'

'I dunno about love, Rishika. But you certainly are' said Jignesh and switched off the overnight lamp.

Rishika who was trying to read was annoyed. 'You always do this.'

'If you must read, the drawing room is all yours.'

'I bet Rahul doesn't treat Sweety this way.'

'Yeah, imaginary boyfriends are always more considerate than real life lovers,' retorted Jignesh.

Months rolled by and there was no sign of Sweety. Rishika felt restless and strangely enough, a tad let down.

It was in November sometime when she saw two teenagers, a boy and a girl, standing outside Sweety's house.

'May I help you? I am Sweety's neighbour,' she said in her friendliest tone.

'Sweety's our mother. We have come to get her stuff,' answered the boy gruffly.

'Is she okay?' asked Rishika, alarmed.

'Fit as a fiddle. What could happen to her?' answered the boy churlishly.

His elder sister admonished him. 'Please, Monty. Not now. Not in front of a stranger.'

Rishika shook her head sadly. 'I wasn't a stranger to her. I suppose you could say we were close. She used to tell me stuff all the time...'

The boy butted in, 'Bet she didn't tell you she was going to elope with a guy half her age.'

If he wanted to shock Rishika, he was in for a huge surprise because Rishika's face split into a broad smile. 'What!'

The two teens stared at her as if she was stark raving mad. Rishika rearranged her features and ventured, 'Sorry, I mean... when did this happen?'

'Oh, months back. That useless no-good sailor of hers landed up and whisked her off. God knows where they are. She hasn't even bothered to write to us since,' the boy hissed.

His sister, who seemed more sensible by far, took his arm, 'That's enough.' She looked at Rishika with a sad smile on her face. 'Now if you'll excuse us, we have things to do.'

They brushed past her, but Rishika was beyond caring. She was right! She was right all along. There was love, after all. And it was blind. She let out a whoop and jumped up and down and stopped only when she saw Sweety's bewildered son staring at her from the window.

Invisible Touch

JAIRAJ PADMANABHAN

When the IT company Xpanxion International Pvt. Ltd came to their campus and made her an offer she couldn't refuse, Smitha knew that the time had come to be on her own for the first time in her life. The placement was in Pune. Her dad found her a PG accommodation with the Dandekars—a small piece of verdant heaven that the retired school principal Dandekar had created on a small plot of hard-earned land.

The cosy cottage had a separate entrance for Smitha's room—a room with a view. A view of the mini botanical garden that the Dandekars tended to with a lot of love and care—a riot of pink, violet, white, red and orange flowers. Every morning she would choose a colour and decide to look for a flower of that colour—and, voila, she would find it. Inside, it was just another room. Her room had a bookshelf cluttered with books, a small cupboard for her clothes, an iron cot and a stool. Smitha was always anxious about the prospect of their son returning and her having to find another house. She didn't know anything about him. The Dandekars kept to themselves—she was rarely invited for a cup of tea. Not that Smitha was painfully inquisitive about their private lives. But staying under the same roof and sharing a wall, her natural feminine curiosity had started asking questions that were not being answered.

With no social life to speak of, she was as good as married to the computer. Like the other species of the nerdy planet, she too found the logical machine more interesting than irrational human beings. Hence, the only thing the room meant for her was dropping dead on her cot and getting up again the next day for another day of bits and bytes. Sundays meant washing clothes, perhaps catching up with reading computer literature and indulging herself in the luxury of sleep—much needed to rest those eyes, weary from blinking at cathode ray tubes.

Three months passed. The novelty of being in a new place, being on her own, and suddenly having so much money to spend on herself waned. Life settled down into monotony. Her indolence had taken its toll. Cockroaches and mosquitoes had begun infesting the place. When the creepy creatures decided to crawl all over her bed and onto her face, she decided she had to wield the broom, and thus began Smitha's exploration of the room.

The top cabinet had plenty of files, neatly arranged. Files full of paper invariably turned her off. She wanted to throw them out but that might've meant her being thrown out of the house, which was something she did not want to risk. So she grudgingly let them be. The three shelves were loaded with books, most of them without covers. These were books she had always wanted to read, but never had the time or opportunity to. Jane Austen, Tolstoy, P.G. Wodehouse and D.H. Lawrence. Couplets by Mirza Ghalib and the works of Gulzar jostled for space with pornography, MAD and Tintin comics. There were also a few diaries through which she casually flipped. Done with the P.G. Wodehouses and Gulzar—and an occasional peek at the pornography—she picked up a translation of the Sanskrit work Mrichakatikam. No dog ears, no underlined or marked paragraphs, no initials of the book owner. As she began to read it, scribbled on a ruled page nestled in between the pages, she found a perfect piece of calligraphy in English that read:

Life is a quiver full of emotions.
Each arrow wasted on the wrong target.

She didn't know whether the reader or owner of the book had stumbled upon it somewhere and noted it down, or had composed it himself. She kept reading till her eyes drooped and she drifted into dreams.

The next evening, it was Ogden Nash's poems for her. Again, there was a piece of calligraphy with a couple of lines:

Till there is but that last arrow
which one wastes on oneself.

She didn't understand what the writer was trying to communicate through these lines. It looked like the author had misplaced the piece of poetry he was trying to compose and had written it again and left it in another book. She was amused as much as she was bewildered. She next discovered a pink chocolate box full of reptiles. Lizards and snakes piled upon one another. She dropped the box in horror before realizing they were lifeless rubber toys. He must surely have been a naughty kid, frightening people around him. She found a box of seeds clandestinely held between the books. She recognized that they were seeds that popped in water. Then she discovered a box of coins. Such a fantastic collection! Also, two lines scribbled on the wall:

Yesterday and tomorrow shook hands today
to decide that fleeting moments cannot stay.

At work, the room haunted her. The face to those aspects of personality eluded her. The Dandekars were a mysterious couple. There would occasionally be arguments, Mrs Dandekar's sobs, and then everything would return to chilling tranquillity. They didn't have any immediate neighbours. Smitha never saw a guest coming in. She did try to intrude upon their castle of privacy, but in vain. She was always politely rebuffed. She occasionally saw them exchanging a few words as they tended to their garden. Every day she looked forward to the evenings. She imagined them as her dates with the invisible inhabitant of her room, where she investigated more into the faceless character's life. One evening, she stumbled upon a diary full of exotic recipes. So he is a good cook too, she smiled to herself. From then on, he cooked for her on their dates.

How could a man have so many hobbies, she often wondered. She had only known her office colleagues and they had only two hobbies: computer games and cigarettes. What did he study? What subject did he major in? Maybe he was an introvert, lost in these creative pursuits. She stumbled on notes and books about tending garden plants and also a book of poems written in that beautiful handwriting. The poems were full of love for life. A few spoke about his obsession with death and one about suicide. Smitha got really upset with that poem. That day she sulked in her office.

Evenings, she would go back to her rendezvous with her date, and they had an intellectual intercourse. She probed and he answered. Sometimes, she found she was talking to herself. 'Go tell it to someone else.' 'I am like that only, I don't agree.' She asked herself, 'Am I in love?'

She did not sleep that night. Gosh, was she really in love? She didn't know what he looked like, what he did, how old he was and if he was married. She knew she was going crazy.

The Dandekars left for Tirupati—a long-planned pilgrimage. Mrs Dandekar asked her to take care of the plants in their absence or their son would get upset. It rained at night. The jasmine flowered. The roses bloomed. The tamarind trees spread out like the open arms of a lover seeking love. She jumped up to pull a branch and the branch shed its wealth of droplets on her. She was in love with them, with herself, with everything life had to offer. She watered the plants, tended the earth as the worms crept out to celebrate. She talked to the plants like she would to children. She received letters from her parents, discovering a new zest, a new spring in her words after the earlier letters describing her solitude.

Finally, one day, her perseverance paid off. Her jackpot was a pencil sketch that she thought could have been Dandekar junior. Facial hair was just sprouting on his pimpled face. Maybe that was what he looked like a few years ago. Behind it was written, 'To RD from L.'

'So your name starts with an R. Rahul, Raj, Rajat, Rohan—what's your name?' she wondered. She ran through the gamut of names starting with R, deciding she would call him Rohan till she got to know his real name.

The last drawer was the only one left to explore. The wood had expanded due to the rains, and Smitha had to use all her strength and knowledge of physics to get it open. She hoped that she had breached the last wall of Rohan's enigma.

She found two files there. One was full of medical prescriptions and receipts. The other looked like letters on yellow pages, followed by pink and then blue. The final one was an inland letter. She desperately tried to find the address, to find the name. It started with 'Dear RD' and was signed 'L.' As she read on, she realized they were all love letters.

'L? Who the hell was L?' she wondered. 'Hey that rhymed,' she smiled to herself. Lalitha, Loveleen, Lily? She had already thought of twenty-five names starting with the letter L. 'I could write a book of baby names starting with the letters R and L,' she thought to herself. The handwriting looked a bit laboured. 'Whoever wrote love letters in this age of sms?' she wondered. The yellow letters indicated that love was blossoming. By the pink ones, love was in full bloom. She became jealous. 'How dare you do this to me, you cheat?' she shouted to herself. She couldn't control herself and she broke into sobs. 'What a fool I have been.' But these letters were old and she hoped that he had moved on. She told herself that she had to stop reading the letters, but she couldn't resist.

The two letters in blue hinted that the relationship was strained. The final one was the parting missive. She had walked out of his life. The letters were very indirect. They seemed to be written in a private language which only two lovers who perfectly understood each other could decipher. Lovers who shared the same latitude of thoughts, who saw things through the same eyes, holding hands, staring at the firmament and the horizon, the vastness and limitations of any human relationship. Smitha felt like an intruder into their lives. But she was happy that the relationship was over.

Two days later, the Dandekars came back. The next day, Smitha went to her parents. She was moody, constantly brooding. Her parents were looking for a match. She said she was not ready yet. Her understanding mother enquired, 'Are you in love? Is there somebody?' She had no answer to that. An affirmative reply would be followed by a string of questions to which she had no answer. She suddenly felt lonely. She had to let off steam, but couldn't. The world would laugh at her. She had to break the ice with the Dandekars. She had to come out of her dream world and know the truth. She wanted to know the true RD.

She dreamt of RD holding out his arms for her, asking her for a dance, and when they hit the floor the whole world cheered them on. And when they walked out of the ballroom, the people arrayed themselves to applaud. She couldn't take it anymore. She had to do it.

The next Sunday, Smitha woke up early and went out into the garden where she knew she would bump into the Dandekars. She felt they both looked older than their age. Aged from pain and suffering. 'I hope I have looked after your son's pets well.' Her voice forced itself out from her throat. Mrs Dandekar didn't reply. She held Smitha's hands, her cold hands melting into their warmth. Then she ran her fingers over Smitha's hair.

'How are your parents?'

'Oh, they are quite good. They asked about you.'

Mrs Dandekar nodded and started towards the door. Smitha was not one to give up easily. She continued the conversation.

'It must have taken years for your son to collect and tend to these plants.'

Mrs Dandekar again smiled enigmatically. A film covered her eyes. She noticed Mr Dandekar giving his wife a stern look as she held back her tears. She couldn't understand their silent dialogue. She didn't know if she had upset them. Had RD married against their wishes and never come back? Was RD missing? She raised an eyebrow at Mr Dandekar, who merely winked at her to keep her worries aside. She asked Mr Dandekar if she could join him for his morning walk. She was politely refused.

The next morning, after a few formal questions were asked, to which the predictable answers were given, Smitha decided to use the opportunity and slowly confessed.

She told him she had fallen in love with their son, who had begun to fill the void in her solitude. He had been the missing link. She wondered if he had a girlfriend or was perhaps married. Mr Dandekar patiently listened to her.

'Smitha, I know what you are going through,' he smiled with pain in his eyes. 'My son Rishi studied in Wadia College. He was an average student, never good either at studies or sports. He had wanted to be a free bird, trekking through the mountains, cycling down the ghats and swimming against the rough waters. Doing what he wanted and when he wanted. He did read a lot. Now, Rishi is that free spirit, having shaken the burden, the obstacles the world keeps impeding us with. Rishi is no more, Smitha.' There was a long pause, a silence Smitha couldn't bear. She didn't know how to react.

'He was seventeen when the doctors told us that he had cancer. It was already eating him away, bit by bit. But Rishi fought, he loved life. He wanted to see the world but he couldn't get up from his bed. His hobbies only grew until he left us. He died when he was twenty. He was our only child, but he was not born to us. We adopted him as a one-year-old when the doctors pronounced my wife barren. My wife did not know of the pain, the pangs of his birth, of carrying him in her womb and nurturing him till he opened his eyes to the world. But she sure has gone through the pain of his death. And those love letters you mentioned, well, they were written by Rishi himself. The girlfriend you mentioned was no girl, but his own life, with which he had a love affair.'

She remembered the letters. Life. L for Life. That explained everything.

The Girl on a Train

ROHAN SWAMY

This is perhaps the most unusual location ever. I am seated at a roadside joint near the NH4, with a can of very cold Carlsberg beer, a new Macintosh notebook, and a basketful of memories. The night is cold, the beer even colder, Ol' Betsey stares at me from the parking lot and a broken down radio plays an old Mohammad Rafi song called 'Dil Tera Deewana Hai Sanam' as I sit down to hum it, much to the chagrin and amusement of truck drivers, and some 'respectable' families who are out for late night drives here.

It has been a long hard day, coupled with that déjà vu feeling of the winter of 2008, which left me broken in spirit at a railway station and then took me to the edge of the crevasses of the Grand Canyon during autumn this year and brought me back. I am ready to forget it all, but those old shadows are really long. Hence the late night drive out on Ol' Betsey. It is to drive away all these old shadows and give myself a chance to write a new story. Something to do with irrationality and finding breathing space in those millions of little joys that we experience every day, and forget to hold on to.

The phone beeps while I am lost in my own thoughts. Once, twice and then for a third time before I finally check the message it has for me. It is from one of the ex-interns at work. I take a moment as I patiently go through the message. It had been her last day—she was a nice, warm person, who disguised her emotions with a carefree smile and played a funny 'time' game with me. I smile as I remember arguing about finding traces of irrationality, with the Masai tribesman, in her.

I am glad that I have been right. I do not really know how but I think I have a knack for it. It is wonderful to meet people of your own kind. It is one of those feelings that you cannot put down in words, but only experience. Brushing it all aside I come back to the present. She has left work and yet kept me in the loop by giving me a sweet chocolate bar laced with rum outside that sepia-tinted work station of ours. She says it was a wonderful thing that I made her time here easier and better. I am glad for her, as well as I am for the fact that people still find time for these simple things.

I understand that these simple things don't mean anything to most. I mean a lifetime, or four seconds; they mean nothing to the vast cosmic mathematician who weaves on those looms of time. But for those irrational enough to rely on the simple joys in life, it is a moment to stop, smile, ponder about the futility of explaining these simple things to the rational world, and then move on hoping to experience something like this again. It's like the rituals of the Aztec people, something to do with the Navajo chants to the sun.

The song changes to a lighter tune by another old world singer, I smile as I repeat each word of the message before settling on something to talk about. It reads, 'Forgot to pick up headphones from you…I am getting bored and feeling sleepy in the train… :(and there is this little girl who keeps coming to me and smiling and tugging on my sleeve who is really cute… :)'

The cold winds blow into my face. I have found my story in the little girl. As I bring the Mac to life my fingers start finding the letters and the images on their own. I type down a beginning for the story. I am sceptical about using names; I have recently been subjected to a lot of mordant words from people, about an old tale that bore some faint semblance. Clearly it's a rational world. And each time I keep bumping into someone who wears one of these masks and fools me, I understand how different my world really is, and how futile an exercise it is to show people those simple things without being tortured, or raped and mutilated in spirit and soul.

Shaking it all off, I send a reply to her asking for a sitrep (situation report). Her reply comes back immediately with a small pang of guilt for me: 'HEADPHONES...:(well at least I get to see Ol' Betsey again...:) the little girl has the most adorable smile... reminds me of a carefree childhood...I am sleepy...waiting for dinner, and now the little girl wants to play with my hair...: P.'

I start laughing at the response; it's funny. I wonder how children can be so irrational and free. Why do they lose this freedom when they grow up? I wave out to Betsey and she acknowledges the wave permeating from the message. The little girl talks to me. She is merely an illusion, and yet tells me that it is normal for the world to scoff at these things. She puts it down for me in simple words, 'Happiness reverberates in your soul. And most of the times people cannot interpret it. And what they cannot understand they hate, rape and burn. It gives them a sense of victory. But that doesn't mean that you falter; on the contrary, it means that you have to keep trying harder to eradicate this hatred.'

I do not understand the message that the little girl is trying to convey with her carefree smile. I am sure there is something wise in it. It is just that I cannot see it. In order to decipher the hieroglyphics, I write back to my ex-colleague asking what the little girl means. This time the answer is not forthcoming. The wait is long.

The wind stings my face and I take a swig of the cold beer to reiterate that cold feeling. I feel sad and disgusted with myself. Taking a look at myself I go back to the crazy month of August when it all happened. The dreaded phone call; her sweet voice; her complex way of explaining why it could not be. I try to shake it off but the old shadows grip me again. A series of coughs rattle my ribcage. I remember that I am still recuperating, from my near-fallacy about ending it all with a permanent solution. The scars that my lungs and the paper-thin veins beneath my pale white wrists bear are dark testimony to the stupidity I have endured. I hate myself for all that occasionally. Mohammad Rafi sings another song about old unfulfilled dreams as two thin lines find a way down my cheek to fog the Scott Harris's mounted on my eyes momentarily.

As I finish wiping the glasses, her reply comes. 'There are these three teenagers... And a wannabe youngster who is trying to make 'English' talk with me...the little girl keeps running to me and touching my nose...:P. Occasionally she also feeds me food with her spoon...and there is an old lady who always smiles at me...I think she is remembering her younger days...:)'

I am lost. Helplessly. My fingers struggle to find letters this time on the board. And I keep erasing and re-writing them. The little girl comes up to me and looks into my eyes. I have too much to ask her. But without being asked she replies back, 'Sometimes you have to learn hard things the hard way. Maybe there is a reason why all this happened. You don't know it. I don't know it, but you have to endure it. In the meanwhile, that girl in our compartment is eating plain white rice, and no chicken; can you help her out?'

I again have a reason to smile and laugh. As I key in another response on my cell phone, asking for more, like Oliver Twist did when he was hungry, I decide to reconstruct a meandering course of what I guess this irrational ex-colleague from work is.

There are no replies forthcoming. The cold beer has long been replaced with a cup of hot coffee laced liberally with rum as the cold out here in the open gets unbearable. 'I haven't interacted much with this intern, but I am pretty sure of her irrationality just as these people born of the sea are of the earth, the sun and the moon,' I say to the Masai warrior who patiently nods his head.

I guess she has been around, seen life the way we have. You know; seen things closely, and yet never mentioned it to anyone. Our discussion continues; the Masai warrior asks me to divulge more of what I can only term as surmises, which I readily do. I see her walk in her college campus, with a lot of friends; she is polite and unobtrusive with all of them, but reserves her confidences for a few. I continue; she oscillates between two extremes, one thoroughly confused trying to comprehend her own lost emotions and the other, having a balanced head ready to solve the mystery of life.

Leaving behind the interiors of the parking lot, both the Masai and I perch ourselves on the high rock where I was first baptised as an irrational cowboy, who sang a haunting tune on his violin for a lost angel. I see this colleague of mine somewhere far off. I do not know anything about her, but I do know she is irrational. She cannot distinguish complex things, and yet her emotions are beyond the comprehension of most. We sit on the ledge watching—the Masai and I. She shows a range of colours, the rainbow of life, unlike the two of us; we live in blacks, whites and greys. She lives in blues, greens, reds, yellows, and the season of spring.

And yet somehow we both come to the conclusion that there is something missing—the irrational element. Like alpha without omega, Yin without Yang. The Masai tells me she has been in places where even the strongest haven't ventured, and has given up more than most. 'Remember the time you had said that giving up the lost angel was important, because her smile was worth walking over the Grand Canyon?' he asks me. I have no answers. 'She has done something akin since the inception of time, when the cowboy had to give up the lost angel and cry aloud at the merciless wail of time.' I feel sad; I have not met many who think like this. Even though our conversation borders on the surreal and the mere assumption of thoughts and a mass of ideas that are thrown in from a few observations, we both cannot help but welcome another of our clan into the clan.

'There is an old woman…who remembers her days of carefree happiness as she keeps staring at me…occasionally she speaks long distance to her little grandchild, and the little girl keeps coming up to me and insisting that I play a movie game with her…: P. So cute…she has learnt my name now, and has been running through the aisles yelling it loudly…: P.'

We both cannot be wrong in our predictions, the Masai declares, many moments after coming back to the parking lot. A dog straggles past us languidly; the time on the IWC reads 11.30 p.m., as I take a swig of the coffee again. This time I stare emptily into the Macintosh. That folder, Picture Perfect is empty, and so is the night sky. I feel lucky that my colleague has a little girl whose eyes sparkle with the brilliance of a midsummer night's dream, to bring the colours back into her life again. The little girl sings a new film song at the top of her voice as I smile at her. The old woman, brows knit, stares at my quiet face. She knows what I am trying to disguise under it—burnt, raped memories and the loss of innocence. I have no words. The last time someone stole glances at me in a manner like that, I felt I was being stripped in the market place. This feels different however. Like the old woman and the little girl are both taking turns at soothing my wracked body and speaking the Sun Chants, trying to bring me back to life, cursing all those Old Shadows and their haunting grip.

My colleague speaks this time, as both the Masai and I hear. She speaks of a happy child growing up, christened the 'black sheep' in her family. We break into silent giggles occasionally. She tries to finish unfinished sentences but is held back. We both understand. She talks in metaphors and we do not reply. She talks of many moods and many emotions that she struggles to comprehend— love, hate, jealousy; that life feeling, that void feeling (something that both the Masai and I have been accustomed to living with), of selfishness; of being arrogant and stuck up; of thanking people who made her what she was. Sometimes she doesn't speak, but her eyes speak volumes. The old woman and the little girl come out occasionally to see me stare at the blank Mac screen; they wipe away tears as I keep breaking down repeatedly, over and over again. The old woman offers wise counsel, 'You gave up someone for her own happiness, which is a great sacrifice.' And yet she understands how difficult it actually is to implement a decision taken on the spur of the moment for generations to come. As all of us are lost in our own worlds; the phone beeps again.

'Ohh god, that wannabe is trying to get fresh… :(impressing me with all kinds of fancy gadgets… :(the little girl enquires about my shoddy phone… :(the guy tries to flaunt his Englishtaani at me… I wish the world were a little more honest like the little girl, her eyes, and the old woman… :|'

I wish I can explain it to her; this is how the rational world functions. But I can't. Just as I cannot make someone far away at work see light. Just as I cannot get that same person's barbed words, that course through my veins like some unclean liquid, out. I tell her it's hard to make them understand. The little girl who I christen Rain and the old woman who I christen Drizzle, take turns at explaining these things to both of us. 'It's a rational world. And people of your race do not belong here. There is no magic here. But precision is there.' She looks at me and says, 'And you my son, are the unluckiest of all, like the priest Judas who was condemned to be hated across the span of time, till the day of reckoning comes. You have to be abhorred, hated, traumatised, raped, looted and plundered, over and over again beyond the beliefs of sanity, and yet you have to endure it. You have to do it for that vow that you have taken; for that one thing that you have been asked to protect with everything you have.'

As she finishes talking, the comet streaks across the sky. 'Lost Angel,' the Masai warrior whispers, I know that this is why I have to endure it all. In the meantime, the little girl comes and offers me curried chicken and rice and pokes my nose. 'She is still eating plain rice, and no chicken,' shrugs the little girl as I laugh, and key in another response.

Her last reply comes in moments later.

'The old woman has gone off to sleep... Rain alters between compartments, occasionally touching my nose and calling out my name... :P amused at how I can eat plain rice and carry a cell phone that resembles her ragged doll... the three teenagers are cooking up stories, and one is wearing dark brown glares... the techno wannabe has given up trying... And ohh look, Rain's mother finally coaxed her to sleep for some time... she feels like a symbiotic association of the wind and light... :) Ohh and wave Betsey good night from my side... I think we both clicked well...'

I look at the peaceful late night sky. Ol' Betsey stares at me with her angular looks. I feel helpless again as there is no Rain or Drizzle to wash away the burns, and their marks. Masai reminds me of the theory of Judas. I resign myself to it. I close my eyes momentarily, and everything flashes by. The intertwining of fingers; the silent giving up of the world; the cauterization of the raw wounds and the acerbic language of the rational. It all comes back and it all has to be endured. As my colleague and I speak for one last time, I tell her this is the end of everything. She sounds unhappy and says I shouldn't be giving it up. I don't know. I wonder at times why the best decision and the right decisions cannot be one and the same. I have no answers, just as I didn't that night at the station, or my colleague didn't when she stopped speaking of her emotions. We are meant to swim a way out of this huge vortex created by the rational. This is a tad tougher in my case as I have to stay right in the middle till the end of time.

As we both part ways finally, the last song on the radio station catches my ear. It is the same song from that night at the rail station when I saw her for the last time. Something to do with the words, *I see God in You*. As I grab the duffel and the Mac, the Masai bids adieu to go back to his uninterrupted sleep. I am left standing thinking about a million unspoken emotions. As I consider walking back to Ol' Betsey little Rain comes up to me, pokes my nose out of nowhere and smiles the sweetest smile ever. In a mystic juxtaposition of images, I see the lost angel in her face, but she is not crying: she is happy. She waves out to the cowboy as our fingers touch and intertwine and pass all those million unspoken emotions to each other as the world becomes still again. The smiling image of little Rain fades into oblivion. Somewhere, far away, a train nears its destination as my colleague pulls off sleepily. And I am left standing in front of Betsey with a long highway beckoning me.

A wry half smile makes its way to my lips as I mount Betsey and gallop off in search of the lost comet and the crying angel.

The Jhalmuri Seller

BHABANI SHANKAR KAR

'Yaar, these onsite guys are so impatient, they want everything in ten minutes,' cribbed Aslam as he took a drag from his almost finished cigarette and went downstairs. Then he threw the butt away on the roadside.

'Haan yaar, they won't do anything themselves, but they'll scream at us,' added Ronojoy, as he continued smoking and walking with Aslam towards the chaiwallah nearby.

Aslam and Ronojoy were typical IT professionals, working for an Indian IT giant in Kolkata. Like lakhs of others, their day was not complete without the regular two-hourly breaks for tea and cigarettes, between the mundane code-call-code-meeting-code-call job from 10 a.m. to 8 p.m. every day.

While Ronojoy muttered, 'Duto cha, dada,' Aslam was still ranting about the idiocies of the onsite guys. Around him was a typical snapshot of the scene outside any big office in Kolkata. Well-dressed young men and women, primarily in their twenties and thirties, with ID tags hanging from their necks, the men with a hint of a potbelly and the colourful women with various kinds of hairdos into which they put most of their salaries. There were the jhups—the huts selling everything from chicken biryani to steaming momos—the chaiwallahs, the sugarcane-juice sellers, yellow age-old Ambassador taxis, and the entire area covered in a light haze of cigarette smoke. Yes, if you are in Kolkata, you can't escape the omnipresent cigarette smoke. Any Kolkata resident worth his salt, be it Bengali, Marwari, Punjabi, Oriya or Tamil, has a cigarette in his hand while he is in the open. And yes, there were sellers of jhalmuri (puffed rice with onions, chillies, mustard oil and a host of other ingredients), and hawkers selling miniature dictionaries and baby care books, and the humble agents selling credit cards and mutual funds.

As Aslam was sipping his tea, Ronojoy got a call from his manager. He rushed back to join a conference call. Aslam continued with his tea and lit one more cigarette. As he threw the tea cup away, he walked towards the jhalmuri seller across the road. A puny, old, weather-beaten man, the jhalmuri seller seemed to come straight out of an R.K. Laxman cartoon strip. Balding, and clad in a dhoti and a dirty chequered shirt, he was the common man personified—Laxman's gift to the average Indian. He drew a lot of people every day, who crowded around him for five-rupee paper cones of his wares. Like a lot of others, Aslam too was a regular.

Aslam waited behind the small crowd, and then he too became a part of it after finishing his cigarette. He always hated the loud chattering of such small crowds, mostly girls. These girls chirped away in their quest to be the first to order, customise, pay and leave with jhalmuri—for themselves, as well as for their friends standing some distance away. Aslam somehow hated getting into this rat race for a fistful of the stuff, pushing, nudging and elbowing the others in the sweaty crowd, while waiting for the old man's attention.

Just as he was throwing away the cigarette butt, his gaze landed upon a group of young girls standing a couple of feet to his left, who were there for the same reason as he was. One of the gang was supposedly in the crowd, while the rest were lazily waiting for her to get back. The butt that Aslam threw fell near one of the girls. She gave him a disgusted look and muttered something in Bengali, which he neither understood nor had the patience to try and understand. He said a nonchalant 'sorry' and stepped into the crowd, seeing no chance whatsoever of it thinning out.

While jostling for space, he noticed a girl in the crowd who was finding it difficult to make her voice heard. It was five in the evening and, at that time of the day, business for all vendors was the most brisk. He saw how she was making futile attempts to ask for five jhalmuri cones 'without oil and chilli'. She had tried three times already and was meekly making a fourth attempt. Clad in a light blue salwar suit, with a temporary ID card hanging from her neck, it was evident that she was a new trainee in the company two floors above Aslam's. He estimated that she must not be more than twenty-three years old.

As the jhalmuri seller finished handing over his cones to a group of people and looked around for the next order, Aslam hurriedly ordered one for himself. Somehow, he found himself adding, 'And five for them, without oil or chilli.' He couldn't believe what he had just said, but now that he had, he looked casually at the old man who had already started picking the various ingredients of the jhalmuri and dropping them into the aluminium container which served as a mixer, making a tat-tat-tat sound in the process. Through the corner of his eyes, he saw the hint of a thankful smile on the face of the girl who seemed to have been equally embarrassed at the goings-on. In a minute, Aslam took his jhalmuri, handed a five-rupee coin to the old man and ran back to the fountain in the office building without a word. One thing he couldn't get out of his mind, though, was the image of the coyly smiling girl. There was something in him that made him want to look up and find her smiling.

Once in his seat, he looked at his mailbox and opened the database to start fulfilling the onsite demands in the next hour. The incident from ten minutes ago was soon out of his mind.

A few days passed. The code had been delivered and the deployment was done. There wasn't much work, and Aslam's team had gone out on a Friday lunch party. As they were returning in the manager's car, he spotted the girl—she of the jhalmuri incident—going into the office building. She was dressed in a light blue shirt and jeans. His eyes sparkled.

Towards the evening, he and Ronojoy were out for tea again. Finishing the tea and popping Chloromint into their mouths, they walked slowly towards the jhalmuri seller who was busy making the regular tat-tat-tat sound. The crowd was sparse today, as people were eager to finish their work and leave to enjoy the weekend. And there she was, the meek girl from that day, standing nearby with two more girls and a boy. Their eyes met for a flirting moment, and she gave a smile of acknowledgement for the favour from that day. Aslam didn't know how to react. He nodded and moved on. There was magic in her smile, something that made it stick in his mind for hours without any reason. He shrugged to himself. He looked at the jhalmuri seller who had seen him shrug. The old man, flashing a toothless smile, prepared his aluminium can for the next round of frenzied tat-tat-tats.

In his room that day, Aslam couldn't take the image out of his mind. The blue salwar suit, the shy smile, the coloured hair flying into her eyes with the evening summer breeze, and the way she freed her hand of her dupatta to push the lock of hair back where it belonged, behind her ears. He found himself opening his diary and picking up a pen to make an entry:

They say bliss is not captured, it is felt, and they say beauty can't be portrayed, only enjoyed. They have not seen you, or thought of you. A serene whiteness, and a glow so pure. A song of love, lips that kill—a joy, a thrill… I smell the hair and feel the skin. A lightning in me, a desire for sin. Oh what are you, some fairy-tale?

He then closed the diary and typed the same into his Facebook status message and started chatting. In half an hour, he had five likes and three teasing comments.

The next day, around four o'clock, when he went down for tea, his gaze inadvertently wandered to the jhalmuri stall which had only a couple of customers. He didn't see her there, nor anywhere nearby. He searched some more and looked back just in case she was near the fountain. No. He went to the jhalmuri stall, ordered one and was looking around, when he was startled by the old man's smiling question, 'Without oil and chilli?' He shook his head and smiled. The old man had caught something in him that he himself didn't know. The toothless man had made him realise what he had been reluctant to face all along—he was in love! Not at first sight, but almost.

Aslam was in a strange situation. He was in love with her, he knew that. He wanted to see her again, he knew that too. But he didn't have an answer to who this 'her' was! He had no friends in her company and had no idea what her name was. He only had the jhalmuri stall which had twice served as a meeting place for him and her. He had no idea what to do next, so he just brushed aside the thought and went back to his desk.

In the next few weeks, they crossed paths several times at the jhalmuri stall but, strangely, never anywhere else. Aslam smiled at her a couple of times, in reply to her smiles. Every one of these times, he fell in love with her all over again and wanted to talk to her, but could never muster the courage to speak. He went so far as to force out a 'Hi' once, while on his way back with Ronojoy, but she had moved on by the time he opened his mouth and Ronojoy made fun of him.

It was a Tuesday afternoon, and he was at the jhalmuri stall waiting for his turn. As the crowd withered away, he found himself alone at the stall for a couple of minutes with the old man, who was busy pouring the muri into a cone for him. He suddenly heard him speak, '*Dada, didir naam ta Rehaana. Ekdum bhalo meye. O bikele paach ta ye ashe.*' Aslam couldn't make much out of it, but caught the words 'Rehaana' and 'paach ta'. Ronojoy translated the sentence for him: 'Brother, the girl's name is Rehaana. Very nice girl. She generally comes at five in the evening.' He couldn't resist laughing out loud, as if to show he was least concerned, but deep in his heart he couldn't thank the old man enough.

The old man's sentence changed Aslam's itinerary for good. He made it a point to take a break every day at five and, more often than not, he managed to find Rehaana at the stall. The meetings—rather, the sightings—became more frequent. And the smiles they gave one another grew cosier and wider. Once at the stall, he even managed to read her name tag. 'Rehaana Banerjee,' it said. But they never spoke. He couldn't manage enough courage to say another 'Hi', and she wouldn't raise her eyes long enough to encourage any chivalry in him. Their encounters were momentary and unexpected, but always cherished.

Then the monsoons came. It rained like never before. Afternoon after afternoon was spoilt, and numerous occasions for meeting were lost because of the rains. Aslam was heartbroken. He rarely saw her anywhere else.

One day there was no rain, but a slight drizzle. Aslam ran out.

There was the old jhalmuri seller, with almost no crowd around him. As Aslam raced to him, he could see him shivering. He had a fever it seemed. Aslam felt pity for the old man. He had to come out in the rain to sell his wares, even with a high fever. He took a jhalmuri cone and handed the old man a hundred rupee note. The man looked at him blankly, as if to say he had no change. Aslam said, 'You can give it to me later,' and raced back. The old man called after him, but he didn't stop. Later, Ronojoy informed him that the man had asked for his phone number and that he had given it to him. He cribbed a bit, thinking maybe the man would ask for more. Then he forgot.

A couple of weeks went by. It rained continuously. Some days it drizzled, some days it rained, and some days it poured. The evening tea breaks were now mostly confined to the cafeteria. The few times he went outside, there were no vendors and no stalls. He cursed the rains, smoked and came back.

After a particularly frustrating onsite call one day, Aslam was starting for the cafeteria with Ronojoy when he got a call from the security guard at the gate. Someone had left an envelope for him. On an old brown envelope sealed with glue was his name in Bengali—or at least that's what the guard told him. He said it had been left by the jhalmuri seller who sat across the road every day.

He came back to his seat and tore open the envelope. A crisp hundred rupee note fell out, with a dirty piece of paper wrapped around another crisp fifty rupee note. It had something in Bengali written on it. The hundred rupee note he understood. The fifty rupee note, he did not. He called out to Ronojoy who was waiting for him outside the cubicle. Ronojoy grumbled. Nevertheless, Aslam called him again and he came. Aslam handed him the slip of paper to read out. What that translated into left both of them looking at each other. It read:

Sir, I might be old, but I was young once, and the ways of the world are known to me. When you saw me shivering that day, I had not come there for want of money. I was there out of habit. Staying at home irked me, and so I came. I knew why you ran back after handing me the money and I am thankful for that, but I didn't need it. So I called after you, but you didn't stop.

Sir, a didi also came that day, after you went. She didn't have change either. She gave me a fifty rupee note. I asked for her number. She gave me the number and left.

I was ill after that day. I recovered yesterday, but the rains make me stay at home. I have become old. I don't think I can sell jhalmuri anymore. The time has come for me to rest, and my younger son shall be the next jhalmuri seller at your office, once the rains stop. As a favour to me, please call the didi on 8016000123 and return the fifty rupees to her. God bless you.

Aslam felt sad at the thought of not being able to see the old man again. He felt sad at not being able to look at Rehaana's shy smiles for some time. He decided to wait till the rains ended to try his luck with the new jhalmuri stall. But he decided to call up the number in the note and hand over the money immediately. He dialled and asked the female voice at the other end to come to the seventh floor elevator. Ronojoy asked him to come to the cafeteria after giving the money. He rushed out.

He was waiting at the elevator and realized that there were many other people there, looking at the rain outside through the glass. Just then, he got a call. He answered.

'Hello?' he said.

'Hi. I am waiting at the elevator. You had just called regarding the money,' a sweet female voice said.

'Oh, but I am there too,' he said and turned back.

As he turned and realized where the call had come from, he

was stunned. With her hair falling over her face—which she was pushing back behind her ear—stood Rehaana, staring at him with a phone in her hand.

They smiled.

Sleepless by Night

MONA RAMAVAT

Pragya was named after her maternal grandmother, but any similarity ended right there. Her parents had apparently argued for days over whose mother's name she should be given. 'Pragya Joshi,' said all her official documents. Among friends, she was simply Prags and at the pub, DJ Prags. At nineteen, she looked a reluctant sixteen, mostly because of a petite build and baby-soft, pale, round cheeks. A put-on, worldly-wise expression only added innocence, to her utter frustration. She never quite liked DJ Prags that much, but DJ Pragya was worse. She had nearly wept when someone suggested DJ PJ. But at least she wasn't named after her father's mother. Else she would have been Sarita Joshi which, according to her, sounded more gynaecologist than DJ.

Her parents found out about the whole DJ deal when they saw (with much silent horror) her picture on page 3 one morning—in a shiny, leather tank top, eyes closed in music-induced ecstasy. What they didn't know, however, was how she did this every weekend. To the best of their knowledge, she had simply dined out with friends sometimes. When had she been sneaking out, and how?

They were upset enough with the tattoo—and now this! Had it not been for the tattoo, by the way, they wouldn't have figured it was her in that picture. How ironic, she mused in complete, parent-defying satisfaction.

But that was the end of her cool life, because Prags was soon sent off to stay with an aunt in Bangalore, away from her useless friends, who they thought had put this whole DJ bug in her head. Since old habits die hard, Prags snuck out every night. But this apartment complex didn't have a bribe-taking watchman. So, instead, she walked within the compound. This wasn't even the second-best option, but she didn't know what else to do. Chatting with friends at home was too tame. So she walked. She couldn't sleep. After walking every night for a month, she had discovered every nook and cranny in the place. But tonight, there was someone else who couldn't seem to sleep.

She stopped short when she saw him sitting, leaning against a pillar within the parking area, one long leg stretched out, the other folded at the knee, with his arm resting absently on it. He was dark and the dull halogen light made him look swarthy. Blue jeans and grey crinkled shirt, head rested back, neck craned, eyes closed, bare feet. Thirty-something. Her first instinct was to introduce herself. Good sense told her that perhaps it wasn't such a good idea to mess with insomniac strangers. But according to Prags, good sense was only for the very boring. So she went to stand three feet in front of him.

'Hi!'

He heard someone, but was not sure. When he opened his eyes—not exactly with reflex action speed—he saw a girl (perhaps a schoolgirl) who was now kneeling before him. Her skinny bare knees touched the concrete. She was wearing ill-fitted yellow shorts. The faded green spaghetti top completed the stick figure look. Her hair was braided in many thin tight braids (some looked red), all clasped back together. But his eyes settled on the artfully abstract black butterfly tattooed at the base of her neck, above the left collar bone. The size of a thumbnail. His. He had big hands.

'Hi,' he said after long seconds.

Settling cross-legged in front of him, she extended her hand.

'I am Prags.'

Sighing, he looked away, before moving his right hand off the knee and taking hers, somewhat reluctantly.

'PS.' He withdrew his arm, blinking his bloodshot eyes. He sat a little straighter. Slowly again.

'Do you do everything like an afterthought? Which is why you are 'Post Script?'' she guffawed helplessly.

This time he turned sharply, arresting her laughter.

Silence. Only raspy night insects could be heard somewhere.

Lips pursed, she looked around, as if the deserted compound was full of topics for small talk.

'New?'

'Yeah.'

'Where are you from?'

'Mumbai.'

'Hey, me too! Greenwood Apartments. Churchgate. You know what? I was a DJ at...'

He glared again, quieting her. But only for a bit.

'A friend from college taught me all about turntables,' she volunteered. 'I helped him with math in return. We were friends with benefits, you see.' She laughed at her own joke. He didn't. 'Hey, don't I look like I can help someone with math?'

'Don't I look like I want to be left alone?'

'No!' she laughed, bringing her palms together in an excited clap. Sigh.

'What do you do?'

'I am a photographer,' he said irritably after a while, his watery eyes not focusing anywhere.

'Why can't you sleep?'

He looked like he'd say something but sighed again. His nostrils flared briefly.

'Hey, do you want to play a number game?' she beamed.

'No. Please leave,' he said emphatically.

After a while. 'How badly would you like to sleep, PS?'

He looked back at her, involuntarily this time, staring with something like slowly rising incredulity.

She grinned. The moment was over. He broke eye contact.

Sigh.

'Like my tattoo?'

His eyes found it.

'Well, you see, my ex's girlfriends were anybody who offered their bodies to him.'

He frowned and turned with an angular jerk to stare at her.

'Gotcha! Haven't I?' Laughter squirted out between those words.

Sigh.

'Ok, now don't look at me like that, please. My ex was this Chinese-looking chef at the Chinese place next door to my pub. Between lunch and dinner, he was an aspiring tattoo artist. He made this one for me.' She pointed to the tattoo. 'You know why we broke up?'

'Why?'

'He wanted to make one on my right shoulder blade. A biggish mermaid or something. But that would have gone over my favourite mole there.'

'Here, see?' Instinctively, she reached for the right strap to slide it down and began turning her shoulder. He froze her with a glare.

She sighed dramatically.

'You know, he was seeing the hostess, who looked like his feminine version. By the time they broke up, she was practically his design catalogue!' She rolled over on her side, shaking with uncontrollable laugher. That's when she noticed the bandaged square on the sole of his foot.

'What is that?' She reached out to touch it.

'Don't!' He held a palm firmly between them, pressing the other on the ground to get up. Wincing, he pressed his good foot down first, and then the injured one.

She got up too. He was holding the pillar for support, half-facing it.

'Hmm... goodnight,' she said tentatively.

He shook his head emphatically, eyes squeezed shut, pained frown, fist clenched against the white pillar. He banged his fist again and again on the pillar.

'I killed her. *I* killed her.'

◆

Annette died while he was asleep. A piercing sob woke him. Her mother had a shrill voice, but she sat in immovable silence across from him in the hospital lounge outside the ICU. Annette's grandmother was sobbing uncontrollably in a chair beside hers. He looked from one to the other, disoriented. Panic rose in his stomach and up to his throat. A different line of fear throbbed down the back of his skull.

He moved urgently across to where they were sitting. 'What happened?' He squatted before Annette's grandmother, shaking her chubby forearms forcefully. 'Tell me what happened. What happened? Please tell me!' She sobbed louder and shriller, drowning out his voice.

'We are going back now. We don't want you at the funeral,' Annette's mother said instead, with an eerie calm, staring ahead.

'Funeral? What are you…'

'Annette is dead!'

'No. It can't be! No!' He shook his head, running towards the ICU. Stopping before the glass oval that separated her from him, he stood staring inside. His sweaty palms kept slipping away from the glass. There were no monitors or drips connected to her. Lying on the neat blue bed, she looked at peace. Asleep.

'See? She's only sleeping,' he shouted. He couldn't take his eyes off her. 'Ann is sleeping…'

When they were taking the body away, he wouldn't let them.

'Where are you taking her? She's my wife. She's my wife! She's mine… She's mine! Ann! Ann…' It took three particularly strong ward-boys to hold him back. He passed out soon after.

Till death do us part.

He regained consciousness early the next morning. As soon as the memory rushed back, he got up and ran down the ward shouting her name. Before anyone could reach him, he found a scalpel from a sterilization tray. But a rushing doctor managed to take it away from him before it could make contact with his wrist. A hospital is not the best of places for suicide, anyway. But he was not turned in to the police.

He went into a police station voluntarily, telling whoever might listen that he had killed his wife. The last dialled number on his phone was the pub manager's, who came over and explained that this man was in complete shock. The death was an accident. The manager saw it himself. There was no trial. There was no complaint made by Annette's family.

He never went back to the pub. He barely went out at all. A few weeks later, he left his home in Mumbai, where he and Annette had lived, and moved to Bangalore for a part-time job at an advertising agency. He didn't have to go to work every day. On his days off, he stayed home but never drank. He cut himself with a blade instead. Usually on the arms or feet. When he had to go to work, he bandaged the wounds. At night, he went out to walk.

◆

Prags didn't see him the following night, or any other night. She asked around, but nobody seemed to know of a PS living there.

'I killed her. I killed her,' he'd kept saying, pounding his fist against the pillar. After a while, his voice was barely audible. And then, only heavy breathing. Abruptly, he limped away without looking back at her. His injured foot had seemed quite bad.

When she went back to Mumbai, she got in touch with the guy who had clicked her page 3 picture. Did he know of a photographer who went by the name PS? No, he didn't—but he could find out. There was no lead for a long time until, one night; she received a text that said someone had known him. Turned out he was a freelancer who dabbled in food photography for a while. Although quite talented, he never really got the right breaks. He was last found bartending at a pub. Her ex—a fulltime tattoo artist now—helped find out which pub PS had been working at. She met the manager the same night.

◆

Annette moved in with him rather early in their relationship. Three months. He was doing an assignment for the campus beat of a magazine. He saw her sitting alone on a rock, busy with a laptop. Hers was the most photogenic face around, he decided. Taut skin, sharp nose and brownish hair falling in elongated waves sensuously down her elbows. He photographed her without her knowing, then with her permission. They got talking, they went out the next day, and he fell in love the same week.

She divided her time between home in Panjim, her PhD in Mumbai and her new boyfriend. Their first serious argument followed his drinks-menu photo shoot at the pub a few months later. He got real interested and took up mixology classes to work alternate weeknights at the same pub. For him, it was a new skill and extra income; for her, loneliness.

Lately, he had been spending more time at the pub than with her. The weekend they were supposed to go to Panjim to announce their relationship, he was asked to fill in for someone at the bar. It was a big party that Saturday. He said they could leave early Sunday morning.

Annette showed up at the pub after hours of being alone at home. He'd had back-to-back photo shoots through the day. She chose a table far away from the bar. He was thrilled to see her, but surprised when she ordered a mojito with a Russian sounding name. She had given up alcohol after her father died of cirrhosis of the liver. He made it anyway, with lesser vodka. Three drinks down, and he was worried. When she asked for a fourth one, he sent a mocktail instead, with 'Annette pomegranate' scribbled on a paper napkin. He smiled from across the bar. She complained to the manager and got exactly what she wanted. The party went on for longer than he'd estimated.

Annette was guzzling down her seventh drink when the party finally ended. She wobbled down to the bar and picked up a beer jug. He tried to take it away from her, but she was holding it surprisingly tight. He yanked it from her hand with some force. She staggered back uncontrollably and crashed head first against the wall. A tiny trickle of blood stained the wall.

He rushed her to the hospital. She slipped into a coma on the way. He couldn't stop crying. Just before they took her into the ICU, he slipped the ring on her finger, choking over wedding vows. He had planned to propose in Panjim, before her family.

You may now kiss the bride.

He gently pressed his lips against hers, before they took her away.

He had been awake for two nights straight. On Monday morning he fell asleep in a chair at the waiting lounge. Annette died while he was asleep.

◆

The manager gave her the home address, although no one lived there anymore. She arrived with no difficulty. Prags was good with directions.

It was a smallish, independent house with red-framed window panes. The rest of it was weather-worn white. The front door was locked, but a window on the side—hidden from immediate view— had a cracked glass. She smashed it with a stone and unbolted the grill, inserting her hand.

Prags slid into what looked like the bedroom. There was an empty cupboard and no bed. A wall mirror was smashed. There were two other wall mirrors in the house—both broken. Shards of glass were everywhere. The empty walls had marks where picture frames or art may have been. She found one frame still hanging, with the glass broken. It was him for sure—a much younger version, holding an outdated looking camera. Her eye fell on something on the floor below the picture. She bent to pick up a brown-beaded rosary. It looked like it had fallen off rather than being left here. She held it, feeling it in her palm for a long time before putting it away in her satchel. She went out as she had come.

♦

The recurring dreams had stopped finally. He would dream of a miniature him falling into a huge margarita glass filled with pink drink which would eventually turn into blood. Or him getting squished between wine flutes. The worst had him at the bar in an empty pub, when suddenly there would be ear-splitting, piercing sobs. It was almost impossible to go back to sleep after one of these.

These days, he had turned into an early riser and slept early too. Every night he couldn't help but think of the skinny schoolgirl from Bangalore. Even ten years later. He could never recall her name though. *How badly do you want to sleep?* He had wanted to, very badly. Badly enough to leave for Panjim the next day. Annette's mother had refused to even see him. After months of dedicated requesting, she had relented. After a few years, she had finally begun to trust him fully.

Annette's father, James, had a flourishing sea-food packaging business. When James died, Annette was still in college. She gave up studies and took on the business. A few years later, she completed college and went to Mumbai for her PhD. After she died, there was nobody to look after the business. But since the day Annette's mother agreed to have him stay with them, till a decade later, the business took up his every waking moment. He brought it to a level that James (and Annette) would have been proud of.

He more or less gave up professional photography in the meanwhile, doing Goan skyscapes or the odd tourism project. But, now, he wanted to get back to it, at least over the weekends. His old contacts in Mumbai had promised to keep him in on freelance assignments. One such was coming up that Saturday, for a magazine. He had to photograph a young music therapist with some fancy degrees from abroad, and a special interest in music therapy for autistic children and comatose patients.

◆

For some reason, he imagined the music therapist would be a dude with a ponytail. The PR person had said she would meet him shortly, as he waited at the hospital lobby. He smiled at the thought. He no longer felt suffocated in hospitals.

She walked in briskly but gracefully towards him. He set the camera bag aside and rose.

'Pragya Joshi.' She extended her hand, smiling brightly. Something about her seemed vaguely familiar. But he couldn't figure what. She was a good foot shorter than him and had straight, dark, chin-length hair framing her face. Down on her neck, there was the black of the tunic she was wearing, but his eyes settled on the artfully abstract black butterfly tattoo. The size of a thumbnail. His.

He was holding her hand in a firm but gentle grip. Clean shaven, clear eyes behind stylish, black-rimmed glasses. He looked well rested. Well slept.

'Pragyan Sharma.'